THE NILI SPIES

Sarah Aaronsohn

The Nili Spies

ANITA ENGLE

With an Introduction by Peter Calvocoressi

FRANK CASS
LONDON • PORTLAND, OR.

First Published 1959 by The Hogarth Press, London
This edition first published 1997 by
FRANK CASS & CO. LTD.
Newbury House, 900 Eastern Avenue,
London IG2 7HH

and in the United States of America by
FRANK CASS
c/o ISBS, 5804 N.E. Hassalo Street,
Portland, Oregon 97213-3644

British Library Cataloguing in Publication data

A catalogue record for this book is available
from the British Library

Library of Congress Cataloging-in-Publication data

A catalog record for this book is available
from the Library of Congress

ISBN 0 7146 4803 5 (cloth)
ISBN 0 7146 4293 2 (paper)

Printed in Great Britain by
Bookcraft (Bath) Ltd, Midsomer Norton, Avon

Introduction

Peter Calvocoressi

TOWARDS the end of 1956 an article appeared in the *New Statesman* in London about Sarah Aaronsohn. The name meant nothing to me but after reading the article I wrote to its author, Anita Engle, asking her if she had any plans to expand it into a book and might care to send it to us at Chatto & Windus where I was at that time a partner. I also showed the article to Leonard Woolf who had an obvious special interest in the story it told and was, as it happened, about to pay a visit to Israel where, I had discovered, Anita Engle lived. Leonard Woolf, besides being the founder with his wife Virginia of The Hogarth Press, had become a partner in Chatto & Windus when the two firms merged after World War II. In Israel Leonard met Anita Engle and her husband, and made a contract with her for what became *The Nili Spies*. On his return Leonard recorded the deal in an internal memorandum, adding with characteristic brevity and effacement that he was "inclined to think it (the book) should be a Hogarth book". Which it became.

Anita Engle's manuscript arrived in our office in March 1958 and soon afterwards I wrote to say that I was reading it "with growing absorption" and was sure that, details apart, "the heart of the matter is here". There followed a copious correspondence – on our side mostly with Leonard Woolf – about the content and shape of the book, and the vexing matter of a title; the title which eventually emerged made its first appearance in a letter from Anita to Leonard. The book was published in April 1959. We printed 3,000 copies and sold all but 500 within about a year. There were more than 40 reviews in Britain with a number more in Israel, South Africa, Canada and Australia, but we failed to persuade any American publisher to issue a separate American edition.

The Nili Spies is a tale of the First World War but also a tale about a very small number of people in a limited area which was only on the fringe of that war. It is a work of chiaroscuro, vividly focussed but set in a wide context of which the actors in the story could see and know little. The NILI spies numbered at times no more than five or six people. Two of them – Aaron and Sarah Aaronsohn – were of the essence of the group in the sense that without them there would have been no NILI spies. Their parents were Rumanian immigrants who had settled at Zichron Yaakov a few miles north of Caesarea in the early 1880s and had brought up six children there. The oldest, Aaron, born in Rumania, became world-famous as a botanist and agronomist, the discoverer of wild wheat in Palestine and the founder of an Agricultural Experiment Station (the first in the Middle East) where he hoped to develop ways of making deserts bloom and his fellow Jews less miserably penurious. He was by all accounts a man of outstanding intelligence and inescapable force of character, but also somewhat superior and, some said, arrogant or prickly. Brilliant and selfless, he sometimes comes through as the sort of man whom lesser men do not find easy to like or live with: a man who invites you to keep your distance.

Aaron shared with his sister a passionate love for the Yishuv, the Jewish community in Palestine, and an absolute conviction that it was in imminent danger of total extinction by the Turks. This was not just some paranoid fancy. They had seen what the Turks were doing to the Armenians, and the Jews had good enough reasons to fear that the attempted genocide of the Armenians would be followed by genocide of the Jews. Their fears were sharpened by the fact that the Turkish Governor and Commander-in-Chief in Syria was Djemal Pasha, a man both brutal and scared. They reckoned that time was not on their side and salvation lay only in action against the Turks and their German allies in Syria: action which could only come from the British in Egypt. They therefore resolved to help the British by collecting military intelligence or, in other words, by spying. Their assessment was probably correct: it was certainly compelling. But their understanding of the British position was quite wrong. Egypt was far away and the central zones and strategies of the war were beyond their ken.

They did not doubt that the British, who had virtually bought the Suez Canal a generation earlier and were obsessed with the imperial importance of the Middle East, would take the offensive against the Turks and the Germans in Syria. They were amazed and dismayed when the British landed in Gallipoli in 1915, and concluded that the British were hopelessly ill informed about the position of Syria and would with better information see their errors, reassess their opportunities and switch their efforts to Palestine. They were expecting this to happen in 1916, when in fact the British were reducing their forces in the Middle East and sending them to the Western Fronts in France and Flanders. It was not until October 1917, after Allenby's capture of Beersheba (which was greatly assisted by intelligence from NILI about the wells in the area) that the British advanced seriously into Palestine: their advance began three weeks after Sarah committed suicide. And finally, the NILI group failed to appreciate how insignificant a small group of Jews seemed to the British in Cairo who had plenty of other groups – Arabs, Armenians, Kurds, Greeks – to choose from if and when they wanted local help. The NILI spies did provide a steady flow of information about the enemy's strength, fortifications and morale, but to the British it was no more than an uncovenanted bonus towards a problematic and subordinate venture. The British were not even coordinated among themselves. Absalom Feinberg, the third of the groups preeminent trio, was rejected when he offered his services to the military in Cairo but, proceeding to Port Said, was taken on by Lieutenant (later Sir Leonard) Woolley of the Royal Navy who thus inaugurated, in late 1915, the shuttle service of the fruits of NILI's espionage from the coast of Palestine by sea to Egypt. (Half a century later, in 1967, Absalom's bones were found in the Sinai desert where he had been killed by Beduin while trying in 1917 to renew the broken contract with the British. "A fine palm tree", wrote Anita Engle to Leonard Woolf, "was growing over the grave and must have sprung from the dates which Absalom was carrying on him as rations".)

These miscalculations created the tragedy which this book recounts, honours and celebrates. It would be wrong to resume the substance of this tragedy in an Introduction – doubly wrong since Anita Engle's telling of it, vivid, judicious, committed but controlled, could not be bettered. And tragedy it is, since on the human scale the Aaronsohns' miscalculations are as nothing compared with their heroism. Above all Sarah's. Before war came she was, or appears here to have been, unremarkable. Unlike her brother Aaron, Sarah was born in Palestine. She loved her family, particularly the incomparable Aaron, and next to her family her community and heritage. Early in 1914, and chiefly to clear the way for the marriage of a younger sister, she accepted an arranged marriage with a prosperous merchant from Istanbul who had come to Palestine in search of a Jewish wife. When war came a few months later, she left her husband, who never saw her again, and fired by the danger of the Yishuv, rushed back to Zichron Yaakov. She came as Aaron's helpmate, but a long break with Woolley in Egypt convinced Aaron that he must face the hazards of making his way to England to re-establish it; and so Sarah became NILI's chief. Her personal courage, determination, exertions, and gift for leadership, and her cool head when alone and in danger were all extraordinary. Her death by her own hand, when she feared that she might no longer be able to keep silent under torture, was grisly and protracted. Like Aaron she aroused suspicions and even hostility among the people whom she was risking her life to save, for she too gave an impression of aloofness which aggravated the trepidation and distrust of her neighbours. This was another aspect of the tragedy. It partly arose, or so it has been surmised, from the entrenched gap between the First Aliya and the Second, between the pioneers of the 1880s and the later, more numerous and by then poorer immigrants of the next generation. But there was also a deeper source of conflict, one which has not been confined to the Middle East or the First World War. The anonymous review (in fact by Stewart Perowne) of *The Nili Spies* in *The Times Literary Supplement* was headed "Was it Worth it?"

This is a question which has been posed by historians writing about the resistance movements of the Second World War whose heroism is easier to appreciate than their effectiveness is to assess. The information sent to Cairo by the NILI spies was substantial and accurate but it was marginal, and those who provided it were all rounded up by the Turks. Valuable though NILI's work was to Allenby he would have entered Jerusalem anyway. Most critical and most difficult to answer is the question whether NILI did more to save the Yishuv or endanger it. Many in the Yishuv stigmatised Aaron Aaronsohn as the "man who endangered the Yishuv". Unwillingly but inescapably embroiled in the clash of Great Powers, Zionists at large and in the Yishuv in Palestine were disposed by tradition and by prudence to keep their heads down, trust in God and hope for the best. The Aaronsohns and their friends were the minority who judged this attitude craven and unrealistic. They feared that merely hoping for the best would lead to the worst – that is, to the total extinction of the Yishuv. Activists of this stamp had in theory two choices. They might try to get the Turks' German allies, who had troops and designs in Palestine, to intervene to moderate the wrathful prejudices of the Turks. But many regarded the Germans as barely less racially prejudiced than the Turks and they resolved to turn to the British and declare open support for them and their allies (even Russia). This was the choice of the Zionist faction led by Vladimir Jabotinsky who wanted to offer Britain a fighting force of Jewish legionaries. But Jabotinsky was disowned by the Zionist movement and slighted by the British. His scheme fell on deaf ears in London and in Cairo, and produced only the short-lived and non-combatant Zion Mule Corps. It was not until 1917 that the British agreed to the formation of Jewish Battalions – disguised under the name Royal Fusiliers – and not until August 1918 that any of them saw action. Within Palestine and entirely unrelated to Jabotinsky or any other group, the NILI spies judged that the salvation of the Yishuv demanded concrete and immediate cooperation with the British. The majority of the Yishuv judged on the contrary that NILI was up to something which would accelerate their destruction. In the event the NILI spies, not the Yishuv, were destroyed. But subsequent events and the hazards which shape them are not the best guide to pronouncing on the actions of people who find themselves forced to decide and act in a crisis.

One consequence of these disputes and troubled consciences was the virtual deletion of the NILI spies from the historiography of the First World War. They were no doubt marginal, but so were many other tributary streams (including T. E. Lawrence and the Arab Revolt), and their spirit, personalities, motives and fate are the stuff which makes the record of war something other than pitiful and squalid. Apart from two books in Hebrew, both mentioned in Anita Engle's Acknowledgements, Zionist and Israeli works ignored or belittled NILI until the appearance of *The Nili Spies* in 1959. So too did the official British histories. There were in London, during the war and after it, many who looked on the Jews through romantic spectacles. Just as Philhellenes contrived to see Greeks as descendants of Pericles and Socrates, so Jews evoke images of Patriarchs and Prophets. But to Generals and Staff Officers and war historians, they were, more pragmatically, few and discordant and of little obvious usefulness. So they got lost. That loss may be a minor blot on military history but in the broader annals of humanity it is a grave offence. Anita Engle did much service by recovering and recounting an uplifting story. In welcoming its reappearance I lament also the sad fact that she did not live to see its resurrection.

Bath, England
November 1995

CONTENTS

THIS BOOK
IS DEDICATED
TO THE
SPIRITUAL HEIRS
OF NILI

·

THE
YOUNG PEOPLE
WHO FELL
IN THE JEWISH
WAR OF
INDEPENDENCE

ACKNOWLEDGEMENTS

I WISH to express my gratitude to those who have provided me with information, and permitted me to use diary notes, letters, reports, and other documents, some of which have not previously appeared in print. Chief among these are members of Nili, particularly Liova Schneersohn, O.B.E., Mendel Schneersohn, and Raphael Aboulafia; and also Dr M. Neumann, Leibel Bornstein, Nissim Rootman, Toba Rootman.

I have to thank members of the Aaronsohn family, particularly Miss Rivka Aaronsohn, who has provided me with material and much information during the course of several years; and Mrs Cela Shoham, who made me acquainted with the life and writings of her brother, Absalom Feinberg. I have to thank as well the Lishansky family, Dr Y. Ben Harozen, Mr Arieh Samsonov, Mr S. Tolkowsky, Mrs J. L. Magnes, Mr Norman Bentwich and Mr Douglas Duff for information and material.

It is with pleasure that I acknowledge the friendly co-operation of Dr A. Bein, Director of the Zionist Archives in Jerusalem, Mr B. Guriel, Director of the Weizmann Archives, Rehovoth, and Mr M. Palmoni, Director of the Jabotinsky Museum, Tel Aviv, who have permitted me to make use of letters and documents contained in their files. I am also indebted to Mr Palmoni for the use of the pictures which are reproduced in this book.

I take this opportunity of thanking Sir Leonard Woolley, who, through the kind offices of Mr Leonard Woolf, has supplied me with information; and the correspondents who were kind enough to write to me following my request for information, which was circulated through the Press.

Further letters and diary notes have been gleaned from printed sources, chiefly articles which have appeared in the Hebrew Press during the past thirty years; from Mr J.

ACKNOWLEDGEMENTS

Yaari-Poleyskin's book *Nili*, and Mr Y. Slutsky's account in *The Story of Jewish Self-Defence*. I wish to pay special tribute to Mr Yaari-Poleyskin's book, which has kept the story of Nili alive; and to the well-documented and unbiased account in *The Story of Jewish Self-Defence*, published in 1956, which is the first official recognition to be accorded the work of Nili.

Additional thanks are due to Mrs Cela Shoham, Mr Liova Schneersohn and Mr Y. Slutsky for kindly reading my MS. and offering numerous useful suggestions; and to Mrs Mary Hart for her assistance in translating from the French and in preparing the MS. for the publishers.

This book was written with the constant advice and encouragement of my husband, Nelson Berkoff, who also made himself responsible for a large part of the research and the translations from the Hebrew. Our sons, Jonathan and David, took an active interest throughout.

ILLUSTRATIONS

GLOSSARY

Aliyah: *Immigration into Palestine*

Fellahin: *Arab peasant*

Galuth: *In exile; a general term referring to the dispersal of the Jews outside Palestine*

Halutzim: *Pioneers*

Hamsin: *Hot wind from the desert*

Ha-Shomer: *The watchman's organisation of the W[C] ment*

Kaimakam: *Turkish government official in charge of a town*

Mukhtar: *Head of a community appointed to be responsible to the Turkish authorities*

Shalom: *Literally "Peace"—the traditional Jewish form of greeting*

Shomer: *Hebrew word for a watchman*

Vali: *The civil governor of a Turkish province or vilayet*

Yishuv: *A Jewish community in Palestine. The whole of the Jewish community in Palestine is referred to as the Yishuv*

Introduction

IN SEARCH OF SARAH

BEFORE I came to Israel I had only the vaguest knowledge of Sarah Aaronsohn. Even in Israel there was little more to be learned, for to most people she was only a symbol. She was a heroine, everyone knew that; a heroine of the early days of modern Palestine. She had led a spy ring against the Turks and helped the British in the First World War. She had worked with Lawrence and he had fallen in love with her. When? Where? What were the circumstances? Why was there only the barest mention of her in Zionist annals? Nobody knew.

The Aaronsohn family had come from the mountain village of Zichron Yaacov, I was told, and the old house was still inhabited. And so one day I found myself walking up the main street of Zichron in search of Sarah.

The village of Zichron Yaacov spreads among vineyards and olive groves on a stony ridge of Mount Carmel some four hundred feet above the coastal plain. In front, the Mediterranean flashes in a magnetic curve against the horizon. Behind, the blue hills of Ephraim swell up in waves against the sky.

The little main street goes shambling along the mountain ridge, indifferent to progress, planning, or civic pride. Half-way up the street, hidden by a hedge and surrounded by a freshly painted wall, stands the strange, beautiful Aaronsohn home, set in a courtyard where even the palms have the lustre of well cared for heirlooms.

Entering that courtyard was like sweeping aside a curtain against which one has seen a shadowy figure, and finding oneself in a room with many people, all of them animated, vigorous, passionate. For within this restricted rectangle, only the past is real, and everything centres on the joys and the sorrows, the ambitions and the animosities of the men and women who had lived out their lives there forty years before.

That was my introduction to the Aaronsohn family. It was in

this house that the matriarch Malka and her pious peasant husband, Ephraim, had brought up their six vigorous, independent children to love the soil and to work for its redemption. Here I found Sarah, for it was in this, her parents' home, that she had lived and died.

There was a Brontë-like quality about the Aaronsohn family, a mystery of nature's workings, which defied explanation or analysis. But while the Brontës were sickly and wasted away in the shadow of their dream world, leaving only figments of their imagination behind them, the Aaronsohn's came of hardy stock; and though at last two died in the creation of their dream world, they left it peopled by a reborn nation.

These two stood out from among the Aaronsohn family; Sarah, the heroine, and her brother Aaron, a man of giant stature, who towered above the Palestine scene for almost two decades, and then, as though a rushing torrent had been suddenly sucked underground, disappeared from life and public record, leaving a mysterious silence.

A third stood beside them, not of the family, but linked to the Aaronsohns in life and death. This was Absalom Feinberg, Aaron's disciple, and forerunner of our own generation of Israeli youth who are so careless of their lives in the interests of their homeland: a beautiful and ardent young man, the first poet of modern Palestine.

It was only by chance that I was able to get a glimpse behind the curtain on my first visit to that secluded courtyard, for the fog of secrecy which surrounds the Aaronsohn family is almost as impenetrable as that which obscures Lawrence of Arabia. But so compelling was their story, and so incomprehensible their fate, that for four years I kept coming back to this house of mystery, trying to piece together the history of the enigmatic dead, whose pictures look down at one from every wall in every room.

Chapter 1

GROWING UP IN ZICHRON

THE parents of Sarah and Aaron were among the founders of Zichron Yaacov, one of the first settlements of modern Palestine. The settlers, humble trades-people, had come in a group from Rumania in 1882. There were only a few dozen of them and they hardly knew what Palestine, then a remote, neglected Asiatic province of the vast Ottoman Empire, was like. They had no adequate means of their own. They knew nothing about agriculture or colonization. They knew not one of the languages spoken in Palestine. They were simply filled with love for the land of Israel, with a desire to redeem its soil, and with it their lives and the lives of their children.

When their ship entered the port of Haifa, they were greeted with the newly issued edict: "It is forbidden for Jewish immigrants to land on the coast of Syria, and it is absolutely forbidden for them to live in Palestine. This prohibition is final."

The Sultan had become suspicious of the attempts suddenly being made by various European bodies to buy large tracts of land in Palestine for Jewish settlement. According to a law forced on the Turkish Government, nationals of other countries could remain under the jurisdiction of their own, or a patron government, no matter how long they resided within the Ottoman Empire. The Sultan feared that a large, organized immigration would give the European powers a pretext for getting the toe-hold in Palestine which they had been seeking for years.

In particular, hidden British interest was suspected. Disraeli had purchased the Suez Canal shares seven years before; a year later Lord Shaftesbury openly began to declare himself in favour of a return of the Jews to their homeland; and Sir Laurence Oliphant was one of the most enthusiastic sponsors of this first emigration to Palestine.

Although the Turkish Government never officially lifted its

17

restriction, the Aaronsohns and their friends—the founders of Zichron—after wandering from port to port for forty days, eventually found a way to land. They entered a country which lay steeped in the torpor and disease and neglect of centuries. The only habitation on their hill-top was a hamlet of half a dozen primitive Arab huts, occupied by the fellahin who had worked the land for its former owner. The Arabs remained as labourers and co-partners in the cultivation of the soil until the city-bred Europeans had learned enough about agriculture to do for themselves.

At first the Jews lived like the Arabs, in booths made of oak branches covered with mud and roofed over with straw matting. Their first permanent houses, of stone, had to be built by stealth, for it was against Ottoman law for non-citizens to build houses, and these could be destroyed up to the moment when they had a roof on them.

The settlers soon found that the rocky strip of land which their emissaries had bought for them was unfit for agriculture. The plain that stretched between Mount Carmel and the coast was dotted with swamps, breeding-grounds for the malarial mosquitoes which hummed unceasingly round the settlement, sapping the life from young and old.

The Aaronsohns and their comrades had regarded themselves as the vanguard of a great movement of pioneers from Rumania who would soon follow them. Funds had been pledged and families organized. But the difficulties made by the Turkish authorities increased, and the way to America became easier. The organization in Rumania fell to pieces, and the pioneers in Zichron were left to fight the afflictions of hostile nature and an evil government alone.

The disaster which faced the new settlement after its first year was averted by the appearance on the Palestine scene of the French philanthropist, Baron Edmond de Rothschild. With his financial assistance and the agricultural instructors whom he provided, the pioneers were able to adjust themselves to the harsh conditions of their new home. They soon adjusted themselves as well to the maze of restrictions which the Turkish authorities continued to wind round them, for there was no restriction which could not be circumvented by bribery.

Aaron was six years old when his parents brought him from Rumania to Palestine. The others, Zvi, Shmuel, Alex and the two girls, Sarah and Rivka, the youngest of the family, were all born in Zichron. By the time Sarah was born in 1890, there were some hundred families in Zichron, their whitewashed stone houses huddled close together for protection against Arabs, who at first menaced the life of the new colony.

Like the Brontës, the Aaronsohns grew up on their high hill-top passionately attached to each other and to the wild country-side in which they lived. Nourished on the Bible and their parents' ideals, the Aaronsohns too created a dream world far removed from the grim realities surrounding them. They did not see themselves as the children of struggling Jewish farmers in a malarial outpost of a decadent Ottoman Empire. They saw themselves as the heirs of an ancient people and a noble heritage. They were ambitious and had grandiose ideas, not for themselves, but for the future of Palestine: the agricultural revival, the education and the self-defence of the Jewish State which they saw in their dreams.

Aaron, as they used to say in Zichron, was a genius in his mother's womb. He understood the new life the farmers were trying to bring to fruition in their ancient land, and their aim became his goal. He had a powerful personality, and while still attending the little village school he was showing evidence of the phenomenal intellect and scientific capacities which were to make him one of the world's outstanding agricultural explorers. He was not yet ten when he began to identify the plants of Palestine with the Hebrew names of the Bible. He taught himself these, as he taught himself many things, by working with and observing the Arab fellahin who were employed at Zichron. His quick ear caught the echo of the ancient Hebrew names in the names which the Arabs used, just as later he began to catch the echo of Biblical agricultural practices in their primitive routines.

The Hebrew language was just emerging reborn from the stagnation of centuries, during which it had been reserved almost entirely for the purpose of prayer. Eliezer Ben Yehuda, the writer and lexicographer, was leading the fight for its revival, but scientific classification still remained a thing of the future.

Aaron was the idol of the family, influencing in particular the three youngest ones, Alex, Sarah and Rivka. Zichron was far from the cultural centres, at that time Jaffa and Jerusalem, and these lively minded young people, like the Brontës at Haworth, wrote long letters to people of the day. When the first modern Hebrew dictionary appeared, Sarah, then fourteen, and Rivka, who was twelve, wrote to Eliezer Ben Yehuda informing him that the Aaronsohns too were trying "to make our language a living language, a spoken language. None of the children in our settlement know the names of the flowers and plants, the birds that fly, and the insects that hum around our ears, so that we can recognize them when we go for a walk, like the children of other nations know theirs, as far as we can judge from their books.

"The usual excuse is that the poverty of our language is to blame, but this is not right. If we pass a view without looking at it, it isn't because of the poverty of our language, but because we haven't been taught how to observe. We know this is right, for we have seen this in our own family. Our big brother never goes out on any of the many journeys which he makes all over our beautiful land, even the trips he makes around our farm, without coming back laden with plants and stones, and everything he comes across. He guards them as though they were pearls, writes down on a nice card the place where he found every single thing, and calls them by names which sometimes have a strange ring in our ears. We can almost say that he embraces and strokes them. He loves their company. It is a great pleasure for him just to sit amongst them and read about them.

"Slowly this disease has affected us as well. We also have begun to bring home different kinds of things from our walks. He helped us at first, and began to write names on the cards for us too. But now the thing has developed until we are the ones who write down, and he has given us the work of sorting and arranging the plants and stones in his collection."

When the Baron de Rothschild had come to the assistance of the pioneers he had recruited agricultural instructors for them from the French North African colonies. As the most promising boy in Zichron, Aaron was co-opted to work with them when he left the village school at the age of twelve, and for six years he smouldered under their contempt for the Jewish settlers, their lack of love for Palestine and their misunderstanding of its agricultural needs. Aaron longed for the authority to become his people's teacher in agriculture.

Unexpectedly, when Aaron was eighteen, it looked as if his opportunity had come. The Baron, who had always taken an interest in him, sent him to an agricultural school in France. He needed farming instructors for the new settlements he intended to found, and wanted to train local youth to replace the foreign instructors about whom the settlers were continually complaining.

Grignon, with qualified teachers, organized instruction and laboratory facilities, was like manna to Aaron, and he believed that now he would gain the scientific basis and the status which would enable him to initiate new agricultural methods in Palestine. But this was not to be. Although wise and practical himself, the Baron's aid was administered through a rigid network of petty, intriguing officials, who tried to humble all and to break the spirit of anyone who opposed them. The administrators wanted to be sure that the students whom they sent to France would return to Palestine, and that once there, they would find it so difficult to obtain work that they would meekly submit to the official régime.

One month before he was to receive his diploma Aaron was hastily summoned back to Palestine. These two years at Grignon were the only formal scientific instruction he was ever to receive, although he later developed into an internationally known scientist in three fields: agriculture, botany and geology.

In Palestine Aaron was sent to be agricultural instructor at a new settlement the Baron had founded at Metullah, up in the wild hills of Galilee, bordering on the Lebanon. This was a fine post for a young man of twenty, and eventually he might have attained a position of considerable influence if he could have blinded himself to the way in which the settlement was administered. But this was impossible for Aaron. Practical, bold and energetic, he soon came into conflict with the officials, and he was forced to leave. Even before the young man got back to Zichron, where everybody, including himself, had such high hopes for his future, the rumour had reached his family that he had been expelled for stealing.

"Do you believe them?" Aaron demanded, startled at the possibility that people would not judge between honesty and dishonesty, between right and wrong. Ephraim Aaronsohn said that Aaron should have tried to get on with the head people, like everybody else did. He didn't like quarrelling. "How are you ever going to do anything if you quarrel with everybody?"

It looked as if Aaron's dream of becoming his people's teacher in agriculture had come to an end, for there were few prospects in those days outside the Baron's bounty. This was a bitter time for Aaron and his family. Zichron was a small village, close-knit and malicious, as such communities are, and the slander was continually being thrust at them, particularly at the younger children, who retaliated with typical vigour. Finally, through the director of the school in Grignon, Aaron became overseer of a great estate in Anatolia. In spite of his youth they gave him a free hand, and here his colossal energy found full expression. The feats, the character and even the appearance of the bulky, ruddy-complexioned, virile young man were of just the type to capture the Eastern imagination, and the Turks admiringly referred to him as "Sheitan"—the Devil. Aaron learned to speak Turkish fluently and got to know the Turks well from the peasants, wily and unwilling to work, to the intellectuals, members of the Young Turk Movement, even then plotting rebellion. He met government officials, and from them learned that bribery was their means of existence and that the corruption and inadequacy of the Turkish Army were only comparable to those of the central government itself.

After two successful years his work there terminated abruptly as the result of treachery on the part of a friend whom he had brought out to help him, and he found himself back again in his parents' home in Zichron. For the next six years he wandered around, trying many things but unable to find a field into which to put his energies and knowledge. When his money ran out, his father helped him. This was the blackest period of Aaron's career. Nevertheless, at the same time it was one of the periods richest in scientific discoveries. It was then that he undertook the many trips of exploration which helped to lay the foundation on which is based present-day knowledge of the flora, fauna and geological structure of Palestine and Transjordan. Aaron's knowledge became encyclopaedic. Up till now there has been no one person who has had such a wide scientific knowledge of Palestine and its produce as Aaron.[1]

Always Aaron's search was directed towards one aim: to find the secrets of nature, the methods of agriculture, which would restore the fertility of the arid land of Palestine. His intensive study of ancient writings, Hebrew, Greek, Latin, and his detailed knowledge of the countries of the Middle East had convinced him that the waste spaces were not barren by nature. From that region had come the produce which had maintained the Roman Empire. It had been agriculture which had supported the rich civilizations now scattered in ruins over the deserts of the Middle East. There had been no change in the climate or the soil itself. The area had become barren through centuries of neglect and the disappearance of the people who had understood the secrets of tilling these arid lands.

Aaron saw that Palestine could never be revived as long as it remained under the rule of the slothful, destructive Turk. He had come to recognize that the régime which barred Palestine to Jewish immigration and settlement was rotten to the core; that it was only a matter of time until the disintegration of the Ottoman Empire, which had begun in Europe, would extend to Asia; and then, by some strong, imaginative action on the part of the Jews, Palestine could be freed. Aaron visited and observed those areas of the Middle East and Africa where the European powers had penetrated with varying degrees of authority, studying their merits as administrators and their devotion to the interests of the governed with an eye to finding the most suitable patron for the Jewish revival.

In the meantime, although things seemed hardly to change, conditions in Palestine were never static. A tenuous fabric of Jewish life was being constructed in little oases throughout the country, with the incredible feats of pioneering and defence which were a commonplace to the settlers of Zichron. How else could settlements be established?

Aaron was working for the time when Herzl, the founder of

[1] Prof. H. R. Oppenheimer, *Florula Transjordanica* (Genève, 1931)

the newly organized Zionist Organization, would obtain from the Sultan the Charter for Palestine which he was always on the verge of getting. This would loose a flood of immigration to Palestine, and Aaron expected to direct the settlement of the country on an organized, scientific basis. But when the second wave of immigration finally did start, some twenty years after the arrival of the Aaronsohn generation, the new immigrants came believing that nothing of any importance had ever happened in Palestine before their coming.

Only a few could appreciate Aaron. A man of science was something rare in the upbuilding movement which had philosophers by the score; where every leader was at least a journalist, if not a writer; and all were orators, continually called upon to inspire themselves and their listeners with idealistic speeches. Committee meetings and conferences—these were the daily bread of the Zionist Movement, and to achieve sufficient agreement for the passing of a resolution was a major and fatiguing triumph. "The committee sickness", Aaron called it. A full-blooded son of the new country, he had a completely different approach from that of the intellectuals who had come, from the cities of Russia and Europe, to a country which was foreign to them in all its physical manifestations. Backward and fossilized as Palestine was at the beginning of the twentieth century, it was nevertheless a land of wide open spaces, every prospect a challenge to enterprise and vision. Aaron was of the calibre of the great pioneer builders of America whose vision and vigour a hundred years ago flung railways across mountains, and built dams, and created teeming cities on desert wastes.

He had taken part in a partial survey of the natural resources of Palestine and had wide-scale plans for exploiting them for the development of the country. He was outspoken in his condemnation of the officially recognized leaders who interpreted their task of national development in terms of buying small tracts of land and building a few houses on them.

The Second Aliyah brought another, more important, form of immigration. It consisted of Russian intellectuals, young men and women who had come to create by their own labour a new and better society in Palestine. They had grown up in the revolutionary movement in Russia. Many of them had taken part in the first, abortive, attempt at a Russian revolution in 1905 and had witnessed the pogroms with which it was temporarily diverted. They no longer believed, as did many of their comrades who remained in Russia, that the overthrow of the Czarist régime would better the position of the Jews. They believed that the Jewish problem was a world-wide one, and could only be solved when the Jewish people had been rehabilitated in Palestine and again rooted in the soil as an agricultural people.

There should certainly have been a bond between Aaron and these young people, eager for work and sacrifice. On the contrary, there was an unbridgeable gap. Although they called themselves "the Workers", and were known in the settlements as "the bare-footed ones", for they were very poor, they were far from being humble. They were steeped in the new socialist ideology and were convinced that they, and they alone, knew the method and should control the means for building the still very ephemeral Jewish National Home.

The newcomers believed that above all the Jews must avoid again becoming an economically dependent section of the population, easily harmed by every circumstance, as in Russia and Europe. Settling in Palestine was not enough. It was not enough for the Jews to be colonists, dependent on native labour, like the French colonists in Algeria. Palestine, to fulfil its function, had to change the whole economic structure, the very psychology of the Jewish people. They must become workers in every branch of the national economy, dependent on no one's labour but their own. The old settlements, like Zichron, which had grown up on the Baron's bounty and now maintained themselves on cheap Arab labour, these epitomized the evils of the old society. The Workers of the Second Aliyah—there was a fiery young man called David Ben Gurion among them—fought them tooth and nail. They formed an organization to unite the workers in the task of national revival according to their socialist programme. Their strength lay in the fact that they had a programme and devoted themselves to carrying it out with a zeal and a devotion which amounted to religious fervour.

25

Aaron tended to brush aside the claims and the imported ideologies of the young halutzim. Not because he was actively anti-socialist but because he considered them irrelevant to the problem of rebuilding Palestine. He could not see how meetings and interminable discussions about ideologies and principles could do the job of building up a country that needed vast resources and assistance on highest governmental levels. Iron of will, aggressive in his ideas, and four decades before his time, Aaron found himself swimming against the tide, without recognition in Palestine or any likelihood of official backing to carry on his researches or put his schemes into practice. At the age of thirty he was still dependent on help from his father and perpetually harrassed by debts. The only aids to scientific exploration which he owned were a magnifying glass which an uncle had given him for his thirteenth birthday, a small camera, a gun and half ownership of a pure-bred Arab mare. Whatever the state of his finances, Aaron would never ride any but a mare of noble breed.

His family suffered with Aaron in his bitterness and despair. At last his dark days, his solitary struggle and his frustrations, powerful as his ambitions, drew to a close. Aaron had made two trips to Germany to classify his botanical collections. Among the outstanding scientists whom he met in Berlin were three botanists who were absorbed in the mystery of the origins of wheat. Barley, oats and rye in their wild form had already been discovered, but apparently nothing existed in nature which could be considered the prototype of wheat. Until 1902, when Aaron was introduced to the problem, nothing more conclusive had been reached throughout the centuries than the fact that wheat had been cultivated since the dawn of civilization. Even the country of origin of this ubiquitous cereal was unknown. The belief that it had come from such countries of ancient civilization as India, China or Egypt had been disproved in the course of time.

Because of its long cultivation, wheat had degenerated and become easily subject to disease and unable to withstand rigorous climatic conditions. It was hoped that if the plant could be found in its original wild form, cross-breeding would produce a hardier species of cultivated wheat. Encouraged by the German scientists, Aaron began to look for wild wheat in Palestine. For two succeeding summers he searched in vain. Then, in June 1906, he found it growing in the mountains of Upper Galilee and along the slopes of Mount Hermon, as finely developed as cultivated wheat, although produced with little soil and less moisture.

Aaron's discovery made him world-famous. Within a few months he had been approached by the United States Department of Agriculture and asked to provide them with useful wild plants from Palestine and the neighbouring countries for cultivating in their arid areas. Aaron responded by describing, with the ardour of a young man writing about his sweetheart, the useful plants he had found growing everywhere in Palestine. The land which other people found desolate and barren, Aaron found to contain more than 3000 varieties of plants, more than even Germany possessed.

Aaron wrote his first letter in December 1907. In 1957, the newspapers carried an item announcing that in December of that year, Israel's Ministry of Agriculture would be planting an experimental range of *atriplex leucoclada* in the Negev in an attempt to turn the Beduin of the Negev into cattle ranchers. "The bush has been found to be ideal for grazing purposes in arid zones," the papers stated.

Exactly fifty years before, to the month, in his letter to the U.S. Department of Agriculture the young Aaron, who had nothing more to go on than his love of Palestine and his enormous powers of observation and common sense, had suggested this same plant as being useful for America's arid areas. "I have yet to come across an *A. leucocladum* plant that has not been partly chewed by camels or goats which are very fond of it," he added.

The wild wheat which Aaron was cultivating in the Aaronsohn fields at Zichron was of particular interest to the Americans, for it was hoped that the new strains would flourish in the semi-arid land of the Western States without irrigation. Not long afterwards Aaron was invited to go to America for consultation, and he spent two years there. He astonished them all with the extent of the knowledge he had gained by his powers of observation and his ability to make use of the past for the living present. "Aaron's mind had the fearlessness of a real mutation which knows it is different from the mass," said David Fairchild, chief of the Plant Exploration Department, who became his devoted friend and patron.

The vigorous, self-taught young farmer from Zichron could have made a brilliant career for himself in the United States, but he refused all offers, including a Chair at the University of California. Although happier than he had ever been before, he was only interested in harnessing his tide of fortune for the development of agricultural research in Palestine. In 1910, at the end of his first visit to America, he returned to Palestine with his life's ambition realized. American funds and backing for an agricultural experiment station in Palestine. Up to that moment, every plan he had ever had for the development and improvement of agriculture in Palestine had been frustrated. Now, at the age of thirty-four, in the full force of his terrific energy, at the height of his phenomenal intellectual powers, his life's work stretched ahead of him.

The Jewish Agricultural Experiment Station which Aaron built up in the course of the next four years was unique in the Middle East. For his experimental fields he selected a spot known all over the country for its sterility—Athlit, on the coastal plain of Sharon, at the foot of Mount Carmel, where sand dunes alternated with malarial marsh. But all around were signs of past populations, and Aaron knew that they could not have settled so intensively if the earth had not been able to support them. The massive ruin of a medieval castle loomed up from the coastline, the last outpost of the Crusaders in Palestine. On the mainland was a rounded hillock that had been a city when the harbour of Athlit had been a place of commerce and seafaring more than 2000 years before the Knights Templars had settled there. The vast Roman city of Caesarea spread beneath the sand dunes along the coast to the south of the Experiment Station, and the Phoenician port of Dor lay in between. Behind, on the slopes of Carmel, were prehistoric cave dwellings. Later excavations proved their inhabitants to have been the earliest known agriculturists, probably the first to have cultivated the wild wheat of Palestine some 8000 years ago.

Aaron chose this spot because he wanted to prove that there

was no such thing as worn out or sterile soil. Perhaps other men might not have succeeded, but Aaron did. Set in palms, and joined to the main highway by the only strip of macadamized road in the country, Aaron's station was like a Garden of Eden. There was something in fruit or in blossom the whole year round. In drought or rain, his fields of wheat and oats and barley flourished, yielding many times more than those of his neighbours, although he used no fertilizer and exactly the same implements as the Arab farmers. Aaron maintained that he had discovered the secret possessed by the ancient cultivators of the Middle Eastern regions. This was nothing more nor less than the rational application of the techniques of dry farming.

His friends in the U.S. Dept. of Agriculture came to feel that "on the eastern, Oriental end of the Mediterranean there was coming into existence a type of experimental agriculture which would be epoch-making, and that Aaronsohn was the man destined to bring this about."[1]

Members of Aaron's sponsoring committee in America came out to visit the Experiment Station. Among them was Nathan Straus, who had introduced pasteurized milk into the United States as a means of combating tuberculosis. Aaron induced him to set up an experimental health centre alongside the agricultural research station at Athlit, and the first scientific investigation into the causes and control of malaria, then the scourge of Palestine, began under Aaron's supervision.

[1] David Fairchild, *Journal of Heredity* (U.S.A., June 1919)

Chapter 2

ABSALOM AND SARAH

AARON drew around him a small group of young and devoted disciples to work with him at the Station. One of these young people, most beloved of Aaron, was himself great of mind and vision. This was Absalom Feinberg. Absalom was a hero straight out of a romance—tall, handsome, ardent, a writer of poetry, a lover of music; wise, witty, a crack shot, a dashing horseman, and so fearless that the Arabs had adopted him as their own, giving him the name of Sheikh Salim.

Absalom was born in Palestine. His parents were Russian intellectuals who came to the country with the first organized group of pioneers in 1882, the same year as the Zichronites, but unconnected with them. They are famous in Zionist annals as the Bilu, the name they chose for themselves from the Hebrew initials of the verse, "O House of Jacob, come ye and let us go" (Isaiah ii. 5).

They settled at Rishon-le-Zion, the first Jewish settlement in the south, between Jerusalem and Jaffa. This was one of the settlements which Baron de Rothschild had adopted, and just as at Zichron, a set of tyrannical officials administered the village's affairs and directed the settler's lives. Absalom's father, Israel Feinberg, a giant of a man, handsome, brave and fiercely independent, led a protest against the officials and was expelled from Rishon together with a handful of others. For the sake of their independence, they faced the deadly hardships of un-assisted settlement which kept so many other families mute under the tyranny of the officials. They moved farther south to found Gadera, an arid, sandy little settlement on the Philistine coast. Here Absalom was born.

Israel Feinberg was the pioneer personified, always thrusting out farther, always ready to conquer new areas. He left Gadera when he got a call to come to a place that needed him even more. This was Hadera, set in a festering sore of swamps on the

30

Plain of Sharon. Here a dozen or so families, Absalom's among them, tried to eke out an existence while they set about draining the swamps which would provide rich land for further Jewish settlement. This was the first step in the peaceful conquest of their homeland. To those who expressed horror that anyone should settle in an area so disease-ridden, their reply was: "Do we shun a mother because she is ill? We will bring her back to health again."

Aaron had become friends with the warm-hearted and big-minded Feinbergs of Hadera some twelve years before, when he himself had braved the domination of the Baron's administration. Absalom, their only son, was then ten, a skinny, black-eyed son of the settlement, as much at home with the neighbouring Arab children as with the Jews. His father, wise in the ways of the Arabs and much loved by them, put Absalom as a small child in the care of an Arab scholar who had a little school. "He is your son," he told the Sheikh, "teach him." Absalom learned the Koran and could talk and read Arabic as well as any Arab. This was in addition to the instruction which he received from his mother's father, Meier Belkind, an inspired teacher and Biblical scholar who made the Bible a living thing for him.

Poetry welled up in him like a spring, or as music from a bird. It was an expression of his passionate, vivid, impulsive, melancholy nature. In spite of his gaiety, a spontaneous, childlike gaiety, he was melancholy to the point of morbidity. The sorrow of the Jewish people, the injustices against them, their perpetual homelessness, formed the background of his existence, while his pride restlessly forced him to seek the solution. When once he saw a play in Jaffa where Russian hooligans were hitting Jews, he jumped on the stage and refused to let the performance go on. He could not bear to look at Jews who turned their backs on blows. At the age of fifteen he was sent to France to study, and remained there for some four years. All the time he was away, Absalom thought of only one thing, of getting national rights for the Jews, just as other young nations were getting their freedom, "and we are so far from it", he wrote to his family. "Why should the Greeks and the Bulgarians have a state, and we who have given so much, cannot get a state?"

He returned ill and unhappy. His parents were worried

about their gifted, impetuous son who could not find his place anywhere. He had continual arguments with his father, whom he thought conservative. Israel Feinberg believed that the Jews could manage very well under the Turks. With baksheesh to the authorities it was possible to buy as much land as one wanted. What the Jewish people bought, they would own. That was how Absalom's uncle, Joshua Hankin, was at that very moment acquiring the tracts of land throughout the country which later formed the basis for the Jewish State. Lack of money was his only hindrance.

Absalom hated the slow method of buying the homeland acre by acre, and depending on the compliance of corrupt officials. He saw how Egypt was developing under British rule; he read Oliphant and George Eliot's *Daniel Deronda*, and he believed that Palestine's future lay in the overthrow of Turkey and the protection of some benign power like Britain. "I would set fire to the Turks, as one lights a candle, and send them up in flame, if it would achieve our aim," he declared. "Either we're facing our end, or our rebirth, If our end, let us die like heroes; if our rebirth, then we don't have to be Turkish politicians."

There were moments when he was overcome by loneliness and sadness, and he felt how brief was one life to carry out the task of national redemption. "The hours are burdened with their paltry business; the wind is howling its terrible song, and the tick tock of a clock is burying my life. We are passing like a cloud, like steam which disperses, and our song dies away without even an echo."

When Absalom was twenty-one, Aaron set up a branch of his Experiment Station in Hadera. Absalom was put in charge of it, and a new period began in his life. Everything he needed and had been looking for he found in Aaron, and he dedicated himself to the older man. "If I do something for Aaron," he once wrote, "I feel I do something for my homeland; the homeland which he loves above everything, and pays homage to, like a poet, like a priest; the homeland for which he gives his whole life." Aaron loved Absalom in return, as a man loves a younger brother, a teacher his disciple, and together they travelled throughout the country, dreaming their dreams of national redemption and making their plans for the future state.

Aaron was so absorbed in his work that it never occurred to him to introduce his ardent young disciple to his two sisters, although he often mentioned him. They met by chance at a Purim ball in Zichron, an hour's ride from Hadera along the spur of the Carmel on which Zichron was situated. Sarah was by this time a fine-looking young woman, tall, full-bosomed, straight-backed, with strength and goodness shining from her pleasant face and wide-set blue eyes. She had been to Germany, Switzerland and Italy, for Aaron wanted his sisters to see the world. But only in Palestine did she feel content—in her home, with her vivid, satisfying family, the bare hills of Ephraim, and the blue sweep of the sea. Sarah helped her mother in the house, while Rivka was the zealous custodian of Aaron's private herbarium at Zichron and the expanding Station herbarium at Athlit.

Bleak and remote as their village might be, it never seemed so to the two sisters, for their days and nights were filled with interest and variety. Household work, in spite of the primitive conditions of the farmers' homes, was no drudgery for Sarah. Working by the side of her mother, she cheerfully washed the stone floors, scrubbed the wooden table and benches with sand and water, whitewashed the walls, and sewed for the family. Sarah loved ministering to others and enjoyed seeing her father and her brothers eating with zest the hearty meals and the great batches of bread she made for them in the iron stove which poured out charcoal fumes from the corner of the kitchen.

In the afternoon, when work was finished, Sarah and Rivka would dress up and go for a walk, like the other girls of the village. Their dresses were simple, of Sarah's own making, but she had an innate sense of style and her straight back and proudly poised head gave her an air of distinction. The doctor's wife and the ladies of the Administration, who used to go abroad every year and bought their clothes in Paris, would admire Sarah and say that if she were to go to Paris and specialize in dressmaking she could compete with Fakken, the famous tailor. In Zichron there was no higher praise.

Like all the Aaronsohns, Sarah was a fine horsewoman. It was Alex, virile and daring, who had taught her to ride and shoot, to know her way among the valleys of Carmel, and not to fear the night. Always full of energy and ready for adventure, she rode any time of the day or night, as the spirit moved her. She spoke Arabic from childhood and trusted to her quick wits or, if necessary, her pistol, to get her out of danger.

Sarah was the feminine counterpart of her brothers Aaron and Alex, and all three of them took after their mother in appearance and strength of character. Rivka was quite different, tiny, and very fair, with a quaint little face which reminded Absalom of Rembrandt's Saskia. He was enchanted with the two sisters and often rode over to Zichron to join them. There were lovely things to do—dancing and singing at the village threshing-floor on the hot, clear nights after the harvest; picnicking and swimming in the ancient harbours of Caesarea and Tantura; or galloping off in a group with other young people to parties in distant settlements.

At first Absalom was drawn to Sarah. He called her Sarati—my Sarah—as the family did. Both were high spirited and enjoyed pitting themselves against each other in horse racing or in swimming or in argument, for they were at the age when every idea and principle was thrashed out and hotly contested. Rivka, whom they called "the little sister", although she was only two years younger than Sarah, was always with them, made much of and teased by Absalom, as she was by her own family.

Rivka existed only in the orbit of Sarah or Alex or Aaron, and had a sense of inferiority which nothing could dispel. Sarah too was humble. All the Zichronites had been tradespeople in Rumania, and her family prided themselves on being hard-working, God-fearing Jews without any intellectual pretensions. "What do I need learning for?" Malka Aaronsohn would say bluntly. "Give me character." There was no thought in the old-time Jewish atmosphere of the Zichron farmers that girls should have another concern than to be good housewives, subordinate to the men.

Sarah's only schooling had been the village school, which she finished at the age of twelve. Although she continued to study at home and read with equal ease in Hebrew, French, German and Yiddish, she was far from the sophisticated culture of the Russian intellectuals who admired exalted ideas, asked melancholy, unanswerable questions and talked interminably about the mysteries of life, while scorning the practical details of everyday existence. Sarah, who read avidly, always searching for and deeply moved by beautiful ideas and heroic deeds, could only listen with silent admiration, for she had no facility for expressing the deep and fine things which lay buried in her heart. Absalom had shown that he understood her strivings. But although he was like a hero straight out of the romances which she loved to read, Sarah refused to let herself be swept off her feet. She could not escape the feeling that he was mocking at her, as he mocked at himself and the whole world, when his feelings grew too intense. What was she to make of his poems and letters, one of which she received after a stormy episode? Perhaps it was not clear to Absalom either.

"Sarati—In spite of everything, here we are, still friends, and I love you with all the strength of my heart. But you make me furiously angry, and for that you are a naughty girl, Saraleh, my darling. I would like to enjoy a quieter happiness, so I ask you to send me quickly, in a registered parcel, your little sister. We will talk about you here, I promise you, and think of you when the sun goes down. In the moonbeams we will see something of your dreaming eyes, and in the flame of the setting sun your ardent heart."

Absalom did not realize that he had only to storm the natural defences of a proud and independent woman. Or perhaps the turn of attention was organized by Sarah herself, for she saw how Rivka felt about Absalom. Whatever the cause, as Absalom's visits became more frequent, to Rivka's amazement and unbelief she found that when the gallant young man came dashing up on horseback to the Aaronsohn home and remained until the small hours of the morning, his visits were directed to her. Before long it was accepted by the two families that Rivka and Absalom were engaged. There was no talk of marriage. Rivka could not marry before the elder sister, a Jewish tradition that was old when the Biblical story of Rachel and Jacob was written.

They were a closed society, sharing their dreams and their plans only with each other, and their close associates. An incentive and a pungency was given to their exclusiveness by the fact that the community of Zichron had joined in the malicious attacks on Aaron when he returned from Metullah. In fact, some of the leaders of Zichron, and in the country as a whole, who felt that Aaron's proud independence and his phenomenal success were a personal affront to them, never ceased their attacks on Aaron and would have been glad to have penetrated the armour of the Aaronsohn pride. But they presented a united and unassailable front to the public—if a family, or any human being can be said to be impregnable to the attacks of a community.

The chink in Aaron's armour was his great love for the Yishuv and his concern for its development. The Aaronsohns could not hide their sadness nor Aaron his bitterness that the magnificent services he had to offer, so valued by the outside world, were practically ignored in Palestine. The European officials with university degrees who had been sent out to head the settlement programme of the Zionist Organization refused to accept the suggestion that a self-taught farmer from Zichron might know more about the building up of Palestine than they. They looked on Aaron as a thorn in their flesh and considered it presumptuous that someone outside official circles should have funds and programmes for the development of the country.

While an outstanding and important élite in America considered Aaron "one of the most interesting, brilliant and remarkable men",[1] people in Palestine judged differently. "An ignorant upstart, out to feather his own nest" was the verdict, some going so far in the attempt to discredit him that they declared he had stolen from a poor Alsatian Christian woman the discovery of wild wheat to which he owed his fame.[2] Knowledge may have its limits, but ignorance knows no boundaries.

Aaron became Enemy Number One to the Second Aliyah when Alex formed a group which he called the Gideonites. It was a watchman's organization and it was in opposition to

[1] Booklet, *Brandeis on Zionism* (Z.O.A., New York, 1942)
[2] Miss Annie Landau's statement, reported in F. E. Manuel's *Realities of American-Palestine Relations* (Washington, 1949), p. 179.

36

Ha-Shomer, the watchman's organization of the Workers' Movement. Ha-Shomer (the Hebrew for watchman) was the first organized attempt at Jewish self-defence in Palestine; later it formed the nucleus of the Haganah, which in turn developed into the Israeli Army. Alex was actively and openly opposed to the Workers' Movement, unlike Aaron who was not anti-socialist and objected to its alien ideologies only because they seemed irrelevant to the building up of Palestine. Alex had been in the United States for some years, as Aaron's representative. When he returned on a film-making mission in the summer of 1913, he found that Ha-Shomer had gained a formidable reputation for prowess in the defence of Jewish settlements. He was incensed at the implication that the sons of the old settlers, who up till then had left defence in the hands of Arab watchmen, were by comparison poltroons, and so he organized from among his own friends, including Absalom, the new Gideonite group for the defence of the Zichron area.

The zeal with which these young men conducted their watch, their knowledge of the Arabs and of every track and cave in the district, brought high dividends at the grape harvest, and the conservative elders of Zichron accepted the innovation of Jewish watchmen. The Gideonites were melodramatic, as were most things connected with Alex, and went in for military discipline, secret initiation and vows of eternal brotherhood. Nevertheless they were a serious group, prepared to do anything which furthered the welfare of the community. Possibilities of work in those days were all too few. As the sons of the land-owning settlers began to take work which could have gone to the new immigrants, who, for all their valour, were still the barefooted ones, the Workers' paper launched a campaign against Zichron, the Gideonites and even Aaron's Experiment Station, although Aaron was busy with his scientific work and had nothing to do with the Gideonites.

Absalom was twenty-three, melancholy at the recent death of his father and fuming at the perpetual frustration of his relationship with Rivka. Sarah was his age, and by the standards of Zichron she should already be married and in her own home. Sarah was only too conscious that she was standing in Rivka's way. But there are some women who seem on a pedestal above the reach of the average man, and such was Sarah. Aaron's status and her own reserve made her unapproachable to the young men of their acquaintance. She had come to be more and more in charge of the home as Malka's strength gave way, and when Malka died at the age of fifty-three, Sarah became the centre of the family, ministering to the needs of the grown-up children and filling the home with her loving presence. She had her mother's strength of character and the same ability to show a calm, cheerful face to the world no matter how great her unhappiness. The family, occupied with their own concerns, had no idea of the pain Sarah was suffering. The idea grew in her mind to run away, to escape to some distant place, so that Rivka could have her freedom and she could hide her love for Absalom.

Her opportunity came. A wealthy, well set up young merchant from Constantinople was presented to Ephraim Aaronsohn as a prospective husband for Sarah. Sarah agreed even before she had seen him. At the betrothal she kissed Rivka gently and asked her to make her happiness complete by joining them in a double wedding. But Rivka, always capricious, refused, saying she wanted a wedding of her own.

In March 1914 Sarah was married and left for her new home in Constantinople. Her marriage hung like a pall over them all that hot restless summer. The family was bereft, not even able to find consolation in Sarah's happiness, for she had none.

For Sarah her marriage had not been a cynical contract, but one into which she had entered honourably, full of good will and hopes that she would be able to attain what she had longed for all her life—a home and children to whom she could devote her strength and her wisdom, and all the love stored up in her heart. She had no overriding ambitions, no wish to dominate, only the desire to work together with her husband, to bend her will to his, and to make him happy. In her husband's home she was relegated to the dim nether world which all women inhabited in the oriental-style ménage of conventional middle-class Constantinople. Her husband, who was genuinely fond of her, had been given a rigid, old-fashioned German education, and his business success had encased him in a male self-satisfaction which nothing could penetrate. Far from being regarded as an equal and a helpmeet by her husband, Sarah's independent ways and free, unhampered ideas were subject to constant correction.

Sarah's lonely letters found an echo in the heart of Absalom. He knew now what he had not realized before. Rivka, who now sat so silent and sad, was the adored little sister. Sarah was the woman he loved. "You do not know, beloved and longed for child," Absalom wrote to Sarah, "and you cannot imagine, what we ourselves did not imagine before, how great a part of my heart you took when you went away. . . . We two who remain are drawn together and try to forget, but someone is missing, missing. But these words are selfish. If we who are left amongst our own, and in our own homes, are so full of complaints, how difficult and bitter it must be for you. For you, poor child, are alone, from morning until evening, alone and unhappy."

Chapter 3

THE WAR

SIX weeks later war broke out in Europe. As was inevitable after twenty years of strong and well-organized German propaganda in the Middle East, Turkey joined Germany against the Allies. Through the slats of her window, barred in harem fashion, Sarah watched with sinking heart the "Conquerors of Egypt", the soldiers of Djemal Pasha's Fourth Army, marching past. She saw this raggle-taggle army as a horde of locusts about to descend on Palestine, for she knew that Zichron and the other settlements would be stripped bare by their pitiless demands.

Detachments of Germans accompanied them. Sarah had the dread of the Germans which Aaron had inspired in all the Aaronsohns, for he hated Germany with a hatred that amounted to foresight. The Jews of Germany had at that time achieved a golden age which had not been equalled since Spain before the Inquisition, but Aaron's uncanny ability to recognize the strains in a plant and its capacities long before it bore fruit, operated in the political field as well. For many years he had been warning his friends in America against the German danger, and in his travels about the Middle East he had watched with deep misgiving Germany's careful and steady plans for eastern expansion. He had long decided that only under Great Britain would the Jews be able to rebuild Palestine. The British had been the first to understand and support the Jewish national movement, and their record in the administration and regeneration of backward countries had shown them to be better equipped for the task than any other European nation. This coincided with Britain's own strategic interests in the area, for Aaron was convinced that Britain's hold on the Suez Canal could never be secure without control of Palestine.

In cryptic letters to her family in Zichron Sarah began to sound out their plans. "Are you interesting yourself in broderie anglaise?" she wrote to her sister in French, which, together with Hebrew, was the family language. "I know how you like flowers. There are interesting things to be seen behind the boul," she wrote another time, using the French word for boulevard which is the Hebrew word for stamp. Under the stamps she gave them the first news of the Armenian massacres.

Thanks to the deep understanding between the two sisters, Sarah was able to keep her family informed of events, and she herself was aware of the troubles and the dangers which had befallen Palestine. Sarah prayed that the Yishuv would be able to hold out until the British came. Like most people in Constantinople, she knew the unpreparedness and the incapacity of the Turkish Army, its lack of organization and even of ammunition, and she watched with growing despair as the Allies suffered their defeat at Gallipoli.

Her husband disapproved of Sarah's absorption in politics. The situation was quite clear and, as far as he was concerned, in order. He was a loyal Turkish subject, and Turkey's ally Germany, whose culture and people he admired above all, was winning the war. Sarah was able to conceal her torment under her habitual silence. "Only God knows how sick to death I am of myself, and the life that I live here," she wrote to her family. "How long? In Palestine hunger and poverty reign, and I sit here for eternity, unable to lift a hand to help my people."

And then suddenly letters stopped coming from Palestine. For three months no news from Rivka, no news from Alex or Absalom. What were they doing was too dangerous to be entrusted to the post in any guise.

When war broke out, Aaron bitterly regretted having to stay in Palestine, for he saw that the time had come for the partnership he had been dreaming of. Aaron was the first, and at that time the only one in Palestine, to recognize the possibility of uniting British and Jewish interests in the Middle East; official Zionism, which had its headquarters in Berlin, still maintained that the Jewish future was bound up with the fate of Turkey. Aaron's responsibility to the institution he had founded forced him to remain where he was, and he soon became involved in the general struggle to safeguard the Yishuv from destruction. The blockade of the Ottoman ports had stopped the incoming flow of commodities and funds on which the Jewish community depended. It was a year of drought, and the impoverished country had now to support the army which extorted to the point of vandalism. Anything that could feed or transport man or beast was taken on the long trek to the south, where, on the sands surrounding Beersheba, preparations were being made for the big attack on the Suez Canal.

Aaron was not so alarmed at the economic situation as he was by the sinister change which had come over the Turkish Government's attitude towards Zionism. Previously, in spite of traditional obstruction, there had been few obstacles to development which money could not overcome. Free to foster their national culture and the use of the Hebrew language, the Jews had felt, if not independent, at least at home in the land of their ancestors. Now they were being methodically robbed of all they had gained. Although few recognized it, this was part of a deliberate policy. The Turks had set out to put an end to all minorities whose national tendencies were a threat to the Ottoman Empire.

Reluctant as the Turks were to co-operate with the Germans in military matters, they eagerly responded in spheres more congenial to themselves, and from the beginning of the war they displayed an organized brutality and an ingenuity quite new in the history of Turkish maltreatment of subject peoples. Aaron, who believed that the German poison lay very deep and that even the sources of German science were tainted, was convinced that the Germans were trying out their more extreme racial ideologies on the Turks, like people who try a new medicine on the dog. Henry Morgenthau, U.S. Ambassador in Turkey during that period and deeply concerned with the Armenian atrocities, came quite independently to the same conclusion, that the Turks were using methods new to them, including—as he wrote in his memoirs—"the idea of deporting people *en masse*, which is, in modern times, exclusively Germanic".[1]

Under a Turkish "specialist" in Zionist affairs, sent from Constantinople, many of the techniques were mobilized against the Jews which later became familiar when the Germans were

[1] *The Secret of the Bosphorus* (Hutchinson, London, 1918)

preparing their second attempt to dominate the world. The Jews were classed as foreigners and traitors who had to be eradicated for the good of the country. Mass expulsions were begun, brutally and without warning, when men, women and children were rounded up from streets and homes in Jaffa and herded off to the port without being allowed to collect their possessions or make contact with their families. The local population was incited by the Jehad, which made it a religious duty to exterminate those of a different faith. This call to Holy War had been thought up by the Germans as a way of rousing the Moslems to fight against the Allies. The Turks were happy to use it as a means of ridding themselves of their non-Moslem minorities, Jew and Christian alike. "Beat them whenever you find them. Kill them wherever you can," ordered the Sultan in a pamphlet which officials circulated among the Arab villages. The German consuls in Palestine had been very active among the Arabs previously, proving that the Germans were a form of Moslem people.

In the months of January and February, when Djemal Pasha was making final preparations for his attack on Egypt, oppression rose to a crescendo. Although the Turks believed that as soon as they appeared to "liberate" them, the Egyptians would rise against the British, there was panic in the air. Detachments of soldiers were stationed in Zichron and Hadera and all the larger Jewish centres overlooking the coast. The possibility of attack from the sea, which caught the attention of Churchill alone among the British military leaders, never ceased to worry the Turks and the Germans until the end of the war. The settlers were ordered to hand over all weapons, a sinister command, for this was their one means of defence against sudden violence. The first news of the Armenian massacres had arrived in Palestine; the Armenians too had been disarmed before being slaughtered like sheep.

Although the official leaders, in a misguided attempt to placate the Turkish authorities, urged the settlements to hand over their weapons, the young people of Zichron and Hadera, like Ha-Shomer, refused to do so. They handed over a few and buried the rest. Someone must have informed on the Zichronites, and Alex and several others were taken off to prison. When three days of bastinado brought no results, the Turks produced their trump card. They would carry off a number of the young girls of Zichron and hand them over to the officers until the weapons were produced. The people of Zichron had no alternative but to dig up the treasured arms and hand them over. "As we came limping home through the streets of Zichron," wrote Alex, "I caught sight of my own Smith and Wesson revolver in the hands of a boy of fifteen, the son of a well-known Arab outlaw. The Turks had not only taken our weapons, they had distributed them among the Arabs."[1]

The Aaronsohns decided to send Rivka to Beirut in order not to have the responsibility of a young girl in the house. She was placed in the American college there and acted as Aaron's contact with the American consul, who had a battleship waiting in the harbour for the protection of American interests.

Aaron turned his semi-official connection into a powerful weapon on behalf of the Yishuv. America was at that time the most important neutral in the world and few realized to what extent Aaron was responsible for the material and political support which came from the United States and enabled the Jewish community in Palestine to survive the dangers and deprivations which ravaged other minorities within the Ottoman Empire. Relief began arriving immediately to the otherwise blockaded country, first money and then supplies. Aaron was appointed from America to take charge of distribution for the northern half of Palestine. When the Turkish officers started laying hands on the supplies, Aaron did not hesitate to complain to Djemal Pasha in person. This was more than a courageous step. It was a very dangerous one.

The powerful chief of the Fourth Army was one of the ill-reputed triumvirate of the Young Turk Movement, together with Enver Pasha, Minister of War, and Tallal Bey, Minister of the Interior. A short, almost hunchbacked man, with ferocious black eyes which glared from a pale face surrounded by a thick black beard, Djemal ordered hangings with the capricious

[1] Alexander Aaronsohn, *With the Turks in Palestine* (Riverside Press, Cambridge, U.S.A., 1916)

irascibility of the Red Queen in *Alice in Wonderland*. He was an open enemy of Zionism and had been jailing and exiling leading members of the community from the moment he arrived in Palestine.

By a happy coincidence, agricultural reform was his overriding passion, and one of his ambitions was to make a reputation for himself as an administrator by improving agriculture in the area under his authority. He had already established several agricultural schools—on paper. Aaron was no European with that automatic assumption of superiority which the Young Turk leaders bitterly resented. He was the son of a Palestinian farmer and an Ottoman subject. His effect on Djemal Pasha was powerful and lasting, and he came to be regarded by the chief of the Fourth Army as one of his most valued colleagues. Eliezer Ben Yehuda has said in his memoirs that Aaron was probably the only person in Palestine at that time, not only among the Jews, whom the despot treated with respect.

From all sides frantic appeals came to Aaron, for he alone dared approach Djemal and tell him of the plunderings of the army and the other outrages which were being perpetrated against the population. Once Djemal, enraged by so much audacity and wondering if he should get rid of so troublesome and popular a citizen, said to him point blank: "I wonder, Aaronsohn, what you would say if I had you hanged."

Not a muscle moved in Aaron's face.

"I could say nothing, Excellency," he replied, "but the weight of my heavy corpse would crack the wood so loud that the sound would be heard in America."

Djemal, under this covert threat of American reprisals, attempted nothing further against Aaron. In fact, he continued to regard him as his highest agricultural authority.

Aaron's success with the Generalissimo strengthened his contempt for the leaders of the Yishuv, and he told them openly: "You know how to listen when Djemal Pasha speaks; I have forced him to listen when I speak to him." Much as they hated this "God's gift to Samaria, and the exponent of American bluff", as one of the leaders of the time has referred to him in his memoirs, they were forced to turn to him with increasing frequency, for it was evident that nothing short of complete annihilation was intended for a community whose European roots and nationalist ambitions must, according to Turkish logic, inevitably make them a subversive element.

Actually, the Turkish authorities, forgetting that 1800 years of exile separated the Jews of 1915 from their last national uprising in Palestine, misread the situation. At no time did it occur to the Jewish leaders to rise in rebellion. They were too well trained in the tradition of rendering unto Caesar that which was Caesar's, and all they strove for was legal and loyal co-operation with the Turkish authorities. This attitude had nothing to do with character or courage; it went so far back that it had become an instinct. From the Roman conquest onward, it had been obvious that any Jewish rising in Palestine could only mean crushing defeat. The leaders and sages of Israel realized that under those circumstances the national spirit might work like a dangerous explosive, causing outbursts which could bring about the extermination of the people. For centuries, therefore, the leaders had tried to subdue the national feeling and enhance the religious side of Jewish life, and so keep alive the nation and its ties with Palestine until the Jews could regain their homeland.

In one short generation the Jewish youth of Palestine had reverted to type. The humble, cautious attitude of the exiles was anathema to Palestine-reared Aaron, Absalom and their friends, and their natural instinct was to revolt against the authority which threatened to destroy their national existence. "It is no people which allows itself to be strangled, and gives itself up to slaughter," declared Absalom. "A people is one which knows how to fight, to conquer, and in time of need to attack. That is the kind of people I want us to be."

There was another group in the country which also rebelled against the conciliatory attitude of the official leaders of the Yishuv, and they too were making plans. The members of Ha-Shomer were secretly accumulating arms and organizing themselves to defend the Yishuv. They also were eager for the overthrow of Ottoman rule, but the 1800-year-old edict of the sages was still in their blood, and they knew themselves too weak to pit their tiny strength against the rulers.

Even if Absalom had known in advance that those who live

by the sword die by the sword, and the weak inherit the earth, it would not have mattered. He had his answer ready when he was 17, still a student in France. "I am prepared to die even tomorrow, and alone, to achieve the Jewish revival", he had written.

It was during the critical month of January 1915, before the attack on the Canal and when Arab incitement was at its height, that a neighbouring sheikh, a quarrelsome evil man, informed the authorities that the people of Hadera were selling wheat to the British. That this was a trumped-up charge was known to everybody, probably even to the German Military Governor of Jerusalem, General Back, who sent a detachment of Turkish soldiers to Hadera one night in blinding rain to arrest thirteen of the young men and bring them to Jerusalem for a military trial. Absalom was one of them. And another was his friend, Liova Schneersohn. While they were rounding up the young men, Absalom managed to slip away in the darkness and galloped through the storm over the mountain top to Zichron to inform Aaron. Alex was there too. It was serious, they agreed. Unless some way was found of intervening, the thirteen were likely to hang.

Aaron listened in silence as Absalom railed against the cautious policy of the elders who expected them to do nothing but bend their backs to the rod and were terrified of disloyalty to the Turkish "motherland". "We can't let idiots dictate our policy. Our worst enemy is the Turk. Now that the hour of his downfall has struck, can we stand by and do nothing? The Turks are right to suspect us. They know the ruin they are planning for us. Anyone who didn't have a rabbit's heart would be proud to spy against them, if it would help to bring the English."

Aaron sent Absalom off into the night again with encouragement. He would immediately contact his friend, the Vali of Beirut, the highest authority in the area. When Absalom was free again they would talk about the next step.

The thirteen were taken off in the early morning, amidst the weeping of the village. Absalom refused to share his comrades' depression. "To the devil with all this sentiment. You have to be ready for the worst. If the time has come for us to die, we'll die. A lot of people are being killed in Europe. Why should we be better than they?" Someone said, "But if we do die, we must die for justice, not because someone has told a lie about us." Absalom turned to him in disgust and pointed to one of the Turkish soldiers: "From this you expect justice? For thinking it you deserve to be hanged."

By the time they stopped for lunch the young men had regained their spirits. They ate, sang, joked, and drank the wine and brandy their families had provided for the journey. All but Absalom. He sat quietly by himself. He was thinking: "Aaron left to see the Vali of Beirut at such and such a time. He arrived in Damascus that evening. Military requisitions, irregular trains, delays. At Beirut, interview with the Vali. If he has won, the Vali is discussing with the military authorities. Bad telegraphic service, long parleys. If the Vali has won out, civil investigation—everything goes well. If there is some error in this calculation: court-martial, order from Back, a dossier from the Kaimakam of Jenin, the Prussian pride; and we're in a pretty fix. The whole business depends on which arrives in Jerusalem first—we, or the telegram from Beirut!"[1]

It was evening when they came to Jaffa, and they were kept there for the night. Absalom developed an attack of malaria. Liova Schneersohn sat beside him, putting cold compresses on his head. Liova's family had lived in Hadera for some years, but Liova had remained in Russia to complete his studies. He was an anarchist and steeped in Russian thought, but the blood of two hundred years of Jewish mystics ran in his veins and he could not turn his back on Palestine. As befitting the descendant of a long line of Hasidic rabbis, he was an irrepressible poet, a dreamer in the early days of the century when there were still new worlds to dream about, and he and Absalom had become fast friends.

"Put a lot of ice on my head," Absalom demanded. "Put a sea of ice on my head. My blood is boiling. All the East is burning in me."

His thoughts were burning in him as well. "You are cold people, people who make calculations. You like mathematics. You cannot understand the beauty of the East. My father was from the north, like you. But I am different from him. I am a

[1] Absalom's unpublished report to Miss Szold, Alexandria, 1915.

Jew of the East. I can understand the mystery, the beauty, the gaiety of the East. The hot nights in summer, the windy nights in winter. I hear the song of the Bedui, the song he sings on the night watch, and it says much more to me than the music of your Wagner and your Beethoven. Wait," he said excitedly, "we'll show the world."

"Absalom, my friend, don't get so excited, the compress is falling from your head."

"Get away from me, you cold man of the north. We'll show all the world what our people can do. I don't mean the 'Jews' from the Galuth, the miserable ones from Berdichev and Mohilev, but we, from the land of Israel, the new ones, the unknown until now. The proud Jews, the brave ones, whose hearts are not eaten by the germs of the Galuth. Don't you feel that a new generation is born? Don't you hear it coming with slow steps, angry, vengeful? Don't you hear, poor thing? Why did you come? Why did you leave your revolutions? Your unsuccessful self-defence? The impossibility of fighting like a man, of dying like a hero? Listen, there's something I want to tell you. I've wanted to tell you for a long time. Don't think I'm talking from fever."

And Absalom spoke to Liova about the war and the chance "for us, the Jews. We can't defend ourselves against the Arabs. We haven't any arms. What are we going to do? Sit with folded hands? Are we preparing ourselves to give help to the redeeming army? It's impossible to remain idle now. We must make contact with the English, somehow or other. Surely we can find brave men amongst us, who will answer the call. I know we can. You wouldn't hesitate for a moment, would you?

"We will go and make contact with the enemy. With their help we will get arms. We will reveal to them the secrets of the country. We will organize the freeing of Palestine. We'll do this in secret, without any committee meetings or discussions.

"If they catch us on the borders, or here in Palestine, they'll sentence us as spies, and hang us. Good. They'll hang us. They'll shoot us. Even if the whole Yishuv suffers for this, we must do it. We must do it, so that we will have the right to tell the world, not only about our agricultural settlements, but that our blood has been spilled for our country. Whoever doesn't want to join us in this can stay at home!"

He was terribly excited. Liova tried to quieten him. "It's not hard to guess what will be happening here in the country. But what if someone finds out what we're doing and informs on us?"

Absalom smiled his wry, mocking smile. "They're already preparing to condemn us to death. And for what? If we must die, better to die for something we've done, as my father used to say. And remember, courage and daring are the decisive things in life!"[1]

Absalom's fever gradually subsided and they fell asleep. The next morning an order arrived from Jerusalem to send them home immediately. Absalom was satisfied with his beloved chief. He had won the race. This surely was a good omen. Absalom and Liova embraced each other, vowed eternal friendship, and were back in Hadera before nightfall.

[1] From the unpublished memoirs of Liova Schneersohn

Chapter 4

REBELLION

FROM the outbreak of war everybody in Palestine had imagined that it would only be a matter of days, or at most weeks, before the British would come and conquer Palestine, if only to assure the safety of the Canal. The Turks, and the Germans too, thought the Allies were preparing to invade the country, and many of their oppressive measures were carried out in haste and panic.

There was little to stop the British from coming through the desert, and less to stop them landing anywhere along the coast. This "obvious manœuvre", for which Churchill was pleading,[1] was dismissed in London as "venturesome and impracticable", although until late in 1915 no artillery existed in Palestine, there were no aeroplanes until even later, and coastal defence was in the hands of a reluctant militia of local Arabs. The fact was, as Wavell wrote, that at least until the end of 1916 "the Asiatic fronts were left to look after themselves".[2]

The population, Druze, Jews, Mohammedans and Christians alike, looked for the overthrow of the Turkish yoke which had lain so heavily on them before the war and was now becoming intolerable. Had the British landed, they would have been hailed as liberators and their ranks would have been augmented from the population—as they were later, though by then two and a half catastrophic years had considerably changed the situation.

It was the advent of the British that Aaron was waiting for. He intended to put himself at the disposal of the invading army as soon as it arrived. But the liberators did not come, and Aaron watched with mounting anxiety as every day, every hour, brought some new and more dreadful blow to the Jewish settlers in Palestine. In April came the incredible news that the British had landed at Gallipoli. They had chosen to pit their

[1] *The World Crisis, 1911-1919* (Odhams, London), pp. 1177-8
[2] Wavell, *The Palestine Campaigns* (Constable, London, 1936), p. 18

strength against the barrier of the Dardanelles when they could so easily have crushed the Turks through Palestine. Difficult as it was to believe, for the omniscience of British Intelligence was almost universally accepted, Aaron was forced to the conclusion that the British really did not know what was happening inside the Ottoman Empire.

It was then, in the spring of 1915, while the leaders of the Yishuv were searching for ways of appeasing the anger of the Turks, that Aaron decided to take the fate of the Yishuv in his own hands.[1] Absalom had been right. The British in Egypt must be contacted and told the real situation in Palestine. Aaron, Absalom and Alex were sitting in the little room at the top of the Station, talking in low voices by the blurred light of coarse home-made candles. Every window was shuttered, and the watch-dog Goliath had been left unchained to prowl along the acacia borders and give warning of any approaching danger.

"Today American ships are sailing in the Mediterranean, and we still have contact with the outside world," Aaron said. "But soon they'll be taking their ships away from here and we'll be cut off from the whole world, an easy prey to the Turks. The English must be convinced that in their own interests they must attack immediately, while the Turks are still disorganized, and the population is still able to help them." Aaron himself would organize the network of espionage which would provide the British with all the information they needed for the speedy conquest of the country. The Station at Athlit would be the cover for their activities.

He had achieved his Station, his life's ambition, at the end of years of disappointment and frustration. But he was prepared to risk it all, after only three years of free, unimpeded work. Many scientists work on through wars, indifferent to corrupt régimes. But not men like Aaron. He would not allow a personal passion for agricultural research to blind him to the needs of his people. And he believed, with every fibre of his being, that a German victory, or even the continuation of Turkish rule, meant extermination for the Jews.

Aaron had no illusions about his status. "If I had left the

[1] Prof. Dinor (Editor), *The History of Jewish Self-Defence* (Tel-Aviv, 1954, in Hebrew), p. 353

country and openly taken service on the English side, it would have been bad enough. My character and my standing would be impaired. But I did worse. I stayed where I was. I organized a whole movement, I became connected with the Intelligence Office, as people who are afraid of words call it. I do not like mincing words. Put it clearly, and say I became a spy."[1]

Spy. That was a word with a terrible connotation among Jews, especially those in Palestine. In the countries of persecution from which they had come, it had meant an *agent provocateur*, someone who betrayed them to the oppressing Government. But as Aaron had said, he was not afraid of words. "I stand firmly before the tribunal of my own conscience."[2]

There was no question of accepting payment for their services. "Nobody can say we are doing this for money. Leave that for Arab spies", said Aaron bluntly. "We needn't expect any honours for our work either," he warned Alex and Absalom. "Nobody is more conservative in this respect than the English, and I don't see them showering honours on spies, no matter how great their services. We can't even be sure that they will have confidence in us. They may think us capable of betraying them just as we are of betraying the Turks. We do not do this for vengeance either. We do it because we hope we are serving our own cause."

Absalom already had plans for getting to Egypt, and it was decided that Alex should go with him. But escape from the country was not easy. One plan after another fell through. At last, in June, the American warship *Des Moines* called to take to Egypt persons expelled from Palestine, and Alex sailed in it with a forged Spanish passport. Rivka was brought back from Beirut to go with him.

Alex was twenty-seven years old, tall, handsome, dynamic and very sure of his powers of persuasion when he arrived in Egypt, hot on his mission to rescue the Jews of Palestine and serve the British war effort. Far from receiving the warm welcome he expected, Alex found himself up against a brick wall. The High Command in Cairo considered that its duties consisted solely of guarding the Canal and keeping order in Egypt.

[1] Letter to Judge Mack, October 9th, 1916. Copy in possession of Mrs J. L. Magnes.   [2] Ibid.

The Palestine sector, which contained the key to the Middle East, was completely overlooked.

In February the Turks had almost caught the British napping in their defence of the Suez Canal, and nothing but their own stupidity prevented them from doing serious damage. A month later representatives of the Palestine refugees in Egypt came to put themselves at the disposal of the British for the conquest of Palestine, which they believed must automatically follow. The delegation, which included Captain Trumpledor, famous Jewish hero of the Russo-Japanese war, complete with two bronze and two gold medals, was told by General Maxwell, Commander of the British forces in Egypt: "I have heard nothing about an offensive in Palestine and I doubt whether such an offensive will be launched at all."[1]

If Palestine did not rate high as a potential battle front, it was of even less interest to the people in charge of Intelligence in Cairo at that time. They were a small group of active and determined people whose interests were concentrated in another direction. A few months later they became the Arab Bureau which, as Lawrence frankly put it, "set out to bend England's efforts towards fostering the new Arabic world in hither Asia".[2] Not unreasonably in a world at war, Britain hoped to gain some military advantage from this. Their sole concern was to jockey the people they had chosen to rule the new Arab world (Sherif Hussein of Mecca, his sons, and the Beduin tribes of the Hejaz), into the rôle of a major threat to Turkish power.

When Alex suddenly appeared with figures to show that the British Army was capable of overcoming the Turks in Palestine, and offered to help by organizing rebellion in the midst of the Turkish Army, he was met with indifference, if not hostility. Nor were the British interested in his offer of an intelligence service providing full and accurate information about the situation in Palestine and Syria. "The Cairo people were very suspicious of Alex, and thought he might probably be an enemy agent" is the explanation offered by Lieutenant (later Sir) Leonard Woolley, who was in charge of Intelligence at Port

[1] V. Jabotinsky, *The Story of the Jewish Legion* (Acherman, New York, 1945), p. 41
[2] T. E. Lawrence, *Seven Pillars of Wisdom* (Cape, London, 1940), p. 56

Said at that time. "They therefore turned him down."[1]

Even to those with an open mind, which the members of the Arab Bureau did not have (as their unceasing hostility to the Balfour Declaration later proved), Alex might well have seemed a very suspicious kind of foreigner to a people notoriously suspicious of foreigners. This suave young man spoke English with an American accent; he was an Ottoman subject, a Palestinian and a Jew. The Jews of Palestine were an unknown quantity, non-existent to most people, and even by the Jews of the outside world they were not considered a factor to be reckoned with in policy making. Whatever the reason, Alex received short shrift from the people in Cairo, and when he wrote articles in the Egyptian papers pointing out the possibility and the necessity of attacking Turkey through Palestine, he was ordered not to linger too long in Egypt. Together with Rivka, he took a ship sailing for Gibraltar. His intention was to get back to America and try to do something there to open the eyes of the world to the Turkish situation.

Aaron and Absalom waited for news from Alex. Hearing nothing, Absalom again began to look for ways of getting out of the country. There were two routes, the Sinai Desert, which was covered by Turkish patrols, and the open sea. The desert route was only feasible in winter, for in summer there was the added danger of not finding water between posts, a distance of thirty to forty kilometres. "And thirst", admitted Absalom, who was prepared to risk the Turkish patrols, "is an enemy that is hard to conquer."

The alternative course, also risky but more easily managed, was to escape by sailing-boat at night from one of the beaches and then head for the open sea until picked up by one of the Allied ships on Mediterranean patrol. With the greatest caution, for any unusual activity would arouse the suspicion of the Arab fishermen along the coast, Absalom set about procuring a boat, a boatman and a trustworthy travelling companion, for the expedition could not be managed alone. Everything was arranged when, at the beginning of August, the French declared a hermetic blockade of the Syrian-Palestine coast and

[1] Interview with Leonard Woolf, reported in a letter of June 11th, 1957 to the author.

announced that every boat, of any sort, would be sunk on sight and without warning.

The situation was tense. No one knew what the next blow would be. It was now three months since Alex had left, and still no news. The Experiment Station's funds were almost gone.

Just at this time the *Des Moines* reappeared at Haifa. This would probably be her last call. Absalom tried to persuade Aaron to leave. He was desperately anxious to get Aaron out of the country, for he attracted danger as automatically as a lightning conductor attracts lightning. But Aaron refused. "I have the responsibility of a captain on board ship. A faithful captain abandons his ship when the waves sweep him off the bridge. I will abandon my responsibilities when I have a rope around my neck!"[1]

Absalom then agreed to try and make his escape by the *Des Moines*. On August 29th, at two in the morning, he said good-bye to Aaron and set off for the harbour alone, in high spirits, making nothing of the danger. "After a series of small frauds, falsification of a Russian passport, a slight disguise, etc., in other words, with not much skill but a lot of luck, I could verify the old proverb that 'Fortune favours the brave'," he reported.[2] At 1 a.m. on August 30th he found himself stretched on a bunk, waiting impatiently for the weighing of the anchor. At last the *Des Moines* moved off. "When the flag was taken down," he wrote, "I think the beautiful stars of the flag were never saluted with so light and grateful a heart, and with such artistic antics, for I got rid of all the accessories with which I had provided myself—a baroque hat, incredible eye-glasses, and a momentary seriousness of mien."[3]

Absalom's luck held. He had the address of an acquaintance, Charley Boutagy, a Christian Arab refugee who was working as an interpreter with Naval Intelligence at Port Said. Boutagy's father, formerly assistant British consul in Haifa, was to have been Absalom's companion in the escape by sea. Instead of contacting G.H.Q. in Cairo, as Alex had done, he went straight to Port Said. There he met Lt. Woolley, who was in charge.

Absalom presented a problem which was far from simple.

---

[1] Absalom's unpublished report to Miss Szold, Alexandria, 1915
[2] Ibid.   [3] Ibid.

The attitude of the Jews to Britain was not clear to the British, nor was it clear what sort of assistance they could provide. But, as Aaron was later to declare, "Lt. Woolley is that rarity among the English. He has intuition. He can sense things." There could be no higher praise from Aaron, for all his life was a struggle against people who could not sense the importance of a situation nor grasp its scope.

Lt. Woolley was deeply impressed by the tall, sinewy young man with the blazing eyes and wide, sensitive mouth. He never for a moment doubted the sincerity of his intentions nor his ability to do what he offered to do. While not prepared to discuss Absalom's plan for armed rebellion, he agreed to use the group at Athlit for intelligence. The warship which passed along the coast of Palestine from time to time to make contact with agents in the Lebanon would call at Athlit as often as signalled. He introduced Absalom to Captain Weldon of Naval Intelligence, a bluff, burly Yorkshireman who was a constant passenger on the ship and gave Absalom signals for making contact with it.

"The die is cast. Our fate becomes more and more linked with the Allied cause," wrote Absalom to Miss Henrietta Szold, the secretary of the American Committee, to whom, at Aaron's behest, he was reporting on the affairs of the Station and the dangers threatening the Yishuv. While Absalom could reveal nothing of the reasons which brought him to Egypt, he could not prevent his love for the English from flowing into words: "If there is a nation whose attitude towards us is even finer than that of America, which is above all praise, it is that of the English nation. For if America offered its bread and its gold to friends who had need of it, England let this bread and this gold into an enemy country; sent it, almost. And with what delicacy, what discretion. . . ."

This confidential report to Miss Szold was a manuscript of 200 typewritten pages, a mixture of statistics, poetry and political analysis, written in exquisite French. Since Counter-espionage was one of the few things which the Turks did well, the report was smuggled out of Egypt in the lining of the suit-case of a Palestinian refugee. It was the first report of this nature to reach America. "This is one of the most excellent and most important documents that I have ever read in my life," declared Judge Louis Brandeis, Justice of the Supreme Court and friend of President Wilson.

Absalom found out from Palestine refugees in Alexandria that Alex and Rivka were in Gibraltar, waiting for a passage to America. America, still neutral, was inclined to be pro-German, a feeling natural among a population so largely drawn from Germany and German-speaking countries. The Jews had an additional reason for favouring Germany. Her attitude to the Jews had not, up till then, gone beyond the usual civilized brands of anti-Semitism, while the pogroms of Allied Russia had been the worst in history.

Alex, who had considerable journalistic and oratorical gifts, had decided that these were the most useful weapons to use against the Turks. He later achieved wide publicity through both mediums and wrote the book *With the Turks in Palestine* which Lord Northcliffe, then head of British War Propaganda, had translated into six languages and circulated in neutral countries.

Alex wrote to Absalom urging him to join him in America, where they could carry on a joint campaign. "I haven't any intention of coming to America, or of getting mixed up in journalism," Absalom replied. "If I have things to say, then I have to say them in the room of the leader, in the office of those of influence and not in the columns of the newspaper. I know that the objective we have set ourselves is difficult, and the way will be long. But that doesn't bother me. My aim is to succeed: either to be victorious or die."

Early in November 1915 the little French warship which was making contact with the spies at Tyre, on the Phoenician coast of the Lebanon, took Absalom with them. In high spirits on board ship Absalom wrote a letter to a Palestinian friend and relative in Alexandria, Raphael Aboulafia. Raphael's mother's family also came from Russia and the Aboulafias were among the oldest and most distinguished Jewish families of the Orient, famous for their rabbis, scholars and statesmen, among them Samuel Aboulafia who had been treasurer to Peter of Castille in the fourteenth century. Raphael was twenty-four, darkly handsome, and as passionately patriotic as Absalom. He had

been sent to the cavalry when war broke out. Determined not
to fight for the Turks, he had escaped from Palestine during the
expulsions from Jaffa and became a regimental sergeant with
the Zion Mule Corps which Captain Trumpledor had formed
from refugees in Egypt to fight at Gallipoli. Aboulafia had been
wounded and sent back to Alexandria, just in time to see
Absalom and hear about his plans.

"What shall I tell you?" wrote Absalom. "Long live the
King, and long live our country! Can you imagine what it is to
travel the whole morning along the shores of our land? At this
moment I could even love sickening Tel Aviv!" Absalom had
told his friends that he was prepared to deliver letters to their
families in Palestine. Only Raphael had responded. "Perhaps
the others haven't any confidence, but I can tell you that in
another ten to fifteen days, mail will be coming and going
between us. I shall be returning in six to eight weeks. You know
my address, of course! c/o Lt. C. L. Woolley, Esq., Headquarters, Port Said."

In the middle of the night, when the moon had gone down,
the ship anchored in the shadow of the old Crusader castle
whose vast bulk rose from the coastline at Athlit, and Absalom
was rowed ashore. He was loaded with presents for everyone
and as gay as a boy on a school outing. The sailors thought they
had never met such a delightful and courageous young man in
all their lives. Leaping happily up the steps to the Station, he
surprised his beloved Aaron, still at work as usual, and gave
him the good news from Egypt. In another ten days, half an
hour after the moon set, a ship would pass that way again.
Absalom would be waiting on the seashore, smoking a cigarette
until a sailor came in a little boat to collect the information they
had prepared.

Chapter 5

CONTACT BROKEN

A ARON had already worked out a vast and thorough scheme of Intelligence, for his powers within the country were fabulous. He had been authorized to direct a campaign against the locusts, a step unprecedented in the Ottoman Empire. Djemal Pasha had learned, too late, that only by drastic measures and complete mobilization could the country be safeguarded from the impending attack and the army saved from starvation.

This brought Aaron into close contact with all the highest military and civil authorities in Palestine, Syria and the Lebanon, and gave him the possibility of opening official doors in Turkey itself. In his possession were military orders, issued by Djemal Pasha, enabling him to have his dispatches and those of his assistants conveyed as war messages with priority over ordinary government dispatches. He had orders to commanders of companies and battalions to move when and wherever he required them. He was authorized to buy out of the army anyone necessary to him in his campaign. Dozens of young men had already been bought out and stationed at important points.

Not all Aaron's supporters were young. Some of them were of professional status; hence the value of their contacts. They included political opponents, "Men who not very long before were opposing me, in mere political trifles, and for this were talking of drawing their revolvers on me, these same men, when they realized I was not playing at trifles, were risking their lives in order to bring me any slight information which might be of value to the cause."[1]

Everything that could be of assistance to the High Command in Egypt, economic and political as well as military, was noted, recorded and deposited in the leather pouch which was kept in a tin box buried in the cellar of the Experiment Station.

[1] Letter to Judge Mack.

Absalom would take the pouch to the seashore with him when the ship called again.

But days passed and weeks, and the ship did not call, although for some time it could be seen crossing and recrossing on its patrol. They signalled, using the code which Captain Weldon had written out for them, even attempting to attract the ship by day as they grew more desperate. At nights Absalom and Liova lay on the beach until dawn, hoping against hope that the boat would turn up. But it was no use. The contact which Absalom had achieved with so much difficulty was broken. The ship never returned again to the meeting-place within the shadow of the Crusader castle.

The British had changed their system of signalling. One of their Arab spies in the Lebanon had been told to inform Athlit. The Arabs decided to get rid of their competitors by not telling them of the change of code. The next time the ship signalled, Absalom did not understand the message or know how to answer, and so it ceased to come. Lt. Woolley, disappointed, decided that the ardent young man had given up the idea, or had been prevented by his family from engaging in such a hazardous undertaking.

Absalom had made a mistake in not arranging to keep in touch with one of his friends in Egypt, someone who could have come to the shores of Athlit and sought him out if necessary. He had been so certain that he would be returning to Egypt immediately, so full of confidence in the British, that it had never occurred to him that such a thing might happen. Although Raphael Aboulafia went several times to Lt. Woolley to ask for news of Absalom, he could not help. He was from Jaffa, and only someone acquainted with the Athlit area could have made the journey at night.

Meanwhile Absalom and Aaron were desperate. If the Captain had not returned, how would they know what form the military activities of the British would take, and what would be the fate of Palestine? Perhaps they were no longer interested in Palestine and Syria? Or did they not trust the Jews at Athlit? At last Absalom's patience gave out, and he decided that he must get to Egypt again and find out why the arrangement between him and Woolley had broken down. He felt it a debt of honour to try and establish contact again, lest Woolley, who had given his moral guarantee, be held responsible. "I don't want the Commander to think that the first young Jew in his service betrayed him", he wrote.

The only way to get to Egypt now was through the Sinai Desert, which stretched south of Beersheba. This meant passing through the Turkish front. Absalom would not let Aaron dissuade him. There was no front, he said, just companies of hungry and lazy soldiers, and after them there were Beduin, and after them the British. Until he got past the Turks he would be a locust official, and when he got to the Beduin, he would be a Beduin, Absalom assured him, and set off on horseback for the south, dressed in the semi-military uniform of Aaron's locust brigade.

These were the activities which were engaging Aaron and Absalom while Sarah sat lonely and longing for Palestine in her Constantinople's exile. Letters stopped reaching her when Rivka and Alex left the country, shortly to be followed by Absalom. Aaron may have feared to write, or perhaps his letters had gone astray. At last she could stand the strain no longer. On November 25th, 1915, she set out for Zichron, travelling for a month through war-time Turkey. All the way from the Taurus to Aleppo she saw deserted villages with only packs of disorderly soldiers, deserters and robbers moving among them like jackals, looking for loot. Sarah saw vultures hovering over children who had fallen dead by the roadside. She saw beings crawling along, maimed, starving and begging for bread. From time to time she passed soldiers driving before them with whips and rifle-butts whole families, men, women and children, shrieking, pleading, wailing. These were the Armenian people setting out for exile in the desert from which there was no return.

Sarah was never to know peace again. "Why are all these people going like sheep to the slaughter? Why aren't they defending themselves? Wouldn't it be better to kill some of these beasts and die honourably? What if the same thing happens to our people in Palestine?" That was the thought which tore perpetually at her mind.

Absalom had gone south two days before she arrived at Zichron. Aaron, in spite of his joy at having her home again, was busy and preoccupied, and merely told her that her "mad one" had gone to the desert to investigate the locust swarms coming from Egypt. But Sarah felt strangely troubled. "I won't believe that boy is safe until I see him with my own eyes," she said. Within a week Aaron was forced to tell her about the work which he and Absalom had undertaken for the relief of their beleaguered people, for news had reached him that Absalom was indeed in mortal danger. He had been caught by a Turkish patrol only a few kilometres from the no-man's-land which bordered the Canal. He was in prison in Beersheba and was to be hanged as a spy.

The Germans wanted to have him hanged without delay, but Aaron had been alerted immediately and gold began to circulate among the prison officials to keep Absalom alive until something could be done for him. The usual methods were used to extract information from him, but Absalom stuck to his story that he had gone into the desert to search for locust swarms. "Tell Aaron that my morale is high," he wrote. "They've examined all they have to examine, and now I'm writing poems in French. Don't worry about Mother. She is the youngest and bravest of all. You can tell her anything, but Sonia Belkind (his aunt), and my sister Shoshannah, best not tell anything."

He was writing to his cousin, Naaman Belkind of Rishon-le-Zion, their agent in the south. Naaman was a gentle, affable young man, not the sort of person to find in a secret organization, but he was so imbued with the patriotism of his dashing cousin that he would have followed him through fire. A Turkish battalion was stationed at Rishon, and Naaman, who worked at the wine cellars there, knew many of the commanders. They invited him to their parties, and he obtained information from them which he passed on to Athlit.

The messages reached Naaman through Yosef Lishansky, a watchman in the southernmost Jewish settlement of Ruhama. It was he who had got wind of Absalom's imprisonment, for this young man was as free as a Beduin and wandered about Beersheba and its military environs as he pleased. He began to smuggle messages in and out of Absalom's cell in the loaves of bread which prisoners were permitted to buy, as a matter of routine, since the prison ration was at starvation level. Danger was the spice of life to the stocky, blue-eyed, fair haired young Yosef, and he immediately associated himself with the espionage.

Aaron could not make a direct appeal to Djemal Pasha for help, but when he found that a local agricultural committee had been summoned to an interview with the governor, he asked one of them to suggest that the matter required Aaronsohn's expert advice. Afterwards, when Djemal asked Aaron to prepare a report for him immediately, Aaron replied that this was impossible; he could not do anything without his secretary, and the stupid Germans were going to hang him any day. Mention of the Germans was all he needed, for Djemal hated the Germans even more than he hated Zionists. He could not take direct action himself, since the case came under the Minister of War, his old enemy Enver Pasha, but he sent a telegram to the military tribunal in Jerusalem asking that Absalom be brought to trial immediately, as he had urgent and important work to do for the state.

Three weeks after his imprisonment Absalom was released. When he turned up at Zichron, bearded and very jaunty, he found a surprise waiting for him. He had not been told of Sarah's return.

Absalom already had another plan for getting in touch with the British—this time through Constantinople to neutral Rumania, where he would seek out British agents. Three days after his release from prison he was on his way north with Sarah to talk it over with Aaron, who was at Djemal Pasha's headquarters in Damascus.

Sarah, Aaron and Absalom were in Damascus for a week. They were never to be so happy again. Sarah's return dispelled the nightmare quality that had hung over their lives since the outbreak of the war, and the two men were as light-hearted as children. When Sarah remembered that she had not written to her husband in the two months since she left Constantinople, they insisted on adding postscripts to her letter. Absalom wrote in one corner: "I swear to you, you won't see her for a long time. The sky was wintry, and now it's bright again."

Aaron wrote in the other corner: "You are permitted to come and see her, but send Sarah to you? Don't even think of it. We love her very much here. Absalom, who is the best of men, asks me not to tell you what we are doing here for fear you will get red in the face, as you used to, when you were annoyed with him!"

Aaron introduced Absalom to Djemal Pasha, telling him that he wanted to send his brilliant young assistant to train with an uncle in Rumania who was engaged in important agricultural research work. Djemal could not give him permission to leave the Ottoman Empire—this came under the department of his old enemy, Tallal Bey, Minister of the Interior—but he permitted Absalom to go to Constantinople and provided him with letters of introduction.

Absalom left for Constantinople. Aaron took up quarters at the headquarters of the Fourth (Egyptian) Army, from which he simultaneously directed his two campaigns—one for the extermination of the locusts, the other for the destruction of the Turks. Sarah returned to Zichron. Her homecoming, for all its joy, was mixed with sadness. Only the old father and Aaron remained in the house which had been so full of life and laughter and vitality when Sarah had left it, and Aaron was now seldom at home. Sarah begged to be given a part in the espionage. Why should she not risk herself? She was strong and had no children. But Aaron would not hear of it. As long as she was at home to receive the messages, that was all he wanted his sister to do.

Absalom wasted almost a month in Constantinople, trying to get permission to leave the country. He received it at last and was preparing to set off for Rumania when a telegram arrived from Aaron asking him to return to Palestine immediately. What could it mean? In an agony of impatience Absalom had to turn again to the clerks and officials he had been worrying for the past month and try to get them to give him a permit for Palestine. It had now become very complicated, for with the end of the Gallipoli campaign troops were again being sent off to Palestine for a second try at the Suez Canal.

British Intelligence in Egypt had begun to get reports from their Beduin spies of tremendous concentrations of troops in the vicinity of the Sinai desert. According to the numbers which the Beduin gave, it sounded as if the Central European Powers had removed their troops from all the other fronts and had concentrated them there for an attack on the Canal. It was realized that while the reports were obviously exaggerated, there might be some truth in them. Lt. Woolley decided once more to contact the Athlit group, and Raphael Aboulafia was asked to look for someone who could make the contact. He found a Palestinian who had been with the Zion Mule Corps at Gallipoli, convalescing in a hospital in Cairo. He had been a coachman in the Haifa-Acre area and knew Aaronsohn and the surroundings of the Experiment Station.

One dark night he was brought to the coast opposite Athlit. He crawled up on to the shore, and moving cautiously from rock to bush, made his ways towards the Station, which lay on the other side of the main highway. At the highway he hid in the bushes, waiting for an opportunity to cross. He had to remain there the whole night, for there was a steady stream of troops and army transport moving southward until dawn. He remained hidden in the bushes the whole of the next day as well, not daring to cross the road for fear of falling into the hands of the soldiers. With nightfall, the troop movements began again and continued until morning. These were reinforcements for the second attack on the Suez Canal.

On the third night Rabin—this was his name—was able to cross the highway. He had just got into the fields leading to the Station when he saw the light of the ship returning from its Lebanon call. If he did not hurry back to the shore, he would be left stranded. Everything was in darkness at the Station. A dog began to bark inside the courtyard. Not daring to approach, he looked around for a place to leave the letter which he had been given to deliver. A plough loomed up through the darkness, and he hurriedly thrust the letter under the cross-bar.

Anything could have happened to the piece of paper thrust so precariously under the cross-bars of the plough; the least likely was that it would be found and delivered to the person for whom it was intended. But Absalom's destiny awaited him in Palestine. Early next morning, one of the workers caught sight of the little note and brought it to Aaron. It was from Lt. Woolley, and Aaron understood, to his joy, that the break in the connection had not been the fault of the British. In cautious terms Woolley wrote that in three weeks' time the ship would be passing again on its way to the Lebanon, and they should contact it, according to the instructions given. This was the note which brought Absalom back from Constantinople.

The moon waned and waxed again, but the ship did not come. Their disappointment was agonizing, bitterest of all to Aaron, who blamed himself for recalling Absalom so soon. Aaron found out later, but Absalom was never to know, that the ship had been torpedoed on its way north. Lt. Woolley was taken prisoner and sent to Turkey, whence he was only to emerge at the end of the war.

Chapter 6

AARON SETS OUT

ABSALOM wanted to return to Constantinople immediately, but Aaron would not hear of it. He had endangered himself too much and was already suspect. Before they could do anything further, they were overwhelmed by the most terrible enemy of all, the scourge of the Bible lands from time immemorial—the locusts.

For weeks swarms of locusts had been arriving from the south, and the whole country was covered with the females digging in the soil and depositing their egg packets. Aaron had dispatched special crews to the edge of the desert to try and stem the onrushing swarms before they could get to the crops. Inside the country thousands of soldiers were set to digging trenches into which the hatching locusts were driven and destroyed. Once the locusts got their wings, nothing could be done to stop them.

It was a hopeless fight. Only the co-operation of every person in the country could have won the day. While in the Jewish villages every man, woman and child worked ceaselessly, the fatalistic Arab farmers sat with folded hands. They could not understand why man should attempt to fight "God's army", as they called the locusts. Aaron had to give up the campaign, and the locusts broke in waves over the countryside.

Every day someone became ruined and impoverished, and the following day it was the neighbour's turn, then the others. Everyone went through it. The sum total was the ruin of the whole village, then of other villages, and then there was nothing left to devour. Everything ceased, everything was dead. In six weeks the locusts turned into ruins what thirty years of tenacious labour had miraculously erected.

By June Aaron could foresee that famine was staring them in the face. The food supplies in the country would not last beyond October. The British had to be contacted immediately, and this time he was determined to make the attempt himself. There was no hope for Aaron to smuggle himself out of the country as Alex and Absalom had done. His only possibility lay through Europe, and he persuaded Djemal Pasha that a trip abroad was necessary for his experiments with a new variety of sesame rich in oil.

Aaron had hoped to lay in supplies at the Station for the entire community against the coming famine, but his funds had given out. Money had ceased to come in from America, and his reserves had gone in releasing Absalom from court-martial. By trading on the good name of the Station, Aaron was able to borrow enough money to leave food for the hundred or more people under his care, but only sufficient to tide them over to the end of October. He expected to reach Britain in time to start his rescue work by way of Egypt before their food gave out.

Before leaving he arranged with Absalom and Sarah a simple system of signalling, inconspicuous and fool-proof, so that ships could not only be informed if there was danger in calling, but at what alternative points along the coast they might safely call. There were to be no more failures. For a year already they had been trying to establish contact with the British in Egypt. In spite of the enormous efforts they had made and the risks run, they were no farther ahead than when they started. Some insoluble obstacle divided them from the Allied ships that passed and repassed in full view along the horizon.

The obstacle was not of the Turks' making. At no time had the group at Athlit been disturbed by a coastal patrol during their long night watches for the British ship. Had a warship arrived, and had a boat, or even many boats, landed on the coast of Palestine in the very heart of the Turkish Fourth Army, there would have been nothing to prevent them.

In July 1916 Aaron set out for Constantinople, taking Liova Schneersohn with him as his secretary. Liova travelled on a forged Spanish passport under the name of Haim Cohen. Aaron covered the same route as Sarah had on her return to Zichron. He saw with his own eyes that she had not exaggerated in her description of what the Turks had done to the Armenians. He saw along the whole route Armenian women and children who had been sold into vice for a few piastres. He heard the cries of thousands of Armenians dying of hunger and thirst, and saw

69

dogs gnawing at the corpses of those who had died. And in his heart was engraved the decision to fight until the Turks and the Germans were destroyed.

Even with his powerful patrons Aaron had considerable difficulty in wringing out of the German authorities in Constantinople the necessary documents for travel to Berlin. Permission for Liova was out of the question. He was left in Constantinople to transmit messages from Aaron to Palestine as long as Aaron remained on the Continent. Afterwards he was to make his way to neutral Rumania, and from there rejoin Aaron in Egypt.

How would Aaron get to Egypt from Germany? How would Liova get to Rumania and Egypt from Constantinople? Where was the money to come from for all this travelling? Neither of them knew. Aaron trusted to his wits, and to the wits of his twenty-six-year-old colleague, to find a way. Aaron was of that breed of men whom Napoleon favoured. He was lucky. The man who was most deeply attached to Aaron, and had aided him more than anybody else in gaining support for his Experiment Station, was Rabbi Judah L. Magnes, leader of the most influential Reform congregation in America. He was in Berlin on a relief mission when he chanced to hear that Aaron was arriving from Palestine. The first person that Aaron saw when his train entered the station was this loyal ally. If Aaron could get to Copenhagen, Rabbi Magnes was prepared to do anything that was required of him.

Aaron's experiments with the oil-rich sesame were of considerable interest to Germany. He pretended to be in need of advice from a seed-breeding station in Sweden and did not hesitate to use the most influential of his scientific friends in Berlin to sponsor his request to the authorities for permission to go there. When it was later found out what his mission had been, he was never forgiven.

All this took time, and even when at last he found himself free in Copenhagen, he had still to be on his guard. There were spies of all nations in that neutral country, and Aaron's position was extremely tricky. He could not visit the British Embassy openly, lest the story get back to Turkey, and anyone he might approach to effect an introduction was just as likely to be pro-

German as pro-British. Finally, through a member of the Zionist circle who was friendly to Britain, a secret meeting was arranged with the British Minister. Even then he did not get far, for at first Sir Ralph Paget failed to see any political importance in Aaron's suggestions. The four months which Aaron had allowed himself for the rescue of his people in Palestine had already passed before an understanding could be reached.

What exactly was agreed is not known. Rabbi Magnes turned up in Copenhagen in October and booked to sail on a Danish ship for New York. Aaron had already arranged to sail with him, although he had no ticket and had no intention of trying to get the visa necessary for one. He accompanied Rabbi Magnes to the ship's side and waited until his friend had passed the ticket inspection and settled his luggage in his cabin. Rabbi Magnes then returned, passed his ticket vouchers over to Aaron and strolled casually back on to the ship. Aaron got on without any trouble and remained concealed for the whole of his journey in Rabbi Magnes's cabin.

At Kirkwall, in the Orkneys, a British naval patrol intercepted the ship and the passengers were interrogated. Aaron was arrested and removed from the ship. He had arranged in advance for the news of his capture to infiltrate into Turkey, so that his disappearance should rouse no suspicion.

In London Aaron was handed over to Scotland Yard. Sir Basil Thomson, then head of British Intelligence, recalls in his memoirs his meeting with the burly, sunburned man with the heavy, determined jaw who strode confidently into his office that foggy November. He brought strange tidings from the East, and unfolded a story that seemed straight from the Thousand and One Nights. Even without the all-empowering documents signed by Djemal Pasha, which Aaron produced as credentials, it was evident to Sir Basil that he had to do with a rare and remarkable individual.

Why had he come to England? His answer was clear and explicit. As a Zionist, he felt his first duty was to his homeland, the Jewish State which was destined to come to life again. He was convinced that this could only come about if Britain were victorious. Therefore he and his friends looked on Britain as an

71

ally which had to be helped to victory with every means in their power. "I offer what I am able to give: my knowledge of the country, the character of the inhabitants, and useful information on the military situation of the enemy now occupying it." In the middle of a statement Aaron interrupted himself to ask: "Why do you bring water for the Army from Egypt. It slows up your progress. There is water right there in the desert, 300 feet down. All you have to do is to drill for it."

"How do you know that?"

"The rocks indicate it," Aaron replied, "and Josephus Flavius corroborates it. He wrote that he could walk for a whole day south from Caesarea, and never leave flourishing gardens. Today the desert sands reach to the walls of Caesarea. Where there were gardens there must have been water. Where is that water now?

"I had the chance to explore the geology of Palestine, and from the rock strata I learned that there is sufficient water there at a depth of 300 feet. Even the whole of the Sinai Peninsula could be turned into flourishing fields of wheat by means of irrigation. There is water there, only waiting for the pipes to bring it to the surface."

"And what can you do?" Sir Basil inquired.

"If I were with the British Army," Aaron answered. "I could show the engineers where to drill. I guarantee that they would find enough water for the Army without having to bring a single drop from Cairo."

Sir Basil sent Aaron to the War Office, and from there he was sent to Egypt. "There he did not find a receptive ear to his suggestions about drilling in the ground on the strength of the evidence given by Josephus," Sir Basil relates, "but Aaronsohn's great obstinacy overcame all obstacles. And eventually, at a depth of 300 feet was found enough fresh water for the needs of the Army."[1]

Aaron was still a long way from that happy consummation. To General Macdonough, Chief of Military Intelligence at the War Office, and his assistant, Colonel (later Brigadier) Gribbon, Aaron urged the importance of establishing immediate contact between Egypt and Athlit. He told them bluntly what he thought of the failures of their Intelligence to maintain contact

[1] Memoirs of Sir Basil Thomson, published in *English Life*

with Athlit, and warned them that owing to the daily deterioration of the situation it would be difficult to accomplish even a tenth of what they could have done before. Aaron suggested that he be sent to Egypt and allowed to supervise the connection with Athlit. His offer was accepted willingly, for the idea was growing that an eastern front would be a helpful diversion from the unprofitable stalemates in Europe.

Although Aaron was devoting so much attention and energy to re-establishing an intelligence link with Palestine, he never forgot that this was not an end in itself but a means of achieving a goal—the national emancipation of the Jewish people under the benign government of Great Britain. There can be no doubt that Aaron Aaronsohn's brief visit to London in that critical autumn of 1916 played an important, although as yet unrecorded, part in shaping the course of events in the Middle East. The memorandum which he wrote and circulated at that time[1] contains within it the germ of the Balfour Declaration. It provides the missing link needed for a logical explanation of how the War Cabinet, engaged in what seemed to be a losing war, suddenly came to have the idea of a Jewish National Home pressed on it as a major instrument of policy.

The generally accepted story is that given by the Zionist historian, Paul Goodman, who was honorary secretary of the Zionist Political Committee for the United Kingdom at that time: "A great deal of the credit for having effectively moved British Government circles in that direction was due to Mr James A. Malcolm, of the Armenian National Delegation, who, with a wide and intimate knowledge of affairs in the Near and Middle East, sensed the extraordinary effect which an offer by the Allies of an autonomous Jewish settlement in Palestine would have on the Jews of America and elsewhere. Through Sir Mark Sykes, of the Foreign Office, who was not only a high authority on Middle Eastern affairs, but a very good friend of the Arab and Armenian peoples oppressed by the Ottoman Government, Mr Malcolm was enabled in October 1916 to bring the matter to the attention of the War Cabinet. . . ."[2]

[1] Copy in Central Zionist Archives, Jerusalem.
[2] Paul Goodman (Editor), *The Jewish National Home 1917-1942* (Dent, London, 1943), p. 30

There is no doubt that Aaron's cogent reasoning left its mark on James Malcolm, who would have been his first contact, coming fresh, as he did, from the scene of the Armenian disaster. All his sympathies led him to associate himself with the Armenians in their plight, and the similarity between their national situation and that of the Jews led him to seek a united front with them in fighting for national aims. The two men later worked closely together in connection with the Peace Conference. It can hardly be a coincidence, therefore, that at just this time Mr Malcolm broached the idea to Sir Mark Sykes, using the very arguments which Aaron had put forward. Sykes and Malcolm then and there began the negotiations with the War Cabinet and with accredited Zionist leaders which led to the Balfour Declaration in November 1917. When it was considered necessary to win the support of the Jews of America for British policy in the Middle East, Aaron was sent to do this, as he had offered in his memorandum of the previous year. Whether Aaron met Mark Sykes during his first visit to London is not known, but Norman Bentwich describes a meeting between them in Cairo a few months afterwards: "We three talked together about Zionist aims, and I realized the influence which Aaron had exercised on the mind of one who had an important part in preparing for the Balfour Declaration."[1]

Aaron's most daring political aim, the goal for which he was constantly manœuvering, he did not achieve. He sought to become the officially recognized instrument through which Great Britain would express her Zionist policy. Aaron was not seeking political leadership. He was hoping, in this way, to force the Zionist leaders in Palestine to accept his authority, and so to bring his ideas to bear in the new programme of upbuilding which he knew was awaiting Palestine. Aaron's claim was that, because he was not bound by any political affiliations to the Zionist Organization, which had adopted an official policy of neutrality, he was able to render Britain a service which the official leaders were unable to render. This involved rousing rebellion in Palestine as well as mobilizing support among the influential Jews of America, almost all of whom were still non-Zionist.

[1] Letter from Norman Bentwich to author, August 30th, 1957.

But there was someone else in England, also a scientist, who had been seeking to bring about a Jewish revival under British auspices. This was the Russian chemist, Dr Chaim Weizmann, who, although not an accredited leader of the World Zionist Organization, was already known as a man of stature, moderate and diplomatic. The British Government chose to work through him.

Chapter 7

ABSALOM'S DECISION

WITH Aaron's departure organization of the work fell to Absalom, and Sarah took an active part. They operated in the north and Naaman Belkind and Yosef Lishansky in the south. Absalom, Sarah and Yosef aimed at rousing an anti-Turk movement in the Yishuv. They were convinced that Aaron would not fail to persuade the British to send them arms and money to organize a Jewish rebellion to synchronize with an Allied invasion of the country—preferably by sea, for that was the speediest, and Aaron was going to press for that as well. Absalom hoped eventually to bring in all the active elements in the Yishuv. The Jews themselves must fight for their freedom, not receive it at the hands of others.

"The rights of every man are measured according to his contribution," Absalom declared. "Now, while we are doubting and hesitating, the doctor of doctors is examining us"— Absalom referred to Britain—"an honest and incorruptible doctor, who could be turned into a friend or an emeny, all according to his diagnosis of the state of our health; and he examines in order to decide whether we are dead or alive. Never in all our existence has the proverb been truer for us: 'he who risks nothing gains nothing'." So Absalom had written in his report to Miss Szold in America, for he had made the same plea to the Jews of America. They too must participate in the Jewish struggle for Palestine. Together with the redeeming army must come battalions of Jews from all the Allied countries to fight together with the Yishuv for the freeing of Palestine.

Rebellion and espionage were many-edged weapons, and Absalom had to feel his way slowly and carefully. After an initial rebuff from Ha-Shomer, he concentrated on the sons of the old settlements, among them friends of the Gideonites and connections of the Aaronsohn and Feinberg families. Some half-dozen young men and women in Zichron were involved in the

76

work, but as they had always been closely connected by ties of friendship and family, the compact little group attracted no attention in the village. Absalom spent most of his time at Zichron now, caring for Aaron's affairs. He filled the place of a son in the house, and by his devotion to the old man, Ephraim Aaronsohn, tried to compensate him for his loss.

Sarah's brother, Zvi the only other member of the family still in Palestine, lived across the street. He was taking part in the work, and so was his wife's sister, Toba, who was Sarah's friend. Toba was a fast writer, and Sarah brought her documents which had to be copied out quickly and returned before their absence was noticed. They never ceased to prepare reports, for they expected the British to be turning up at any time.

They used to meet at Zvi's house in the evening, where Sarah and Absalom lavished their love for children on his small son and daughter. Wherever Absalom was, there was fun and laughter, and no young people in Zichron seemed gayer than the group which centred on the Aaronsohns. This was only on the surface. In reality they were all tensely waiting for the news that Liova Schneersohn would be sending from Constantinople of Aaron's movements.

Absalom's young sister Cela was studying in Berlin, and Aaron arranged that she should pass on to Liova any messages that he sent her from Copenhagen. Aaron had met with delays everywhere. Four months passed before he had any information to send them, and it took another month for it to reach Palestine. Before he left Copenhagen he telegraphed to Cela that he was sailing for America to see his friends. He never expected Absalom to take the message at its face value. It was merely intended to convey the information that he had succeeded in getting away. When the cable was relayed to Palestine, it may have arrived in a garbled version, or for some other reason Absalom misunderstood it. He concluded that Aaron was following in Alex's footsteps, and leaving the field of battle. "He's left us here to fight it out alone!" exclaimed Absalom bitterly, almost beside himself at the defection of his beloved leader. Sarah also failed to understand, but she had her family's unshakable confidence in Aaron. She tried to reassure Absalom, and begged him to be patient a little longer.

But too much time had been lost already. Absalom was responsible to people who had risked their lives for him. Material was piling up, and he was powerless, cut off in Palestine without contact with the outside world, and now without a ray of hope. The fear was growing of a German victory and the destruction of Palestine. Absalom would wait no longer. One morning he informed Sarah that he was leaving for the desert again. There was no other way to establish contact with the British. This time he was not going alone. Yosef Lishansky was coming with him. Yosef had become a leading member of the group. His ability to penetrate anywhere, among Arabs or Turks, was a valuable asset, and he was always ready for anything. But Sarah knew that he was prepared to take risks just for the thrill of them, and his participation in this dangerous mission only confirmed her fear for Absalom.

Ever since Aaron left, Sarah and Absalom had been working together as one. Wise, calm and courageous, her presence was a source of strength and encouragement to Absalom. Their understanding was complete. They loved each other, a great, fulfilling love, a calm haven within the boundaries of the stormy world they had created for themselves.

Sarah regarded herself as married, although with Aaron's departure she had given up the pretence—a pretence to herself as well as her husband—that she was thinking of returning to Constantinople. And Absalom was engaged to Rivka, the little sister pining for him in her American exile. They knew there could be no union for them this side of the grave. They knew there could be no peace for them as long as misery and danger threatened their people. But in their love there was neither melancholy nor pain, for though they went among people, in their hearts Sarah and Absalom had already closed their accounts with life.

And so this too they had to face—that Absalom should ride off to the desert and Sarah should be left alone. Sarah protested and tried to prevail on Absalom to give up this idea. But even as she protested, it became clear to Sarah, like a programme that had been fixed long in advance, that Absalom would die in the desert and she would be left alone.

He left a letter for Lt. Woolley, in case contact was established in his absence. "I have decided, come what may, to cross the desert, and to reach you. I must run my last race, and I beg you to note that I do this in the service of His Majesty, George Vth, King of England, who, in my mind, is already crowned King of Palestine and Mesopotamia. You will hear further details from my friends at the Station, who tomorrow will be your comrades in arms."

When Absalom left, the sole responsibility of the espionage fell on Sarah. From that time onwards she worked daily, hourly, under mounting pressure and constant danger. To her own danger she gave no thought. But she was responsible for the lives of a devoted band of people prepared to go through fire at her command. Even they were not the chief worry. Each one had joined the organization of his own free will and was willing to face the risks for the sake of the Yishuv. The terrible fear which hung over her day and night was that some slip on her part, or on the part of her followers, might bring disaster to the whole Jewish population of Palestine, the very people whom they were risking themselves to save.

She was full of compassion and consideration for the hardships suffered by the families of those engaged in the espionage, for she knew her own loneliness. They had all gone. No word from any of them. Alex and Rivka far away in America. Aaron had disappeared, no one knew where. And Absalom in the desert. It seemed that fate had cleared the stage, so that the fierce light of martyrdom should beat down on her alone.

But Sarah could not sit with folded hands and mourn. She knew that one day contact would be established with the outside world, and so she must prepare herself. She read again the letter to Woolley that Absalom had left with her, in case the ship should appear, or if he failed to return from the desert. She pored over Aaron's maps and studied reports, so that she could absorb all that was happening at the front. She must not shame her brother and Absalom.

These things she did in the long evenings, when she was alone. She was very busy by day, keeping house for her old father and acting as secretary of the Experiment Station in place of Absalom. The land was being cultivated and crops sown as much as possible, and the workers reported to her. The days dragged on, days of worry and expectation. The famine which Aaron had foreseen was upon them. In the cities people were dying of hunger. Even in the settlements, poverty and want were increasing. The authorities were vicious, and the people lived in fear.

One afternoon Sarah was sitting at Zichron, sewing, when Liova Schneersohn turned up from Constantinople. When it had become clear that there would be no more messages from Aaron, he began to try for his visa for Rumania. From there he intended to get to his people in Russia, and then, provided somehow with funds, he would join Aaron in Egypt. It was a crazy idea, but the world they lived in had gone crazy too. When Liova appeared at the passport office in Constantinople, and presented his forged Spanish passport, he did so with confidence. Things had been difficult in Palestine, but with sufficient baksheesh they had been able to bribe their way in and out of almost any situation. But Palestine was a province, administered by ignorant, underpaid and lazy officials, far from the heart of the Ottoman Empire. Things were done differently in Constantinople.

The clerk to whom Liova applied for his visa chanced to be a Jew, a Jerusalemite, whom Liova knew by sight. He took a look at the Spanish passport, then at Liova's Slavic features and blue eyes, and he sized up the situation. He drew Liova aside and said to him in a low voice, "Listen, pal, do you want to swing? Get out of here as quick as you can!"

Liova's funds had run short during his long stay. Without money for baksheesh, and with the falsity of his passport so obvious, Liova found it as dangerous to try and return to Palestine as it was to get out of Turkey. While thinking over the situation, he attempted to earn some money by selling matches at a theatre entrance. He finally turned to an exiled Zionist official from Palestine. The exile, a German, got him a free trip back to Palestine as servant to a German officer.

With Liova Sarah could talk about Absalom, and they bore the agony of waiting together. He remained with Sarah, helping her at the Station and in the work. The daily life at Athlit was sad, lonely and hungry. Their meals consisted of tea made of fig leaves, and bread made of coarse Arab barley. Liova spent most of the morning in Aaron's room at the top of the Station. He wrote, and watched the sea for the ship that would bring the redemption.

Sometimes Sarah slipped upstairs and watched with him. Sometimes Liova must have become so absorbed in watching her that he forgot to watch the sea, for among his diary notes there is a disconnected sentence, like a sketch made by a painter: "I see you sitting quiet and wonderful, with your wonderful white hands, and your slim fingers, of such loveliness and beauty as I have never seen."

He went with Sarah for trips in the neighbourhood, noting the coastal patrols. One morning, walking back from the sea-shore, "we cross the road, approaching the gates of the Experiment Station, and suddenly Sarah says to me 'Look!' We see two carts in the courtyard of the Station, and a man in a tarbush wandering around. There are others wearing hats."

Sarah told him to hide in the trees, and she would go on by herself. "If it is nothing, I will call for you. Otherwise, wait."

Liova hid under the trees, and Sarah went forward, picking flowers and humming to herself, like a lady going for a walk in the early morning. "I watch everything through the leaves. Sarah approaches them. They lift their hats. I think to myself, 'So it's nothing,' and in fact, Manasseh Bronstein runs and whistles to me. 'Sarah says you can come. They're only acquaintances.'"

Nothing but anti-climax. They longed for action, for some sign. But there was nothing.

Chapter 8

AARON IN CAIRO

AARON arrived in Egypt on December 12th, 1916, full of vigour and afire with the prospect of being able, at last, to gear his masterly and meticulous plans to the British war machine. His reception in Cairo was like a slap in the face. Nothing had changed there.

Whatever London may have decided about the imminent emergence of the Palestine front, there were no such thoughts in Cairo. The aim of the High Command was still defence. The skirmish that took place a fortnight after Aaron's arrival, advancing the British lines to El Arish, was only to clear out Turkish-Arab patrol points in the Sinai desert that were encroaching too close to the Canal. Aaron's large-scale plans for a revolt in Palestine, his idea of drilling for water in the Sinai desert—they all fell on deaf ears.

Worst of all, he was unable to arouse any enthusiasm, or even understanding, among the Intelligence for the help he and his people in Palestine were prepared to give. The truth was, they did not take his espionage talk very seriously. They could not believe that there really were scores of people behind the Turkish lines just waiting to risk their lives for the sake of the British, and without payment. It made no sense. His scheme was so fabulous, and what he promised too good to be more than bluff. If it had not been for the letter of recommendation which Aaron brought from the War Office, they would have paid no attention to him at all. As it was, they fobbed him off on one pretext or another, coldly indifferent to the violent scenes he made in his anxiety to contact his people in Palestine.

Aaron, who had endangered himself and had sacrificed everything he held dear in life to get to Egypt and put his services at the disposal of the British, now hung around Cairo doing nothing, bitter and disillusioned. The contemptuous treatment of the Intelligence officers, and the status they tried to impose on him, opened Aaron's eyes to the sordidness of the enterprise he had been drawn into. In America, in Palestine, in Europe his was a name and a status that commanded instant respect. It had never occurred to him that a situation would arise in which they would ever be questioned. But these people could see only a foreigner, an enemy alien, a Jew, who was seeking employ as a spy. They rated Aaron no higher than Abdulla, the Arab boatman from Tyre, and his two sons, who were in the pay of Naval Intelligence.

As soon as Aaron arrived in Egypt, he got into contact with Absalom's friend and relation, Raphael Aboulafia in Alexandria. Trustworthy, knowledgeable and patriotic, Aboulafia became his close friend and helper. "You are fed up with Captains Edmunds, Smith and Jones," Aaron wrote to him. "So am I. Until the moment I started conversations with them, I have never allowed any man to behave to me with such indifference and lack of respect as I allow them, because their ideas and their behaviour are so different from ours.

"But what is done is done. I didn't know the English. I've had experience with all kinds of men, with different governments, but such people, and this kind of government, I've never met before. And this is our catastrophe. Absalom should have warned us. He was with them and saw them in their decadence. But he didn't tell me how thorny the path was. I know that the lives of hundreds of our people are hanging on this slim hope of help we can bring, and I must continue my work, no matter how much I dirty my hands, or destroy my soul. I can't step aside now. Only after I have succeeded in re-establishing connections with Athlit will I have the right to get out of this mire.

"Then I can come before Absalom and say to him: 'If your heart is still strong within you, go and work with them. I cannot. For either they don't need us, which is why they are behaving to us like this; or else they don't understand how faithful we are to them, and how necessary we are to them, and so they don't know how to use us. Whatever it is, we have no part in their work, and the conditions they are making for us drag down our precious idea.'"

Aaron had been in Cairo for a month before he was asked to

submit a memorandum, stating his qualifications for service with British Intelligence, together with references. He might have been applying for a Civil Service post in London in peacetime. One of the people whom Aaron mentioned as a friend happened at that time to be an officer with the forces at El Arish. This was Norman Bentwich, who was requested to come to Cairo "to interview a Jew from Palestine who had told a romantic story, and was recommended to the Intelligence by the War Office. I was to find out whether his story was genuine, and whether he could give service to us."[1]

They spent a day walking together along the banks of the Nile, and Bentwich was able to reassure Intelligence with regard to Aaron's devotion to the Allied cause and the service he could render. Only after that did Aaron realize the chief reason for his troubles in Cairo. He had been dealing with people of no real status. They were merely the officers of the Secret Service. It was not their duty to think in broad, political terms. There was a special branch for that, headed by Brigadier General (Sir) Gilbert Clayton, who had served for fourteen years in Egypt and the Sudan. His right-hand man was Major Wyndham Deedes, expert in Turkish affairs and Turkish language. Major Deedes ordered that steps should be taken immediately to renew the contact with Athlit.

Aaron himself was forbidden to land. It would have been too dangerous. The problem now narrowed down to finding someone who could swim four hundred metres from a small boat let down from a warship off the coast of Athlit, and then make his way inland to the Experiment Station. But it was not enough for a young man to be brave, patriotic and a first-rate swimmer. He had to know the coastline and the Athlit area so well that he could literally find his way about blindfolded, for the work could only be carried out on moonless nights. He could not be a native of the district, lest he be recognized by someone. It took a while to find a person with such special qualities, but nevertheless he was found. Raphael Aboulafia was still in contact with the men of the Zion Mule Corps, most of whom had been Palestinians, drawn from the refugees in Alexandria. He had

---

[1] Norman Bentwich, *Wanderer Between Two Worlds* (Kegan Paul, London, 1941)

found Zvi Rivin for Lt. Woolley, and now he began to search for somebody for Aaron.

Aboulafia turned up with a tall, raw-boned, slow-spoken villager from Petach Tikvah, who had been in his regiment in the Zion Mule Corps. Leibel Bornstein his name was, and he had earned his living by driving a diligence on the Acre-Jaffa route, the main highway which skirted the Experiment Station. He had often driven the famous agronomist, Mr Aaronsohn, and considered it an honour to be associated with him in his patriotic work.

Aaron had the unsavoury task of fixing Leibel's allowance with his friends of the local Intelligence. On the one hand, they refused to understand what Aaron felt was essential that they should understand, namely, that they were not dealing with ordinary spies who were risking their lives for the sake of the money, but with people who were fighting as a group for a national aim. On the other hand, the Intelligence showed themselves remarkably reluctant to pay sufficient money to maintain Leibel's wife and two children while he risked himself in his dangerous work. "The Arab Revolt is being kept alive by a stream of gold," Aaron said to Captain Edmunds with heavy irony. "But we will give maximum value without affecting your cash reserves. We know very well how to appreciate national independence. We don't have to be paid to accept it."

He wrote another of his bitter letters to Aboulafia. "The amount of money our friend Leibel demands is not excessive, but there is an obstacle. Captain Edmunds has found that now is the time to save money. Since we know *how much money is being wasted by the others*, we must understand that our friends really have to economize as much as they can. But it doesn't matter. I am prepared to put up the difference of £10 myself, so that this young man should feel he is dealing with men who appreciate his efforts and are not misers."

Aaron never ceased to fear what the impulsive and impetuous Absalom might have done during the months that had passed since his departure from Palestine. That he had endangered himself, Aaron was sure, but that he would always manage to find some way of escaping he did not doubt.

When Aaron returned to his hotel at five in the afternoon of January 25th, he met Captain Edmunds waiting for him at the entrance. He said to Aaron, in a mysterious manner, "I've been looking for you since the morning. You must go at once to Port Said. One of your men has reached here through the desert."

"Absalom!" thought Aaron. He was terribly excited, but could learn nothing more. "Why are they sending me to him?" Aaron wondered. "Why aren't they sending him here to me? Is he wounded? These gentlemen of the Intelligence get mysterious without reason and without efficiency."

He hurried to his friend Pascal, a man of his own age, whose parents had come with the Aaronsohns from Rumania. Pascal was an orange grower in Petach Tikvah, but he had escaped at the beginning of the war. An hour later Aaron and Pascal were on their way to Port Said. They found that the Palestinian who lay in a hotel in Port Said was Yosef Lishansky, the man who had set out three weeks before with Absalom to cross the desert and make contact with the British. Severely wounded, Lishansky had been picked up by an Australian patrol near El Arish. Absalom he had left behind in the desert, dead.

According to Lishansky's story, on January 20th he and Absalom, dressed as Beduin, had set off by camel from Beertuvia, north of Beersheba. They had with them a Beduin as guide. Neither Army paid any attention to the Beduin, and they moved about without interference. In the night they passed the Turkish lines and reached the no-man's-land in the neighbourhood of Sheikh Zowa'id, not far from El Arish. Then their Beduin lost his direction, or so he said. It was a misty night, without stars, and they had nothing to guide them. Fearing to retrace their steps, they decided to wait beside their camels until dawn, when they would be able to see the British camps.

Suddenly a group of Beduin pounced on them. Lishansky did not know how many, perhaps thirty or forty. They said there was a blood feud between the guide's tribe and theirs, and they demanded that the man be handed over to them. Absalom refused. A quarrel started. The guide darted from their side and ran towards the Beduin. Absalom, suspecting treachery,

brought him down with a shot. Then began a terrible battle
with the Beduin. Lishansky was wounded in the neck and chest
and fell to the ground. Absalom continued to defend himself
until his bullets gave out. "I'm finished," he gasped to Lishansky; "tell Aaron . . ." but he could speak no more.

"I hugged him and kissed him," Lishansky murmured des-
perately. "I didn't want to leave him. Then I fell unconscious.
When I came to again, there were no camels, no Beduin, no
Absalom. Only a great pain in my body, and a terrible thirst.
I crawled along until I met an English patrol, and they brought
me here to die."

"You won't die," exclaimed Aaron bitterly. He could not
control the sick fury that rose in him at the sight of the man
lying there bandaged and limp. Why was it not Absalom to be
nursed back to life? Brutally killed, on Saturday, January 20th—
more than a month after he had arrived in Egypt. If they had
listened to him when he first came, he could have got a message
to Athlit and Absalom would still be alive. Here was the first
result of the lack of confidence of Edmunds and his men.

After a time Aaron asked doubtfully, "You hugged and kissed
him under a volley of bullets?"

"Yes," answered Lishansky, and closed his eyes.

Aaron and Pascal exchanged glances. "And did anyone else
see how all this happened?" Aaron added, fixing Yosef with a
penetrating glance.

"No," murmured Yosef.

"And so Absa, the brave Absa, has fallen by the bullet of a
Beduin," Aaron wrote in his diary, "a low Beduin, looking for
prey; fell, and died, amongst those for whom his contempt was
so great. What appals the mind is that it is thanks to us, to him,
and to me, that he must be left to lie unidentified in the desert;
that he is buried without leaving a trace. For how great would
be the number of the innocent who would have to pay with
their lives if they identified his body. This idea in itself is
enough to send one mad."

Aaron asked two things of the military authorities. That
Lishansky be removed to a hospital and given the best possible
care. And that a patrol be sent out to Sheikh Zowa'id to try and
locate Absalom's body.

As soon as he got back to Cairo next day, he went to Edmunds but Edmunds was not there. Then he went to Major Deedes, who received him immediately, a courtesy which Aaron had not been accustomed to since his arrival in Egypt. "I don't know why, but I feel that I can talk to this dry, brisk man. He is full of understanding. I speak to him with passion and pain, and he listens to me, with all his heart. I am not ashamed to weep, and he comforts me for all the suffering which I have suffered. . . . He also knows and understands the deficiencies of the British organization, to which can be added, in our case, lack of confidence. But Deedes promises me, now that we are going to work together, that there will be no more insults, or suspicions, and we will be able to stride forward to progress. He gets Smith on the phone, and Edmunds too. He is full of energy, and knows how to give orders. . . . When I go out I meet Edmunds and tell him that I consider him morally responsible for our disaster."

Lishansky was taken to the officers' hospital, and he was asked a second time what happened. He replied, "Who knows, perhaps Absalom is still alive." But when he got properly well and was asked again, he repeated the first story with a few unimportant changes. These small changes might have aroused the suspicion of an investigating attorney, but were natural under the circumstances.

If the body of Absalom had been found and buried, perhaps Aaron's heart would have been at peace. But the Beduin whom Major Deedes sent out to look for Absalom came back empty-handed. The desert had swallowed Absalom's body, and the secret of his death. Aaron realized how dangerous would be the repercussions if Absalom's death were to become known. Only a few people could safely be told; one of them was Raphael Aboulafia.

"The inspirer of our idea, the main worker, we have left stricken at the beginning of our work at the very time when his wonderful vitality, his fine soul and his pure heart were so necessary for the success of our enterprise. A sacred obligation remains to us. We can honour his memory and his undertaking only by devoting all our energies and all our abilities to fulfilling the great things that will stand in his name. Oh that we may soon see the redemption of our people and our land!"

Things were going better for Aaron now, since his interview with Major Deedes. He had broken through the solid wall of indifference, and at last had found men with whom it was possible to work, he informed Aboulafia. "It's too early yet to say that we have succeeded, because those who received the reprimand still have their fingers in the pie. We still have an underground struggle before us, but at any rate, I've seen the man whom it is necessary to see, and I know how to force people to open the way I want. I am hurrying, I am trying to get great things. But to behave to us as they have behaved until now will be impossible in future.

When Lishansky got up from his bed, he came to work with Aaron. When Aaron got to know him at close quarters, he was far from satisfied with the blond, dapper young man who would have to take such a responsible part in the espionage now that Absalom was gone. Yosef had a shrewd brain, but not an ounce of discretion. He swaggered, he exaggerated, he liked to cut a figure—in fact, he had all the childish qualities of his American counterpart, the cowboys of the Western range. He had grown up in the mountain village of Metullah in the north, very far from the centres of settlement. The Arabs and the Druze were the only neighbours. He had learned to ride and to shoot just as they did, almost as soon as he could walk, for the Druze had been hostile to the new settlements and the settlers had often to withstand a siege. He was not strong on deference to age or position, and his manner of speech was a compound of freshness, ignorance and genuine belief in the equality of man. The only criteria Yosef recognised were love of Palestine and of his people, and the ability to handle a gun in their defence. Since he knew nobody could excel him in these, his manner of walking and talking conveyed his open satisfaction with himself and his abilities.

Yosef respected Aaron as he respected nobody else, and in spite of the older man's frequent impatience, his twenty-seven-year old partner was proud and willing to fit in with all his plans. By the time the moon was right for another attempt at Athlit, they had agreed on the method of their work. Aaron, in Cairo, would maintain contact between the British and the group in Palestine, directing their activities according to the needs of the war effort. Liova Schneersohn would be picked up in Palestine to serve as liaison between Aaron and Athlit. Yosef Lishansky would return to Palestine and carry out the work there with Sarah's help.

Chapter 9

CONTACT RENEWED

TWO days before they were due to sail, Leibel Bornstein received an order to go to Port Said. On the way, at one of the stations, he met Aaron, who had come from Cairo, together with Lishansky. In Port Said they stayed in different hotels. Their permits to enter the harbour were brought them by the young Christian Arab, Charley Boutagy. He was making the trip too. It was intended that he should swim ashore with Leibel and help him in case of difficulty.

Inside the harbour they were met by Captain Smith, and all went together by boat to a small ship anchored in the harbour. The ship was the *Monegam*, which became known as *Menachem* in the code language of the espionage. After an hour they set off. Dawn found them creeping along the coast of Palestine. Aaron had come to an understanding with his friends, the Intelligence, and arrangements were made according to his instructions. He noted impressions in his diary, as he saw his homeland unfolding before him again for the first time since he had left it eight months before:

"9 o'clock. We're approaching Jaffa. At last I've good glasses, and can see everything. We pass Caesarea, Tantura, and finally, at half-past three, Athlit. At first we didn't see a solitary person at the Experiment Station. Giddiness passed over me. My fear increased when I noticed that the wall of the balcony was black, as though after a fire. A moment of fear, and suddenly I realized that 'it was only the shadow of the Station which was darkening the wall. Then I saw two of our men in the vegetable garden, and two people hanging out the sheet on the balcony. (The ship's smoke had been seen, and the white sheet was the sign that it was safe to return that night.) And so the way is open."

Aaron took Leibel up to the captain's bridge and showed him through the glasses where he would have to go at night. "Here are the ruins of the Crusader castle. At night the ship will be opposite the castle, to cover her outline from the eyes of those on land. But we hope that no one will be watching. See those table-shaped rocks on the shore? You'll go up the shore along-side those rocks, and you follow the wadi until you get to the highway."

"Oh, sure, I know the highway. Many times I've passed over that road at night," said Leibel.

"From the highway you'll take the road that leads to the gate of my Experiment Station, and you'll go to the two-storey house. There you'll call out the name of Rabb, that's the man who works in the Station. When he opens the door, you go in, and give him what you'll get from me. Take what he'll give you. Tell Haim Cohen he's to come back with us to Egypt. Tell Reuven Schwartz (Aaron's cousin) that I want to see him. When you get back to the shore, signal the little ship, and the Arabs will swim back with you. That's all."

The *Monegam* continued north to Tyre to pass the time until nightfall. Then it returned south, and close on midnight it stopped about a mile off shore, opposite the Crusader castle. It was the end of the month. The moon did not appear until almost dawn.

The letters and the money were already prepared and packed in an oilskin package. The boat was put into the water, and Leibel, Aaron, Captain Smith and Boutagy entered it. Abdullah and his two sons rowed it towards the land.

They could not go in as close as they might have done, for fear they would get dragged in with the breakers. There was no knowing how far Leibel would have to swim to shore. It looked a dangerous business, jumping into the stormy, wintry waters. The swim back would be worse, against the tide. And how to find the boat, pitching and moving in the dark?

The two young Arab fishermen murmured that Leibel would not dare to throw himself into the water. Leibel heard, but paid no attention. Boutagy had already decided that he did not like the look of the stormy water, and was not going to accompany Leibel to the shore. Aaron's heart was knocking. Only one person was calm; that was Leibel. The journey was divided into three parts. Sailing, swimming, walking. The first and the last were not dangerous, thought Leibel. Certainly he should be able to manage the second.

Captain Smith heard Boutagy's refusal to go into the water, and thought it was all off. He was going to order the boat back to the ship when he heard Abdullah ask Leibel, "Are you ready to jump?" "Ready," said Leibel simply, as if someone asked him if he was ready to drive them in his diligence to Jaffa.

They both stripped, shivering in the wind. Leibel had fixed on his back the leather sack in which were his change of clothes, the package of papers, an electric torch, a bottle of whisky, and a loaded revolver which Captain Smith had given him. He jumped into the water and swam towards shore accompanied by Abdullah, a powerful swimmer. After a while Abdullah advised him to rest a little on the inflated leather bag. They continued swimming until they felt land under their feet. Abdullah shook Leibel's hand. "You're a hero," he said, and wished him good luck. Leibel asked Abdullah to wait for him on the shore until he came back. He did not see well at night, and he did not know if he would find the way alone through the water.

"That's impossible. I have to return immediately to the boat. When you return to the shore, give a sign with your torch and my two sons will come for you."

On land, Leibel put on the clothes which he took out of the leather bag and warmed his body with another mouthful of whisky from the bottle, as Captain Smith had told him to do. Then he grasped his loaded revolver and the package, and set out into the darkness.

That morning Liova had sat in the little second-storey room, watching the sea and writing his diary notes, that were mixtures of thoughts, poems and events. "February 21st. A month already since I came back from Constantinople! It seems like a year." His depressing thoughts were broken off in the middle, for suddenly a ship loomed up in sight of shore. Sarah flew up the stairs at his call and, startled and excited, they watched the ship. The diary continues:

"Most important to Sarah is the smoke, because the smoke is one of our signs. Thick black smoke pours out of the funnel of the ship. Hurrah, Sarah!

"The ship, when it comes opposite the houses of Athlit, makes a sharp turn, with its prow straight for the open sea. This is the second sign. Tonight, Sarah!

"So we prepare ourselves for the night. We arrange everything in the yard, as agreed before-hand. The workers are working. The horses are in the stables. It's good that Nasir isn't here. We gave the dog to the guard, and sent the guard off on an errand. It's safest that way. Mendel (Liova's brother) comes before nightfall. He's going to Haifa. On his way back, he'll spent the night at Athlit. Some people came, but we sent them away. Visitors are not very welcome this evening. They have found just the right time to come. What is connected with the Herbarium we shall try to arrange and send on to them, with our apologies. Thank God they went away. From Zichron come Itzhak Halperin and Reuven Schwartz. They will go to the shore through the wadi. Baruch and Yehuda will take another route. Mendel will stay at the Station, in the big room. Sarah and I, in the room above.

"We blacked out all the lights in the Station. The two groups have already set out for the sea. Now we are waiting. For whom? For what? We are nervous. The whole business is so full of mystery and secrecy, *and* so dangerous. One careless step, and everything is lost.

"A strong wind. The sea is roaring terribly. The sky is black. Rain, and no rain. The trees are thrashing about in the wind. From the distance we hear the barking of dogs. One hour passes, two hours. Suddenly we hear steps, heavy steps on the wooden stairs leading up to the room. As if a lot of people are going to burst into the room. I jump up from my chair in fright, and fling open the door.

"Into the room burst Baruch and Yehuda, with a creature whose eyes are starting out of his head, whose clothes are in tatters, dripping water at every step.

"Baruch calls to us, pushing him into the room: 'Here he is.'
"Who is it?"

"A man, half-demented, looking with startled eyes at his surroundings, stammers unintelligible words. The smell of alcohol is on his breath, and he is trembling from shock.

" 'Man!' we shout, catching him by the throat, 'can't you talk? Speak up, you rotter, or we'll choke you!'

"He begins to pull himself together, and stammers: 'Aaronsohn, on the ship . . . which will come . . . Schwarz . . . Schwarz . . . where is he? Haim Cohen . . . Where is Haim Cohen. . . . Who is coming . . .''

"As he talks he fumbles in his pocket, produces a medallion and gives it to Sarah. Sarah recognizes the medallion she gave to Aaron.

"They begin to massage him, to bring warmth into his body and revive him. Bring him hot tea, which is already prepared. Anything, as long as it is hot.

"What more did you bring? Who are you? What's your name?''

"His giddiness passed, and he opened his mouth. He was Leibel Bornstein, who once worked with Ephraim Halperin, of Petach Tikvah, as a driver of a diligence. Baruch remembered that he had driven with him several times.

"Aaronsohn is on the ship. He wants Schwartz and Haim Cohen—me, that is—to come to him. That we should come to the ship in a little boat, and that I am to remain on the ship with him. Leibel didn't bring anything. The English, before they let him down over the ship's side, gave him a big shot of whisky. Do you know how important whisky is? The sea was very high, and it was very hard to swim. He came ashore near Bir-Badai. Our people didn't meet him on the way. Baruch and Yehuda found him near the gate of the Station. When they met him, he couldn't speak a word, and they brought him up to the room.

"Excited, and unable to concentrate, we get ready to go to the seashore. Those going are: myself, Reuven, Baruch, the man Leibel. Sarah remains behind. I am to leave with the ship. We take nothing but the reports, in a leather pouch. Mendel remains at the Station.

"Now we are ready. Leibel is already a little rested, and looks more of a man. He tells Sarah about Gallipoli, about Jabotinsky, about the Mule Corps, about Raphael Aboulafia. 'And Absalom,' Sarah asks. 'What about Absalom Feinberg?' He doesn't know. Sarah longs to fly to the seashore, to pull from the waves some news of Absalom. But it is forbidden, Sarah. A ruling is a ruling.

"Now we start on our way. Baruch took his rifle. 'If by chance we meet someone near the shore,' he said to me on the way, 'I'll shoot once, and will shout, "Rehat el bata"—that is to say, "The duck has got away", so that it looks as if we are out shooting birds.'

"Rehat el bata! The bird has flown. There are moments which can raise a man's spirits!

"Leibel has already pulled himself together completely. The Arabs will be waiting for him near the shore. The sea is rough again, and it will be very hard to swim. We have to hurry up, because the sea is getting rougher. We hurry along, crossing the highway, climb the little hills, pass El Bustra and approach the sea.

"The storm is wild. The waves are as high as five-storey houses, and they look as if they would crush us like worms. White foam froths from the mouths of the waves. Terrible.

"Two naked ghosts, like angels of horror, emerge from the darkness. They shiver and chatter with cold. These are Leibel's Arab friends who have come to take Schwartz and me to the ship. Yitzhak and Manasseh appear. They took another route.

"Schwartz took me to oneside and said, 'We are to swim out to the ship at a time like this? It's impossible!'

"I, I'm ready. One of the Arabs wants to take me on his back, and will swim with me to the ship."

"Leibel says this is impossible. If I don't know how to swim, and if I'm dressed in heavy clothes, and can't depend on my own strength, I shouldn't even think of going out to the ship. The Arabs are trembling with fear and cold, and shout, 'Yallah! Yallah! Ya, Leib, Yallah!'

"With all the noise, and the excitement, there isn't time to think anything over with a cool mind. The Arabs have already jumped into the water, and shout to Leibel to do the same. I just have time to shout to Leibel to tell Aaron what the situation is, and ask him to send a ship as quickly as possible to establish contact with us. Then Leibel jumps, and the sea and the wind swallow him in a moment. They all vanish, as if they had never been.

"The wind is so strong that it tears Reuven's black cape from his shoulders, and he has to fight with it. Rabb remains with his unfired rifle, without shooting, and there's nothing left for us but to return to the Station.

"And so I didn't succeed in getting on the ship. With head sunk, saddened, depressed and bitter of soul, I walk slowly in the direction of the Station. I don't pay any attention to the friends who walk beside me. They are disappointed too.

"Who knows if Leibel will get to the ship? If Aaron will get our messages? And where is Absalom? And again we have to wait, who knows how long, to sit in the poor little Station, and wait for the Redemption. Again the connection is broken, the war is going on, and it is so bad and so bitter in our hearts.

"We reach the Station, and I knock on Sarah's door. She is astonished and upset to see us. We talk about our disappointment, of the disappointment of Aaron, and our longing for Absalom. You need luck for everything!

"It is already very late, 3 a.m. The others go to sleep and to rest. In our little room there is a pale light. Sarah and I sit silent. Suddenly a pebble is thrown on the shutter of our window. I jump up, and hurry to the balcony. A low whistle near the door. Sarah whispers 'What's this?' 'Wait,' I tell her, 'I'll go and see.'

"She doesn't let me go by myself, but goes down with me. Down by the door stands a man, stark naked, shining white in the darkness. Trembling with fear and cold, and teeth chattering.

" 'It's Leibel,' stammers the naked figure.

"He couldn't get to the boat. He lost the Arabs on the way. He nearly drowned. He was saved by a miracle. Without any strength to see where he was going, or to care for danger, he plodded on his way until he came to the Station.

"Sarah, full of despair: 'This time all is lost!' "[1]

Leibel did well to return to land, for there would not have been the slightest hope for him if he had not saved himself. One of the Arabs only escaped death by the prompt action of the father who heard his cry for help.

From the light which Aaron saw twice at the window of the

[1] From the unpublished memoirs of Liova Schneersohn.

Experiment Station, he understood that Leibel had achieved his aim, and was now safe at the Station. The important thing was that Sarah had received the signals, and connection was re-established at last.

After nine the next evening, the *Monegam* once more anchored off Athlit. Aaron noted in his diary: "Together with Capt. Smith and Yosef we run over the details of the final plan. At exactly 10 p.m. we leave the ship. Captain Weldon, Yosef, I, and the Tyrian fishermen. The sea is quiet, but there are heavy waves near the shore. Yosef is carried ashore on the shoulders of Abdullah's son. At 10.15 he disappears. Midnight. Yosef has not come back. 12.30. A line of light. Our men are there. Our boat approaches the shore. Three figures wait for us. A wonderful sight. Yosef, Liova, and Reuven. Loiva jumps into the boat, Reuven after him, with the water reaching to his knees. He falls on my neck."

After final instructions Yosef Lishansky and Reuven got off the boat and disappeared in the direction of the Station, while the *Monegam* quickly and quietly set sail for Egypt. Aaron did not permit himself the luxury of seeing Sarah. He had given instructions that she was not to come to the shore. The details of her welfare he got from Liova. But first Liova demanded news of Absalom. Aaron, knowing that he could depend on Liova, told him the truth of the disaster which had befallen their friend.

They both sat miserably on the deck, in the chill light of the early morning. Liova was seasick as well. He sat with his Bible in his hands. It was a gift from Absalom. One of the Intelligence officers, a young New Zealander, came up to Aaron.

"By the way," he asked, "what's your password?"

Obviously they needed a password. How else could they be sure of anyone they encountered on the seashore, on their dark landings? Aaron turned to Liova.

"What name shall we use?"

Liova opened the Bible. It is a common practice among Jews who are devoted to the Bible to form names from the initials of pertinent sentences from the Bible. Absalom's Bible fell open at 1 Samuel xv. Saul comes to Samuel, the priest, who had caused him to be chosen from among the tribes to rule over

Israel. Saul begs him to stay, but Samuel is angry with him and turns to go, saying: "I will not return with thee; for thou hast rejected the word of the Lord, and the Lord hath rejected thee from being King over Israel." As Samuel turns to leave, Saul catches at the priest's cloak to hold him back and the cloak tears. This Samuel sees as an irrevocable symbol, and he declares to Saul: "The Lord hath rent the kingdom of Israel from thee this day, and hath given it to a neighbour of thine, that is better than thou."

Neither Saul's prayers, nor his sacrifices could alter it now, Samuel told him, for: "The Eternity of Israel will not lie nor repent. Is He a person that He should repent?"

In Hebrew, the sentence, "The Eternity of Israel will not lie" is "Netzach Israel lo Ishakare."

"That's our password," exclaimed Liova, "NILI". He pronounced it in the Hebrew way, Nee-lee.

"Nellie?" said the New Zealander. "That's a nice name."

And so Nili became the name of the espionage group, adding a new word to the Hebrew language and a name by which many girls in Israel are called today.

Chapter 10

SARAH AT WORK

THE Nili movement, which worked for the next eight months under the very noses of the Turks and Germans, gathered the information which was to seal their doom in Palestine—this movement was as spontaneous as its name. There never was any formal organization, programme or procedure. It developed of itself, out of the needs of the time and the opportunities found by its members for fulfilling those needs.

The members of Nili, mostly young people between twenty-four and twenty-seven, were amateur spies. They had nothing to go on but their intelligence and their intuition. Each one acted according to his capacities, according to the extent of his ingenuity and his understanding. There discipline was Aaron's commands and the cohesion which Sarah induced in them by her own unswerving faith in the value of the work.

The organization, although it started with vast potentialities under Aaron, had dwindled to a few score by the time work finally got under way. Those who remained were people who had come into the work through love for Absalom, through their relationship to him or Aaron, or through working in daily contact with them at the Station. It was almost a family affair. Yet during the period of its operation, Nili became one of the chief factors in the life of the Yishuv; one of its chief sources of food and money during famine; and its outlet to the outside world, whence came the political pressures which shielded them from the brutal extinction meted out to the Armenians.

And the value of their intelligence work for the British? The answer is given by Lt.-Gen. G. M. Macdonough, Head of Military Intelligence at the British War Office from 1916 to 1919. In a lecture at the Royal Military Academy at Woolwich in 1921, he stated: "English Intelligence was victorious in 1918. You will no doubt remember the great campaign of Lord Allenby in Palestine in that year, and perhaps you are surprised at the daring of his action. The truth is, that it is impossible to anticipate victory in war without being ready to take risks. But all risks have to be logical. Someone who is looking from the sidelines, lacking knowledge about the situation, is likely to think that Allenby took unwarranted risks. That is not true. For Allenby knew with certainty from his intelligence (in Palestine) of all the preparations, and all the movements of his enemy. All the cards of his enemy were revealed to him, and so he could play his hand with complete confidence. Under these conditions victory was certain before he began."[1]

Captain Raymond Savage, Deputy Military Secretary to Field-Marshal Lord Allenby, was more explicit when he told the New York press in 1924: "It was very largely the daring work of young spies, most of them natives of Palestine, which enabled the brilliant Field-Marshal to accomplish his undertaking so effectively. The leader of the spy system was a young Jewess, a Miss Sarah Aaronsohn." The contact with the High Command in Egypt was made solely through Aaron, who was attached to G.H.Q. as a staff officer, and was, as General Allenby has stated, "mainly responsible for the formation of my Field Intelligence Organization behind the Turkish lines".[2]

"General Allenby, who made use of these services in the most brilliant manner, had the greatness of soul to declare that his victory over the Turks had to a large extent been due to Aaron Aaronsohn's incomparable achievements," stated Alex Aaronsohn,[3] who later served as Captain in the Intelligence with the victorious forces, winning the D.S.O.

This conflicts with the statement made by Lowell Thomas in his book on Lawrence, that his hero, disguised as an Arab woman, "penetrated hundreds of miles into enemy territory, where he obtained much of the data which finally enabled Field-Marshal Allenby's forces to overwhelm the Turks". Whatever feats Lawrence may or may not have performed in the Hejaz, which was well outside the area of Turkish army concentrations, he had no connection whatever with the work of Nili.

[1] *Sarah, the Flame of Nili*, by Simple Soldier (Jerusalem, 1943), p. 74
[2] Letter of condolence to Alexander Aaronsohn on death of Aaron.
[3] Introduction *Florula Transjordanica*

The remarkable circumstance of a group of people, voluntarily and without payment, risking their lives in order to place intelligence in the hands of the British must have stirred the imagination of those attached to G.H.Q., Cairo, among them Lawrence. In *Seven Pillars of Wisdom*, which he wrote some years later, Lawrence claimed this as part of his own achievements. "We on the Arab front were very intimate with the enemy. . . . Relations between us and them were universal, for the civil population of the enemy area was wholly ours without pay or persuasion. In consequence, our intelligence service was the widest, fullest and most certain imaginable."[1]

Neither Lawrence nor the Sherifian forces, who constituted the "Arab front", operated in the Palestine sector. The individual Arabs of Syria, Lebanon, and Palestine who acted as spies had direct contact with Intelligence in Egypt. They were paid for this. It is doubtful whether the information they provided could be classified as "the widest, fullest, and most certain imaginable". The civil population of Palestine was not anyone's, for they feared the Turks too much and were glad to keep out of trouble. The amount of information which Nili provided for the High Command might have made it seem as though the whole of the civil population took part in the espionage. In fact, only a small part of the Jewish population co-operated, and the Arab population of Palestine took no part in this or any other form of revolt against the Turks. The Palestine Royal Commission's report of 1937 (which, incidentally, fails to mention Nili's activities) explains the Arab attitude by stating: "But it must be remembered that to revolt in the desert was far easier than to revolt in a country still in Turkish hands, and subject, as the British invasion proceeded, to increasingly vigorous treatment."[2]

All the more remarkable, then, that a group of unarmed young people took on themselves to rebel in those conditions and held to their decision, even when their grim and inevitable fate unfolded like a Greek tragedy before them.

Sarah Aaronsohn was not only the force behind the organization in Palestine. Without her there would have been no Nili.

[1] *Seven Pillars of Wisdom* (ibid), p. 394
[2] Pal. Royal Commission Report (London, 1937), p. 22

Yosef Lishansky and the other members of Nili daily performed deeds of courage and daring. But it was Sarah who was the inspiration, the incentive, the focus for all the activity. Only she could have held it together. Only she had the wisdom, the steadfastness and the spiritual strength to confront the hostility of the Yishuv as well as the enmity of the Turk.

When Lishansky arrived in Palestine he revealed to Sarah, and to Sarah alone, the secret of the death of Absalom. From that moment she ceased to be the gay, tender, reasonable young woman that everyone had known. She became as iron, and there was no human power which could have turned her from her chosen task. "To continue what my dear one began—that is all I wish," she wrote to Aaron. "And vengeance, great vengeance, on the wild ones of the desert, and on the cruel Turk. May God only give us life to continue."

Within a week of Lishansky's return, he and Sarah took the first of their long trips, spreading the network of espionage which eventually reached as far as Damascus in Syria. Sarah had not forgotten that Yosef had encouraged Absalom to make his fatal journey through the desert. But that was past. Sarah knew Yosef's weaknesses, but he had valuable qualities as well. He was daring, he was optimistic, and like herself he was prepared to sacrifice everything for the success of the work.

Composed and pleasant, there was no hint of dangerous enterprise about the plump, blue-suited young woman in the pretty white blouse of her own making who set out sedately from her father's house in full view of the villagers of Zichron. Sarah had often accompanied Aaron on his journeys around the country. Now too she travelled in the carriage belonging to the Experiment Station, driven by Abu Farid, Aaron's servant and trusted friend. Their destination was Jerusalem, with a long detour to include Nazareth, the Turkish military headquarters in the north. From the moment they set out, they began to record everything that could be of value to the British in Egypt—troop movements, conditions of the crops, the mood of the population. ". . . The yield of corn between Zichron and Athlit is small, because the heavy rains delayed sowing. In the Station itself the yield is very good. On the way from Athlit to

Haifa, we met the Arab military coastguards, patrolling, not on the coast, but on the highway!"

In Haifa, their first stop, they were able to co-opt helpers for their work, but failed to receive permits to travel to Jerusalem, which belonged to another villayet (district). Authority had to come from Damascus. In Haifa they could get permits to go no farther than Tiberias, and it was forbidden to take their own carriage and horses. How much baksheesh changed hands was not recorded, but two days later they set out for Nazareth in their own carriage with Abu Farid at the reins, as before, and Jerusalem still their destination.

They picked up information all along the route. With a mejidi (half a crown) they could do anything. With a gold pound they could buy anyone. In one evening in Nazareth they found out that there was a large arms dump in the courtyard of the convent of the Carmelite Sisters. They knew which troops were stationed in the area, where they came from, and who was at their head. Also that the soldiers were starving, for the officers stole their rations and they had to subsist on what they could pilfer from the provisions allocated for the pack animals.

The next morning they were off again, heading for Tiberias. On their way they stopped at Beit Gan, a tiny farming community huddled in a hollow between black hills which rose above the houses like a besieging army. Out of sight of the encircled settlement, the basalt range dropped sheer to the Sea of Galilee, which lay at its feet, 200 metres below sea-level. Beit Gan was Yosef's home, in as much as he had one. He had been one of the founders of the settlement, and his wife's family still lived there. The grim routine of a farmer's life was not for Yosef, and he had turned watchman, working together with a group of Ha-Shomer (the watchmen's organization) who lived higher up on the basalt ridge at a place called Poriah.

They were responsible for the security of the settlements in the Jordan Valley, four or five islands in a sea of Arab settlement. Yosef was always at loggerheads with Ha-Shomer. He wanted to take a strong hand with the pilfering Arabs and teach them a lesson. This was contrary to Ha-Shomer policy. They were too few to withstand a concerted attack and had decided that they must build up prestige by caution and diplomacy. When Yosef killed an Arab in a fracas, he was obliged to leave the area to escape the retribution of the tribe. He was excluded from Ha-Shomer as well. He went off to the south, where he tried to start another watchman's organization from the many independent watchmen who also did not feel at home in the strict and dedicated discipline of Ha-Shomer. It was then that he met Absalom and joined Nili.

Yosef hoped to recruit workers for Nili among his old friends at Beit Gan, but he failed. They did not want to contaminate themselves with espionage. Besides, the farmers in Galilee had managed their relations with the authorities much better than those in the south. It was hardly worth trying to overthrow a government that gave you whatever you wanted for baksheesh.

Yosef and Sarah did not even have to go to Tiberias to get the forbidden permit for Jerusalem. They sent in for it from Beit Gan. "For five Turkish pieces of paper, they did this for us and even gave us an order that our horses must not be interfered with on the way," Yosef wrote Aaron. "From this you learn everything."

Their next call was down the sheer basalt ridge and across the River Jordan. The bridge across the Jordan was so narrow there was no room for the horses to pass. Sarah crossed by boat, while Yosef and Abu Farid drew the carriage over the bridge, all the time in danger of slipping over the sides and falling into the river. Their main reason for taking the long detour was to arrange for an agent at the railway junction of Affulah. This was one of the most important points in Palestine, for all men and munitions from Constantinople, Aleppo and Damascus passed through Affulah on their way to the front.

The chief military doctor at Affulah was a friend of the Aaronsohn family. Sarah brought him a note from Aaron, asking him to take part in their work. Dr Neumann was a cautious, good-living man, a bachelor, who took his mother to live with him wherever he went. When he finished reading the letter that Sarah brought him, he looked up in horror. "But I'll be playing with my head if I do this!" he protested.

Sarah was watching him with her straight, penetrating look. She answered him quietly, pointing to her own head: "You see, my head also sits firmly on my shoulders, but I am endangering it all the time. If you call yourself a man, you should be prepared to do the same."

Dr Neumann became a valuable member of Nili. It was his duty to inspect each trainload of soldiers as they arrived, and from his dispatches the British knew exactly what reinforcements the Turks and the Germans were sending into Palestine. He even went out and measured the railway lines at Aaron's request, so that the railway the British were building to carry supplies and troops through the desert would match up at Affulah and be ready to carry them right through to Damascus.

Eight days after leaving Zichron, Sarah and Yosef reached Jerusalem. It was still light, and they immediately contacted their people. That evening they were able to add, to their report to Aaron, which divisions were in the country, their strength, and where they were stationed. Thanks to one of their informants at headquarters in Jerusalem, Aaron was able to notify G.H.Q. Cairo that ". . . from Shellale and Sharia, and south-east from Beersheba the Turks are planning to hold only a temporary defensive line, and afterwards to retire to the mountains of Jerusalem and Hebron, which they are already fortifying."

In Jerusalem Sarah and Yosef stayed at the Hotel Fast, rendezvous of young German officers who spent their time drinking and arguing over women and the war. Yosef mixed with them at the bar. The German Commander von Kressenstein was staying at the hotel with members of his staff, and from one of them Yosef learned that the German forces in Palestine numbered some 50,000 men. From another source he learned where they were stationed. Sarah sat, demure and serious, in the lounge. She was ostensibly absorbed in letter writing, but jotted down whatever she could glean from the officers talking around her. "The Germans were previously informed by Beduin spies that the English had an army of about 100,000 men in the South, and now after they've made a count by aeroplane, they've decided that the English haven't more than 50,000 there," she noted.

By the time they left Jerusalem two days later they had received a map of the city with all the fortifications marked on it by one of their contacts, who was an engineer in the army. "I will get some more maps from him, and from other places, which will be very interesting and useful to you. We have also contacted another man, very important in the government, and he is prepared to work for us without getting any reward. The population is impoverished and dispirited. Everyone here says that if the English really wanted to come, they would have come long ago. They are certain they won't come now."

At Rishon-le-Zion they called on Naaman Belkind and picked up the information he had collected for them. Naaman was worried at not having heard from his cousin Absalom. Yosef explained that Absalom was busy training to be a pilot, and he had no time to write. Naaman hardly listened to him. He could not stand the way Yosef acted as if he were the head of Nili, and Sarah kept deferring to him as well. He believed that Yosef was taking advantage of Absalom's absence to get control of Nili and had in some unaccountable way won over Sarah as well. Among the papers he gave them was a letter to Absalom.

They left Rishon feeling miserable, and there was foreboding in Sarah's heart. But the calls went on over the rutted roads or no roads at all, for the heavy rains had left quagmires everywhere. At Petach Tikvah they heard a rumour that the Beduin were buying the oranges which had been left hanging on the trees for lack of buyers, and were taking them south to sell to the British patrols in the Sinai desert bordering the Canal. "If this rumour is true," Yosef wrote, "then you want to catch these Beduin and not let them come back, because they reveal what is going on in the English lines. In general, it is most essential not to permit the Beduin from here to cross the border, and not to allow Arab spies to come here, otherwise the English will just be making trouble for themselves."

At 8 o'clock that evening, they arrived back at Zichron after a journey of twelve days. Zichronites, seeing Sarah handed out of the carriage by Yosef, looking so dapper in city clothes, were quick to form an opinion of two people who went off for joy rides in such serious times. Sarah understood the looks very well. Pale with fatigue, but with her head held high, she greeted them quietly and pleasantly and then passed into the shelter of her father's house. There was no one, not in Zichron nor in the whole of Palestine, to whom she could reveal her thoughts, with whom she could share her burden for even a little while. Only when writing her final report to Aaron that night did she permit a sigh to escape her: "The house is always sad and lonely, and all kinds of terrible thoughts come into my mind, for after all, our work is very black, and always in danger. Thank goodness, that until now everything has been all right."

Chapter 11

THE GUESTS OF RAHAB

TOWARDS the end of the month, as the moon waned, Sarah began to watch for the ship on the horizon. An open window in a watch tower in the Aaronsohn vineyard on the mountain top at Zichron indicated to the ship far out at sea that all was well, and that is was safe to return that night. They signalled from the Experiment Station as well by hanging sheets in an arranged order on the clothes line. The sheets for signalling were always kept ready, and when Sarah saw the ship on the horizon, she would quickly wet them and hang them on the line, as if to dry. White sheets for safety, a red sofa cover for danger. The ship would increase smoke, as a sign that the message had been received, and then sail off. The *Monegam* would turn up again after dark and anchor some two kilometres off the shore. Liova, Leibel and sometimes Raphael Aboulafia would be rowed ashore by the Arab boatmen, who would then carry them through the water if the waves were high. Although they no longer experienced the hazards of Leibel's first trip, it took courage to plunge through the stormy water, even on someone's back.

The contact between the sea and the shore, and the shore and the Station, had to be made in darkness. Everyone concerned took his life in his hands. Caution was even more imperative than courage, but how could one be cautious when moving practically blindfold over a kilometre and a half of boulder, steep-banked wadi, open highway and stubble field? Sarah and her helpers at the Station were experts. They had all grown up in the area and could make their way as easily by night as by day. The expeditions soon became a routine, and they assessed by instinct the danger conveyed in every sound. Aaron had forbidden Sarah to make the journey, but she went whenever she could, for she had no fear.

On the nights when the ship was expected, Sarah and a man,

109

or sometimes two or three men, would leave the Station like shadows and be swallowed up in the darkness of Aaron's famous palm-bordered road which ran for three-quarters of a kilometre to the main highway. Crossing the highway was the most dangerous part of the journey. This was the beat of the patrols. Nili had a man in the village who tried to keep the soldiers occupied with drinks and cards when the ship was expected, but it did not always work. There were troop movements too.

They halted in the shadow of the palms to listen. Eyes wide, ears strained, they went forward slowly, silently. Suddenly the silence was broken. The noise came from a field close by. Another moment and a cow leaped out and plunged into the wadi in front of them.

"If a cow has escaped," whispered Sarah, "a man is running after it." She jumped behind a great boulder and disappeared. Manasseh was beside her. The others melted into the darkness. A moment passed and the cowherd appeared, a tall Arab brandishing a stout stick. He found his cow, then came up to the boulder behind which they were hiding. There, on its flat top, he squatted down to "cover his feet", as the Bible puts it, when Saul chose a cave for the same purpose, the very same cave in which David and his men were lying concealed.

Suddenly Manasseh felt that Sarah was moving. He would have stopped her, but he knew that Sarah would never do anything without a reason. Stealthily she rose above the level of the rock, and when she knelt down again the cowherd's cudgel was in her hand. Then Manasseh remembered. Sarah had given her weapon to one of the others when they set out, and she was using this opportunity to rearm herself.

The Arab stretched out his hand to take the stick. He felt all around him. Finding nothing, he let out a few curses and went to look for his cow. "Don't you remember your Bible", said Sarah with a laugh. "I will deliver thine enemy into thine hands, and thou mayest do unto him as it seem good unto thee. Then David arose and cut off the skirt of Saul's robe privily." She leapt up and went on toward the sand dunes.

"Sarah," whispered Manasseh, "don't get too far ahead of us. Wait."

"Quiet," she breathed, and strode ahead. As they mounted

the crest of the hill, the roar of the Mediterranean rose out of the stillness. The episode with the cowherd had lengthened the time of the journey, and the visitors from the sea were already there, anxiously waiting.

The meeting with the messengers from the outside world made up for all the dangers. Short questions and answers, and then the leather bag full of reports and letters was handed over. In exchange, they received a pouch containing letters, newspapers, instructions, materials, and gold for Nili work. They would have liked to prolong the meeting, but not a moment could be spared. Captain Weldon was waiting in the little boat. Abdullah, the boatman, had already given the signal. Shalom, Shalom. And the three visitors strode into the sea and were lost in the darkness.

One night they lay on the cliff waiting for the party. The night was calm and the sea was smooth. About a hundred yards to the left, on the other side of the wadi, there was a water-melon field guarded by Arabs. The people lying on the cliff were out of sight, but they could hear every word the Arabs were saying.

Shortly after nine the little boat approached the shore, and presently they could see the silhouettes of their three friends coming in their direction. One of the visitors stepped on a dry branch, and it snapped loudly. The Arabs immediately seized their guns and began to fire. The people lying on the cliff could hear the bullets whizzing over their heads.

The visitors dropped to the ground, and after a moment the Arabs ceased firing, deciding that it must have been a false alarm. The visitors turned and made for the shore again. Sarah sprang up and gave chase. Feeling themselves pursued, the visitors ran harder, but Sarah, fleet of foot and delighted at the unexpected sport, caught up with them before they disappeared again into the sea.

Once a more serious incident occurred. Again the night was quiet, and the stars shone bright overhead. The people from the Station were early, and they lay on the sands, waiting for the visitors, everyone plunged in his own thoughts. The small boat approached silently, and after a murmured greeting they set to work with feverish haste to unload its contents. This time, in addition to Nili supplies, there were provisions and heavy sacks of gold coins for the relief of the destitute.

They had hardly started on their work when, to their horror, the bells of an approaching caravan reached their ears. There was no time to lose. All the cases and bags were thrown back into the boat, which quickly made off with its party. The people from the Station rushed into the sea, leaving only their heads above the water. There they waited while a caravan of some twenty camels and ten or more Arabs plodded past, unaware of the four pairs of eyes watching them from the water a few metres away.

When the caravan had passed out of hearing, they emerged once more, wet and shuddering with cold. At a signal the boat returned, and they began again to haul off the cases, this time undisturbed.

On another occasion when they were expecting the visit of the *Monegam* that night, they became aware of a German U-boat wandering along the coast. Worse still, the Commander of the U-boat paid a visit to Athlit village. Did it mean that the Germans had received information about Nili's means of communication, or was it purely an accidental visit to the inviting little harbour? The Commander spent more than an hour there, drinking with the officer in charge of the coast patrol, and then left in the direction of Haifa.

From the Experiment Station they kept a close watch over the sea in case the U-boat should return that day. Just before sunset they saw it speeding southward. Their anxiety grew, for one of their agents at Athlit village reported that the U-boat was after a British ship. The *Monegam* was, in fact, pursued by the U-boat, but managed after a lengthy detour to throw it off in time to arrive at Athlit not more than a few hours later.

When Aaron heard that Sarah was endangering her life by going to the seashore, he was much concerned. Her work was at the Station and at Zichron. Going to sea was the duty of the men. Yet even though he scolded her, he could not help praising her bravery. "I really wanted to give you a smack on the face because you went to wait for the boat by the sea. But I also want to kiss you for this. I love you for your courage, Sarati, but a human being mustn't be treated like a rag. Do you remember the tribe of Arab Savia? They had one heroine in their family, whose name was Savha. Until this day, when one of the tribe wants to encourage himself or his brethren, he cries: 'I am your brother, Savha, our sister.' Do you want us to be of the House of Sarah?"

Sarah wrote him a little letter in reply: "You amuse me, Araleh, when you write that my face should be slapped because I go to greet the visitors from the sea. Do you really think this is bravery?"

Soon after connections between Egypt and Athlit were established, the rumour spread in the Yishuv that a dangerous group was in their midst. The actual details of Nili's work were never known, for only a handful of people took part in the contact between the Station and the sea. But the existence of a group of people carrying on espionage and plotting rebellion could not be concealed. Sarah and Yosef Lishansky were striving all the time to bring more people into the work of Nili, and to do this they had to reveal something of their activities.

The continual attempts to widen the base of the movement had, like the movement itself, a drastic political aim. If Nili could be recognized as having acted in the name of the Yishuv, then Aaron would have the authority to stand before the Allied Powers at the end of the war and make his demands in the name of the Jews of Palestine. But the small Jewish community of Palestine already had a recognized body which was doing its best to safeguard its welfare. At the beginning of the war the Zionist and communal heads had set up a Security Committee to organize the Jewish population for the purposes of mutual help, and to ameliorate its lot through intercession with the authorities. The Committee was not democratically elected, and many sections of the population were not represented on it, but because of the seriousness of the situation and the money for relief which had been put at its disposal, chiefly by America, it had wide powers among the Jews of Palestine. (This voluntary discipline, which included self-imposed community taxation and acceptance of political authority, was the beginning of the self-organized community which finally emerged as the Jewish State.)

The Security Committee was a depleted and distraught

body by the time Nili tried to take control of the situation in the spring of 1917, as most of the leading figures of the community had been banished by the Turks. The "guests of Rahab", who now suddenly appeared in their midst, created panic among them. The leaders had struggled all these years to prove to the Turks that the Yishuv was loyal, and they genuinely believed that only by complete loyalty could the Jewish community continue to exist until the storm of war and persecution passed.

It was by no means cowardice which dictated this policy. Ha-Shomer, one of the most courageous groups of men that ever existed, was also dead against Nili. Over a period of years Ha-Shomer had built up a strongly disciplined organization which had taken on itself the task of defending the isolated Jewish settlements. The Turks provided neither law nor order. Every Jewish settlement depended either on the goodwill of its Arab neighbours (which had to be bought), or on force of arms (which Ha-Shomer to a large extent represented). Small in numbers and insufficiently armed, Ha-Shomer could only function under two conditions: non-interference from the Turks, and unquestioning co-operation from all sections of the Yishuv. Nili imperilled both these conditions. On the one hand, if they were caught spying and fomenting rebellion, Ha-Shomer would be destroyed and the Yishuv with it. On the other hand, Nili represented nobody. It consisted of individuals who were acting on behalf of the Yishuv but were not subject to the discipline of any of its organizations.

If Aaron or Absalom had been in the country, the opposition might have been less bitter. Both had undeniable status in the Yishuv, and none could doubt their seriousness or their sense of responsibility. But Yosef Lishansky, who now acted as spokesman for Nili in Palestine and was canvassing for recruits—who was Lishansky? A penniless watchman, a fly by night, always up to some crazy escapade. Could not stick to farming, neglected his wife and two children. People were outraged. Hottest against him were Ha-Shomer. He had worked with them for two years, but they had expelled him from their group for refusing to submit to their discipline.

At Ha-Shomer's headquarters at Tel Adas, in the mountains of Nazareth, they decided that Nili must be destroyed. A messenger was sent to the Political Committee of the Workers' Movement in Jaffa demanding that Nili be broken up. The active members were to be brought inland under guard and forbidden to appear in any settlement near the coast. If they refused to comply, terror must be used against them. In guarded terms, the Workers' newspaper announced its decision: "Our realistic policy in the existing circumstances is complete civilian loyalty, and every activity which removes the Yishuv from this framework must be thought of as a danger to the existence of the Yishuv."

The old settlers too were against Nili. It was too drastic. It was putting all the Yishuv's eggs in one basket. One false step on their part would bring sure and terrible destruction to the settlements which they had succeeded in building up after thirty-five years of toil. It was suspected that the Station at Athlit was the centre of activity. Zichron seethed with gossip, with fears, with prognostications. Ephraim Aaronsohn listened to the talk around him, his gnarled old peasant face revealing nothing to the sharp eyes that tried to pry from him the secrets of his children. Beyond repeating to Sarah any information that could be of value to the British, he never spoke about the espionage, or cautioned her against the dangerous path she had chosen to follow. If Aaron was in it, it must be all right.

Sarah went about her work, shirking no encounters. Ever since she could remember, Aaron, Alex and the Aaronsohn family had been the target of violent criticism and abuse on the part of the Workers' Movement or some other section of the community. Aaron had never let it turn him from doing what he considered right. The beautiful Experiment Station, which had no equal in the Eastern Mediterranean, was the result of his vision and his effort. He had made the whole world of agriculture turn to poor little Palestine to learn the secrets of fertility. Great scientists came to visit his library and to study in his herbarium. All this he had achieved by himself, because he knew more, saw farther; because his love for his country was so deep and understanding that he could see fruitful fields where others saw only barrenness; a proud and free people, where others saw only poverty and helplessness.

Sarah wrote to Aaron: "The Yishuv is all excited and stirred up. Everyone is thinking things about us. For the time being our work is being carried on properly and as it should be, and we have no fear that they will inform the authorities on us."

Less than two weeks later, a blow fell on the Yishuv which made many people in the community look to Nili as the only hope of salvation. On March 28th Djemal Pasha ordered the expulsion of the Jews from Jaffa and its new suburb of Tel Aviv. This followed Gen. Maude's capture of Baghdad on March 11th and the first signs of a British offensive in Palestine, a three-day attack on Gaza on March 27th which the Turks only just repelled.

Djemal Pasha had declared: "I know that the Jewish community in Palestine is waiting for the English like a bride for her bridegroom, but as the bridegroom comes closer, we will remove the bride farther away." The expulsions from Jaffa and Tel Aviv showed that he was really going to carry out his promise. Perhaps Nili could hasten the British victory and prevent the evil designs from being carried out.

Meanwhile the refugees streamed out of Jaffa on foot, and in the vehicles which had been mobilized from the settlements and villages in response to the S O S sent out by the Security Committee, which had been situated in Jaffa. Accommodation was found for them in settlements and villages all over the country. Twenty-four hours after refugees arrived in Zichron, Sarah informed Aaron and Reuter had flashed a message around the world of impending Jewish atrocities.

The Allies—who now included America—were conscious of the moral advantages which had been gained from the German invasion of Belgium and the Armenian atrocities. The possibilities of a massacre of the Jews in Palestine served the same purpose. The State Department and the British Embassy in Washington began a barrage aimed at the neutral countries. The German Government, sensitive to the implications of this diplomatic attack, denied the story but at the same time cautioned the Turkish authorities to be more discreet. The story ricocheted from consulate to consulate, until it arrived back in Palestine in May, just in time to stop the expulsion of the Jews of Jerusalem to the desert of Transjordan, where they would doubtless have died of starvation, as did the Armenians in the Syrian desert.

The Yishuv was not even aware that someone was working on their behalf, and Sarah herself did not know the value of the work she had done. The shock of the expulsions released in Sarah the horror and foreboding which had hovered at the back of her mind ever since she had seen the fate of the Armenians. She never knew that in her heart there could be such compassion. All her love flowed out to the miserable refugees, sheltering in the wine cellars of Zichron, and she became a sister of mercy among them. She longed to tell them the great secret, that they were no longer cut off from the world and surely the redemption would not be long in coming.

She wrote to Aaron, urging him to get money so that she could provide food and clothes for the children. Aaron had already begun to concern himself with aid for the Yishuv and had organized a Relief Committee in Cairo to collect contributions in Egypt. When Aaron let it be known in Egypt that help and messages could be sent to Palestine, he was inundated with things which he passed on to Nili. This was very dangerous and added enormously to the trials and responsibilities of the small group, but Aaron thought it was politically important enough to justify the risks involved in focusing attention on them as the suppliers of the Yishuv.

One day a little man came to the Hotel Continental in Cairo to find Aaron. He would not reveal his business to Liova, and when Liova entered Aaron's room with him and remained there, the little man told Aaron that he had to speak to him privately. Aaron assured him that Liova was quite safe, and he explained his business. He had an almond grove at Kfar Saba. He was not sure that it was being properly taken care of. The trees had been saplings when he left Palestine two years before. Could Nili find out how high the trees were now? Aaron burst into a roar. "They're *so* high!" he shouted, measuring with his hands above his head. The little man, terrified, backed out, stumbled over a chair near the door and ran for his life.

Money began to pour in from Europe and America as a result of the publicity. With America's entry into the war in April, Nili became the sole channel through which substantial help could be sent to Palestine. It was a major triumph for Aaron's powers of persuasion that he could get permission from the British High Command to send quantities of gold into blockaded enemy territory. His status had risen since contact had been renewed with Athlit, and the High Command now had complete confidence in him.

The money was sent to Palestine in the form of gold coins of pre-war mint. In pitch darkness and with agonizing caution the messengers of Nili carried the heavy sacks of gold coins on their backs, through the sea, across the sand dunes, over the boulders, to the Experiment Station. Sometimes there was as much as £4,000 at a time. Sarah and Lishansky had to conceal the sacks of gold until they could be placed, again with the utmost secrecy, into the hands of the Relief Committee for distribution. This was apart from the gold brought in for Nili work, and Sarah kept meticulous accounts of both, passing the receipts on to Aaron in Cairo.

Although Ha-Shomer and the Workers' Political Committee were still dead against them, Nili's prestige rose. Lishansky thought that the time had come "for the Yishuv to know that it is Mr A. Aaronsohn who is organizing the affairs of the country in this moment of emergency". That would assist Nili in organizing groups of young people everywhere who would be under Nili's discipline, "prepared to go everywhere we order them to, and for the time being we will use them as defence forces in the country, for there will certainly be disturbances very soon. And you (Aaronsohn) must remember that we are here without arms, and you must try to send us arms, so that we will always be able to defend our honour against those who will be ready to attack us in our time of need."

Chapter 12

SARAH IN CAIRO

EVER since contact had been established, Aaron had been urging Sarah to come to Egypt. Now that the work was under way, Sarah agreed to come on condition that Aaron promised to let her return to Athlit with the next ship. Liova Schneersohn was mooning about in Port Said, aimless and dissatisfied, when he got word from Aaron to go to Palestine and bring Sarah back with him.

Absalom's vision and fervour had made Liova one of the first adherents of Nili. Now, two months after his friend's death, he found himself dashed from the heights that Absalom's vision had created, into the cold abyss of reality. The excitement over the renewal of contact had disappeared in the days of waiting in Famagusta, in Port Said, in Alexandria, for the moon to go down or the sea to calm. And for all their work and danger, there was no sign that they were accomplishing anything for their suffering people in Palestine.

Liova had no relations with the British officers under whom he worked, and Aaron had snubbed him when he wrote complaining: "They don't understand us. We, Yosef and all of us, we are doing our work for them—but is it meant to be only for them?" Aaron, himself frustrated on his first contact with the British, was very busy now and impatient at being bothered in the midst of his important work by the soul-searchings of a young dreamer. Aaron was a practical man and an optimist. He had no patience with the pessimism and the unanswerable questions of the Russian intellectuals, and Liova felt this and resented it.

There were only two things that he could hold on to. The memory of his friend and his love for Sarah. But thoughts of Absalom only deepened his melancholy, and his love for Sarah increased his despair. What could he hope for from a woman who had been the beloved of Absalom and was herself not free?

But his love welled up unbidden, like his poetry, and his thoughts and his doubts and his worries were all consigned to a little notebook, inscribed on the cover "To Sarah".

"You gave meaning to my life, and courage for my work," he wrote. "Comfort me, Sarah, and help me now. Help to strengthen my faith in Nili, which has bound our two lives together, and taught us to offer ourselves for our homeland."

Aaron's message to go to Athlit and bring Sarah back with him came like an answer to a prayer. The *Monegam* left Port Said on April 14th, and at nine the next morning Liova was out on deck with binoculars and diary. "We are getting nearer Zichron. We wait for the sign. We can make out the house in the vineyard at Zichron—the window, and the open shutters. At 2 o'clock we approach Athlit. We don't see any signals. What happened? Have they made a mistake in the day? We don't see anybody. We sail slowly past, on to Haifa.

"Once again we are sailing for Athlit. It's 9 p.m. now, and we extinguish our lights. Half an hour later we put a boat down and reach the coast. The sea is quiet. We go ashore. We listen. Silence. Leibel follows me. They've not let us down at the right place. We turn north; stones, rocks, difficult going. At last we reach a track we recognize. We've crossed our boundary. The night is hot and pleasant. The frogs are croaking. In the distance we hear the sound of men's voices. We slip silently past the most dangerous place, and at last, on the other side of the highway, we hurry forward. There is light in the house. They must be there.

"I tell Leibel to wait, and enter the house. Who's there on the balcony? Yosef?

" 'Yes, yes.'

"Hurry up then. What's happened to you? Where's Sarah? Why didn't you give the signals?"

"I'm already upstairs. Questions, answers, excitement, discussions. I hand over money, equipment, orders. We collect together the necessary men, and at half-past eleven we finally return to the shore.

"I go first. We reach the sea. I see the outline of the ship. Everyone lies down. I signal, and immediately we feel the boat approaching.

"The captain is very quick. It appears that there are two submarines in the area. A few days ago pirates were seen around the coast of Athlit. We're not going to take the load off today. They'll do that on their way back from Tyre. I enter first, with the leather bag with the papers in my hand, and after me Sarah, Leibel and Yosef."

There had been no intention that Lishansky should accompany Sarah to Egypt. He had his work to do and was even more important in her absence. But the idea of a little jaunt appealed to him—they were only going to be away three days—and he wanted to be with Sarah.

Aaron met them at Port Said. His eyes sought out Sarah, whom he had not seen since he left Palestine almost a year before. And Absalom had left them. They stood looking at each other, too moved to say anything, only their eyes speaking. After a moment he slowly lifted his hand and gently pinched her cheek.

"Are you well, Sarati?"

When Aaron noticed Yosef emerging behind her, he gave him a look of amazement and fury, but said nothing. Port Said was too dangerously public. In his room at the hotel Aaron hit the table a blow that smashed the glass on his wristwatch and roared at Yosef for deserting his post. When Liova turned up early the next morning, with flowers for Sarah, he found the two men moody and silent. Yosef glared at him, and Aaron ignored him.

Aaron's rages were like tornadoes, and even Sarah did not openly interfere with him. She remained discreet and pleasant, silent but friendly, inwardly praying that the storm would subside before Yosef became deflated to the point of stubbornness and defiance. That happened so easily if he thought he was not appreciated. In her dealings with him she had always been meticulous in according him the respect he thought he deserved.

Sarah understood Yosef much better than either Aaron or Liova, and she could appreciate, as they could not, how important his work was for Nili. She did not see how the work could be done in Palestine without his co-operation. She could only go to places where a woman's presence would not attract too much attention. She could not move about on horseback in the wild south, among the Beduin and the army. And none of the other members of Nili had his contacts.

Sorry as she was to part from Aaron, Sarah could only feel relief as the train left the station for Port Said two days later. But here a totally unforeseen calamity befell them. Stormy weather held them up in Port Said until they could no longer leave. They had to return to Cairo to wait until they could try again in another fifteen days.

Sarah stayed at the Hotel Continental with Aaron, and she learned from him the course of his attempts to shape history single-handed. In some respects he had already made consider-able progress. The British High Command had come to recog-nize his value, and work was now piling in on him. Aaron was spending eight to nine hours a day in consultations at the Savoy Hotel, the Headquarters of General Staff Intelligence, and then coming back to his room and working until two in the morning. This was no real exertion for Aaron. In the old days he would sit and work for three days on end, dozing in his chair and waking up to work again. In his eating habits he was like a camel, eating enormously at one time, if food was available, or able to do without for long stretches. But now he kept more regular hours. It was too important for him to be on duty again the next day, always at hand, when those high-ranking officers needed him.

"I mustn't relax my grip for a single moment," he told Sarah. "It wasn't easy to achieve, but the great ones, who have the fate of the whole business in their hands, have begun to listen to us. Now that they've got used to listening, and even to asking for advice, it's my duty to be available all the time, to answer their demands."

The fact was that Lloyd George had begun to press for activity on the Eastern front, and less than three weeks before he had sent a telegram to the C.-in-C. of the British forces in Egypt, Sir Archibald Murray, indicating Jerusalem as an immediate objective for his army. Aaron was an inexhaustible gold-mine for the General Staff. Until he came, they had no more up-to-date source of information on the topography of the territory to be invaded than a survey made by Lord Kitchener in 1878, when he was a subaltern in the R.E. Aaron's reports for the Higher Command contained not only the information which he received from Athlit, but also his own personal knowledge of everything connected with the country. The reports were known as AAG—the Aaron Aaronsohn Group.

Aaron was branching out in other directions as well. "It seems as though I have a hidden talent, as our mother used to say. Strategic abilities have been revealed in me. I took courage and spoke with one of the officers, a person of secondary importance, and of average intelligence. He listened, admitted that he didn't understand all, but suggested that I speak with his chief. And so I went up and up, until yesterday the highest of the high called me to see him, and thanked me for the serious and basic plans I had presented to him. This is not yet action, Sarati, but it is an important step towards action."

Plans were now being made for the future administration of the areas to be conquered. Sir Archibald Murray was so impressed with Aaron's abilities that he declared he would recommend him as director of agriculture not only for Palestine and Syria, but for Mesopotamia as well. Here was a unique opportunity, which Aaron did not fail to exploit, of pressing his idea of linking the Jews of Palestine with British aspirations in the area. The first reaction was always one of astonishment. "But there are no Jews in Palestine. The country is settled only by Arabs!"

Then Aaron told them of the Jewish settlements which had been going on in Palestine for the past thirty-five years. He told them of the founding of Zichron and the heroic struggle of the pioneers, his parents among them; and of his own efforts, through the Jewish Agricultural Experiment Station, to restore the whole area to its ancient fertility. If there was a speck of culture and creation in the midst of the desert, it was due to the sacrifices which the Jews had made for the sake of the national rebirth of their land, he told them. "These dots of culture are very few, because the Turkish authorities put great obstacles in the way of the settlers. But if the country will again come under a civilized government, one which will help towards its development, and which will give guarantees for the national rights of the Jews in the country, then Jewish energy will be able to revive the whole land."

With brilliant simplicity Aaron answered another question which had puzzled many of them: "Are the Jews a nation, or a religion?" It was as a nation that the Jews had been driven out of Palestine, and it was as a nation that they had been kept out of it during all the centuries, he explained. Although a small minority in Palestine at the moment, the Jews nevertheless were the only group of people living there which represented a nation in embryo. Just as the varied physical and geographical characteristics of Palestine made it a mosaic of countries, so its population was a mosaic of the peoples which had passed through it since the dawn of history. The Arab conquest had turned these various residues into Moslems, speaking an Arabic dialect, but they were not Arabs for all that, Aaron maintained, and they represented no national entity.

Aaron's clear policy, and his deep love for the Jewish people in Palestine, proved a source of enlightenment to the young Near Eastern diplomats such as the Hon. William Ormsby-Gore, then in Cairo, and his colleague, Sir Mark Sykes, Assistant Secretary to the War Cabinet. Mark Sykes was the chief motivating force in London behind the British Government's Near Eastern policy in the war. He had known the East from boyhood. A younger man than Aaron, he was brilliant, seemingly erratic but in reality firm in his loyalties and subtle in his tactics. He had come from England in the summer of 1917 to plan Allied policy in the Middle East, and Aaron had won his complete trust. Sykes liked the genuine product, a people of the soil, proud of their own race. "The Jews were to be regenerated, they were to become a nation of genuine peasants and squires, like everybody else, not financiers, cosmopolitans and radicals."[1] In Aaron, Sykes saw the personification of the change which even one generation on its own soil can work in the Jewish people.

Picot, the French signatory of the Sykes-Picot treaty of 1916, which had divided the Middle East into zones of control and influence, had accompanied Mark Sykes on a mission to inform the non-enemy Arab leaders about the post-war plans which the Allies had for the area. Sykes invited Aaron to meet Picot. Aaron debated stormily with him, maintaining that any solu-

[1] Kedourie, *England and the Middle East*, p. 85

The Aaronsohn House

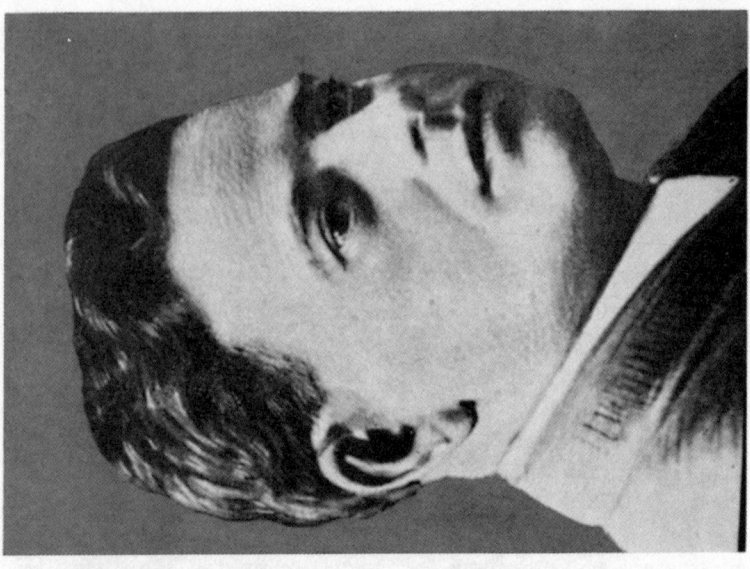

Aaron Aaronsohn

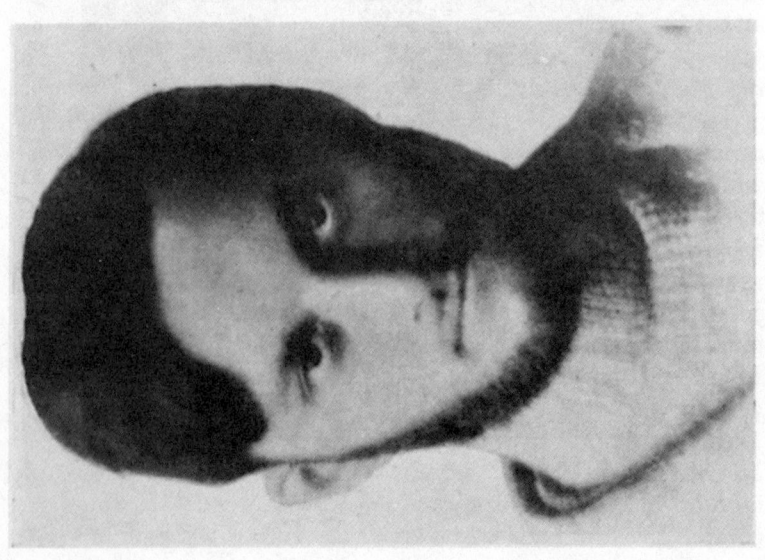

Absalom Feinberg

tion which ignored Jewish demands would be a shame on the peoples of Europe, while Picot kept asking Aaron if he thought of Jewish Palestine as under French or British control. Aaron, whose views on this matter were well known to Sykes, answered with an Arab proverb: "He who marries my mother will be my father," meaning: "He who conquers Palestine will rule us."

Aaron told Sarah, "I am now slowly going forward to the very situation I aimed at: to stand behind the scenes and influence the progress of events, so that they will accept our movement and our aspirations. What I do will not be seen. Only those in the secret know how good this development is for our mutual work. And it is our people who will benefit. The redemption is perhaps a little nearer than before."

"Oh, that it will be," prayed Sarah fervently to herself. She shared in Aaron's satisfaction at his growing success with the British, but his activities bearing directly on the relief of their situation in Palestine still bore no fruit. He still had not been able to accelerate the British conquest or interest the British in making the attack from the sea which would at one swoop free all the big Jewish settlements in the coastal plain and the Sharon valley, cut the Turkish Army in two, and release forces for revolt within the country.

The fact was that while Aaron was a source of enlightenment to those who were willing to listen, the High Command as a whole was not interested in permitting him to step out of the framework of Intelligence. The Arab Bureau thwarted Aaron's attempts to get the British to take account of Jewish military assistance, since Britain would thereby incur obligations to the Jews. The people attached to the Arab Bureau had their own ideas for the reorganization of the Middle East as an Arab Empire, within which there was no place for an independent Jewish entity.

Another handicap which Aaron faced was British caution in accepting a man who put himself forward as a spy, not for money, but for far-reaching political demands—a situation complicated by the fact known to the authorities and avowed by Aaron, that he was working without the support of any representative Jewish organization either in Palestine or abroad. There was, moreover, open hostility between Aaron and the Committee for the Palestine Refugees in Egypt over the handling of funds collected abroad for the relief of the Jews in Palestine. The members of the Committee had been leading members of the Yishuv, and better men never headed a parochial welfare committee. They were of no serious political calibre and in fact had no aspirations in that direction, leaving politics reverentially to the Actions Committee of the Zionist Organization in London. As a result of an appeal to Jewish communities in neutral countries, gold had begun to flow into Zionist headquarters in London and to Aaron in Egypt. Nili was the only means of getting it into Palestine.

The Welfare Committee of the Palestine Refugees in Egypt considered it an impossible situation that they should be taking no part in this important work. Raphael Aboulafia was sent to Aaron with the suggestion that he should form a joint committee for sending help to Palestine. Aaron harshly refused. They had ignored him in Palestine all these years, had never asked for his help before, nor offered him any. Why, just at this moment, did they insist that he should work with them? "I am not a public worker, and I haven't any interest in being one," he wrote to Aboulafia. "What I'm doing, I'm doing as a private individual. That is, the danger, if there is any, I take on myself. The responsibility, however big it will be, I take on myself. The good results, if there will be any—they're the property of the whole nation. I don't know what these people really want—that we should set up a committee of five, and ask the Americans to send us money? My dear fellow, ask your friend and he will tell you that long before his name and the names of the other members of the committee you wished to form were known in America, there were men like Schiff, Rosenwald, Brandeis and others who were in the habit of listening to Aaronsohn and sending him money, great sums of money. I don't need any recommendation from members of the committee to America. I can get the money which we need there without their help. Tomorrow there is the chance to send our dear ones a little bread, a little help. Let's do it. We can do that without a committee."

If Aaron had given in, how much easier his own work would have been. If Sarah had been able to return to Palestine with the gold coming from such a committee, how different her reception would have been and the attitude towards Nili. But Aaron could not give in, and Sarah would never have expected him to.

Chapter 13

THE RETURN

ALL the time Sarah was in Cairo, she was ill and unhappy and longing for Palestine. In spite of her busy days, the time dragged intolerably. Large quantities of gold had begun to arrive for the refugees from Jaffa, and she was eager to deliver it. Nor could she be easy until Yosef was safely out of Egypt. The tensions which had developed between Aaron and Lishansky and between Lishansky and Liova spelled danger for the work.

All the tensions and the conflicts centred on her, and she could do nothing to resolve them. She felt the weight of Aaron's disapproval of Lishansky, and his inability to be at ease with her as long as Lishansky was with them. Liova went around suffering and looking at her with his blue eyes full of pain and longing. Yosef sulked and demanded her attention. He did not show to good advantage among townspeople. He was at home on his horse, in loud, boasting conversations with Beduin, in trials of strength, in rivalries, in dangerous intrigues, and, best of all, in the wide open spaces of the Galilee or the Negev. That was the trouble with them all. They were not at home in Egypt. They missed Palestine. In Palestine, where they could feel and talk normally and be themselves in spite of the danger and the strain, they could have settled their differences; but here they were estranged from each other and from themselves.

Just as Aaron had felt when he first came to Egypt and their aims had to be viewed through the minds of others, foreigners to their people and strangers to their thoughts, so Sarah was appalled at the drabness of their work, the insignificance of the Jews of Palestine in the British scheme. An insignificance which extended to herself and the two young men who each tried never to leave her alone with the other, but never did anything but sulk all the time they were with her.

As the time for her return drew near, Aaron tried to persuade her to remain with him in Cairo. If the existence of Nili was common talk in the Yishuv, the possibility that the Turks would get wind of it could not be ignored.

One evening Sarah, Aaron and Pascal were sitting in the lounge of the Continental Hotel when Captain Edmunds came up and greeted Sarah. "Madam," he said, "the High Command has authorized me to thank you very much for all that you have done for us. They urge you not to return to Palestine. Egypt is open to you. You can stay here as long as you wish. What you have done up to now is valuable, and it is enough."

Sarah immediately understood that Aaron was behind this, and she answered in French: "Please convey to your Commanders my thanks for their attitude, which is very pleasant to me. But I have only one aim. To save my Jewish brothers and sisters in Palestine. That is the reason why I am working for you. I've decided to return, and if mistakes are made, or our secret revealed, then I am responsible, and my blood will be on my own head, and not on others."

She continued, looking not at Captain Edmunds but at Aaron: "If you know me, then give me the means to return. If you don't provide them for me, I'll find my way back myself. If I can't do this, then I'll kill myself."

Shocked by the intensity of her feeling, Aaron gave in without further argument. Sarah had felt that Aaron did not understand her need to be back in Palestine, carrying on Absalom's work, which was her only hold on life. Deep as the love was between the brother and sister, not one word of emotion or sympathy had passed between them during Sarah's stay in Cairo. Many times Sarah longed to pour out to Aaron the bitterness that lay in her heart, but she remembered the edict of the sages that silence was sweet to the wise, and she restrained herself. Aaron, perhaps fearful of the torrent that would be released in both of them, never encouraged his sister to break her silence. Only later, when she was back in Palestine, did he permit himself to offer the comfort that he longed to speak:

"Don't think for a moment that your inability to express yourself in words prevents me from understanding you and loving you. On the contrary, I am proud of you, just because you have such great powers for silence. And believe me, that many many of the bitter and complicated things which were in your heart, and on the tip of your tongue, but which you never managed to get into words, believe me, I read them, I heard them, and they reached my ears. But it was not the right moment to say them, and so I did not press you to speak."

May 13th was the date set for the return to Palestine. Liova came to Cairo the day before to get final instructions from Aaron and to take Sarah and Yosef back with him to Port Said. "I take flowers to Sarah in the morning," he noted in his diary. "At 9.30 Aaron and I go to visit some prisoners, three pupils from the Herzlia Secondary School, who are in the Turkish Army, and escaped through the lines to the English. We get information from them and ask them to join Nili, but they say they've had enough of the Turks."

The next day, when they should have started on their way back to Palestine, they were still in Cairo. "Everything is called off. Yosef refuses to return! Aaron is furious. We've had discussions all day, and everyone is tense and angry." What had happened? Exactly what Sarah had feared would happen if Yosef was not treated tactfully.

"Yosef says that he hasn't received the honour and the confidence he deserves, and under these conditions he can't continue," Aaron wrote in his diary. "He threatens a strike and a scandal. He thought that would frighten me. I left him and reported to Edmunds that it was difficult to persuade Yosef, and I was going instead. There was excitement in the office, but they were forced to agree."

Unless Aaron found some extraordinary way of disguising himself, he could not move a metre inside Palestine without being recognized and hanged. But he was not going to let his plans founder on the rock of Yosef's obstinacy. Nili was his strength with the British High Command, his political weapon for future power.

"Why? What are you doing it for?" Liova demanded of Yosef.

"On principle!" Yosef retorted.

"Just the obstinacy and the impertinence of a Shomer!" Liova recorded in the intervals of furious negotiation. "Aaron must be made to understand once and for all that the greatest power in the world is Yosef Lishansky. Nothing but diseased self-love. I knew that this would break out sooner or later. I agree to take him a letter from Aaron. I speak with him, but he just sulks. He feels that Aaron hasn't honoured him enough, hasn't taken him into all the details of the business, hasn't introduced him to all the generals, and so on."

In the afternoon Sarah went to Yosef, and Liova lay down to rest. But he could not rest. He decided that it was his duty to try and save the man from the miserable situation he had got himself into. He went across to Yosef and spoke to him as a friend.

"Look, you've got to go. If you don't agree, I'm going to take you by force!"

Yosef answered that he had already decided to go.

They hurried with their preparations. The boat sailed from Port Said at dawn the next day. The party spent the night in an hotel at Port Said. Everyone was very nice to Yosef, but it was clear that he was miserable. Well, he could only blame himself for his sufferings, thought Liova. He told Sarah that he had to speak to her. She came into his room and they talked for some time. Yosef must have been waiting in the corridor. When she went out, Liova heard shouts, reviling, abuse, a shocking scene. He remained in his room, shattered.

"And so that's the business," he recorded grimly in his diary. "Now many things are clear to me."

May 16th: "In the morning, everything was known to me. So that's it. Excellent. Yosef goes around with his eyes on the ground, walking like a bear. You are coarse, my friend. It's hard to stand you. We board the *Monegam*."

Liova kept some distance behind Sarah and Yosef as they mounted the gangway. Sarah fell back a moment and waited until Liova came abreast of her. She looked him full in the face, then said earnestly: "If any bad thoughts about me ever passed through your head, it doesn't matter. I repeat it once again. It doesn't matter." Then she moved on to join Yosef.

By 12 o'clock the next day they could see Zichron. The shutters on the house in the vineyard were open. They sailed on. By the time they were opposite Athlit a storm had broken and it was difficult to recognize anything. They went on to Haifa, and returned. When they approached Athlit that night, it was clear they would not be able to land. They drifted around waiting to see if it would be possible to land the next night. If not, they would have to go on to Cyprus.

Sarah felt as if she were caught in a nightmare. She had to get back. The work needed her. She must hurry. But she could not move. The storm held them bound until the moonless nights were ended. They had to return to Egypt, to wait for another two weeks, until the moon was right to try a third time.

On the ship Liova avoided Sarah and Yosef, and Yosef had time to pull himself together. Yosef may have seemed gross to Liova, but he was capable, in his own way, of just as high principles and ideals as Liova was. Like Caliban, he could only express himself in certain ways and was hurt and puzzled by the effect his words had on people. He could not understand why everything he did and said brought forth such harsh reactions. Ever since he could remember, he had been odd man out. An orphan of the Kishinev pogroms, he had been brought up by relations in Palestine who had all they could do to take care of their own children; and now he was being rejected from the close companionship of Nili just as he had been ejected from Ha-Shomer. Sarah understood him, pitied him, encouraged him, made him believe in the validity of their struggle and sacrifice, and he was as putty in her hands. In Cairo they had tried to keep Sarah away from him—Liova, who himself was in love with Sarah, and Aaron, who was infuriated at Yosef's familiarity with his sister. The assurance which he felt in Palestine when Sarah was beside him deserted him in Cairo, and he had gone to pieces.

Self-love was far from being the only reason for Yosef's tantrums. There was something nagging at his conscience. It was the same thing that was nagging at the conscience of Liova, of all the members of Nili, and of Sarah too, but each one tried to hide it from the others like a guilty secret.

Was Nili justified? What certainty had they that their efforts, the sacrifices and the dangers they were bringing on themselves and the Yishuv would bring a reward in keeping with their aspirations? Up to that very day they had not received from the

British a single clear promise. Aaron continued to fight for his place and his influence with the High Command, but he could only give them hopes, not clear promises.

Yosef Lishansky could not tell Sarah his doubts about the ultimate value of their work. Perhaps he feared that she would accuse him of cowardice; of the desire to run away, of wanting to throw off the yoke which had grown beyond his strength. But Lishansky had somehow to relieve himself of the heavy burden which weighed upon his soul. He turned to Liova. Although they had been virtually open enemies in Egypt, he was the only one of the group whom Lishansky felt he could talk to.

Returning from Cyprus to Port Said, Yosef wrote to Liova: "We haven't seen you. Don't you feel good in our company, or rather in my company? No? I was too miserable, wasn't I? But what to do? The whole situation is so complicated, and causes one to think so much. And what's even worse, the more one thinks, the more complicated the situation becomes.

"Again the question arises: What are we doing all this for? You will say 'What, do you want to stop? How can one stop in the middle of the work?' Then not to stop? My head is whirling with worries, till I am nearly mad. It's difficult, my friend, to grope in the dark.

"If I were groping alone, I wouldn't care, but many people are working for me, and I cannot reveal to them what I reveal to you. And so I am deprived of both alternatives. I am working, but with terrible pessimism about the value of the work I am doing. In addition, I am deceiving innocent people, who believe all I say. And how much longer is this going on? I don't think I can stand much more. We have got to get out of this mess somehow or other. Our Jews are being destroyed under our eyes, and we're not bringing them any results. On the contrary, in some ways we're even harming them.

"But I must stop writing. I'm getting upset again, for nothing, for it won't do me any good. Forgive me that you found me in this bad mood. I would like to be at Port Said already, and get the telling off that Aaron will give me, for being under his eyes once again. Poor, miserable chap. He's also justified in his anger. He also has his troubles. But am I to blame for them?"

And poor miserable Yosef. The letter released the pressure on him, and when he and Liova came face to face again, it was as if nothing had happened between them.

While they were back in Cairo, waiting for the wane of the moon, Yosef went every day to learn about the use of explosives. They wanted him to be ready to blow up the Jisr Mejamie bridge over the Jordan, the point of entry for the trains from Damascus which brought all the supplies and men and munitions used on the Palestine front. (This was not the line which Lawrence and the Beduin used to raid. Theirs was a secondary line which ran from Damascus to Medina and branched off well before it entered the battle zone.) Dynamiting a bridge was a complicated operation, not easy for Yosef to understand.

"You'll get a £100 bonus for this job," his instructor, a cheery Scots colonel, told him by way of encouragement. When Liova translated this to Yosef, he leaped up as if stung.

"What? Does he think I'm doing this for money? Does he think I'm a donkey, going because he pushes me? Let him do it himself!" And he flung out of the room and slammed the door behind him.

When Raphael Aboulafia came to visit his friends at the hotel later on, he found Yosef lying on his bed, crying.

"What are you crying for?" Aboulafia asked him, in his quiet, practical manner.

"*We're* risking our lives for a chance to build up Eretz Israel (the Land of Israel), and *they* think it's enough if they pay us to destroy bridges!"

Two weeks later they again left Cairo for Port Said. A hot, dry hamsin wind, straight from the Sahara, turned the train into a gritty furnace. Sarah sat silent, her heart like stone. Liova's stern gaze never left her. Liova had had no opportunity to speak to Sarah alone, for Yosef never left her side. Instead, when they were on board ship, he silently handed her the little notebook labelled "To Sarah" and disappeared into his own quarters.

Again the sea was too rough to permit them to land, and they headed for Cyprus. To take her mind off the agonizing anxiety over their prolonged absence from Palestine, Sarah read and reread the contents of the little notebook.

"Believe me, Liova, if you are sad or depressed about me, you are to blame, not I, because I have remained as I was," she wrote him in reply. "With you, everything is built on fantasies and dreams, and so, when you meet a woman like me, you suffer, because I am too real, because I belong to life, and for you, all that is necessary are castles in the air. All the world is one big lie, and it is good for you that you can have your own world in which you see everything according to your own desires. But I must accept life as it is, and from the bad choose what is good. However little good there is, I am prepared to say: 'Dy-ay-nu. It is enough.'

"It is not in my nature to boast, and I don't like to say good things about myself, but recently I have become aware that I must value myself more highly. Don't think that I am saying this because I agree with the good opinions people have been expressing about me in Cairo. But you should realize that in *real* life there aren't many Sarahs, even like me, the imperfect one. I am forced to bear witness for myself now, but in time you yourself will understand that this is so. From day to day life gets more difficult, more cruel, and the truth is seen less and less. But the day will come when we will see the truth unveiled.

"My head aches so, and the boat is rocking so. If we meet again, we will try to speak at some length, if we have a chance. I'm certain that will not happen. You or Yosef are bound to be in a bad mood, and one will have a bad influence on the other. Once again each of you will sit in your corner, alone and sulking, and I, as always, the go-between. How tired I am of that task. Generally I am not a hypocrite, but there are times when I have to falsify my voice, not to let anyone know how unhappy I am.

"You write that I do not understand you, but you are mistaken. I understand much, and feel even more, but Allah hasn't given me the ability to write or to express myself in words. And so if you see me approaching you, shaking your hand, hugging and kissing you, don't think of me as a woman, and that is my need. Don't dare to think for a moment that I am doing it because you are a man and I a woman. My kisses and my embraces are instead of words. With them I can express better what is in my heart, because I am not good at the use of words. Like a dumb person who expresses his wishes with gestures, so am I. You will understand me, Liova, won't you? Why has God cursed me like this? And why do I see everything so black?"

Stormy seas again prevented them from landing at Athlit, and during the course of the next two weeks Sarah was either tossing about on the Mediterranean in the *Monegam* or spending dreary days in Famagusta waiting for the moon to wane. On June 15th they again approached Athlit. It was two months since they had left Palestine.

The wind died down when they were opposite Carmel; it looked as if they would be able to land. The Captain was new and did not know where he was. He kept rushing into the cabin and consulting his map. "They must be sending messages up and down the coast announcing there is an English ship around," Liova recorded as they waited in a frenzy of impatience. "The captain lights a match. What a fool! They'll see it." At last they were opposite Athlit.

Two boats were let down, Yosef, Leibel Bornstein, Abdullah, his two sons in one boat; in the other, Sarah, Liova, a British sailor and all the baggage. This consisted of supplies for their own work and sacks of gold and provisions for the refugees. Yosef and Leibel went ahead to find out what the situation was. If everything was all right, Sarah would land. Yosef and Leibel approached the shore and disappeared. The others waited. The wind was blowing from the shore, and the sea was quiet. The stars were shining brightly. Complete silence.

Liova and the sailor lay down in the bottom of the boat, and Sarah with them. They lay and looked at the sky full of stars. Sarah found it pleasant to lie in the boat and listen to the waves and look at the sky. Who knew what would be waiting for her when she returned to shore? Why did she feel no fear, Sarah wondered. What was this, bravery or lack of imagination?

They heard the frogs croaking. They got the sign, and the other boat joined them. Yosef was in it, waiting to help Sarah over. Only a murmur from Liova, "Shalom, Sarah." Liova's boat rejoined the *Monegam*. The ship turned and made for Famagusta.

Chapter 14

TROUBLE

IT was after midnight when Sarah and Yosef reached Athlit. They found Reuven Schwartz, Manasseh Bronstein and Mendel Schneersohn waiting on the shore, as they had waited every moonless night during the two months Sarah and Yosef had been away. Sarah embraced her cousin and sought to draw from his strained face some indication of the situation that awaited them. Reuven could only murmur "Bad, very bad," before he turned and plunged into the water to help the others.

Luckily the sea was dead calm, for the five men had a great load to carry from the boat to the shore, and from the shore to the cave among the rocks which was Nili's hideout in stormy weather. The bulk of their burden consisted of grey canvas sacks weighing ten kilos each—50,000 francs in gold coins for the relief of the refugees from Jaffa and Tel Aviv. Even Sarah had to carry two cases, ill and exhausted as she was from her bouts of malaria and the wandering and tossing at sea.

"Ain devar," she kept saying, with a smile, putting heart into them again. "Never mind, it's nothing to make a fuss about."

In the cave she learned that they had returned to chaos. The family and those most closely connected with them had become completely demoralized in Sarah's absence, and the work of espionage had fallen to pieces. As soon as it was noticed that Sarah and Yosef were no longer there, the Zichron Committee called Zvi Aaronsohn and demanded to know what was going on, and where Sarah and Yosef had disappeared to. Everyone was talking about it, they declared, and the whole business would soon get to the authorities. Some people said that the Germans already knew about it.

Zvi was no Aaron or Sarah. He was a humble, peace-loving man, like his father, law-abiding at heart and impressed by authority. He tried to pacify the Committee. He told them that the rumours that were being spread around about espionage were not true, and he promised that everything would be settled quietly. He stopped his own activities and gradually let it be known to all those taking part in the work that it was being wound up. He believed this to be the case, for when such a long time passed without word from Sarah and Yosef, he thought that they had been drowned. He was furious now at the predicament which they had got him into by returning, and demanded, as did the others, that Sarah and Yosef leave the country again immediately.

Sarah relied on the money they had brought for the refugees to cushion the shock of their return. For three days she and Yosef remained hidden in the cave in the rocks, guarding the gold while negotiations were carried on with the Refugee Committee. They desperately needed money. Their head, Meir Dizengoff, was a practical man. He disapproved of espionage but finally agreed to accept the bags of gold which were delivered to him through the medium of a wholesale grocer, stuffed into flour sacks and concealed within wooden kegs labelled salt herring.

Immediately the money was disposed of, Sarah set herself to disentangle the complications which had developed in her absence. Every one of their agents with the army had been transferred somewhere else. Others had stopped interesting themselves in the work when the information was not collected. It still was not safe for Yosef to be seen in the community, and so Sarah had to travel alone, to hunt up her agents, and to see who could be found to replace those who had disappeared from important points. Everywhere that Sarah went she heard the cry, "Where is Absalom? Where is Absalom?"

"The situation is so bad, and so difficult in itself, and here I have to keep a face like a statue and hide the truth," she wrote to Aaron. "Wherever I turn I feel his lack. Everything here reminds me of Absalom, but what can I do? Can I bring him back again?"

While Absalom's family listened in painful silence when Sarah told them wonders about his progress at a pilot's training course in England, at home her father and Zvi gave her no rest. "Why don't you tell us the truth?" they demanded of her, for they were sure there could be no other explanation for his silence than that the boy was dead. Naaman Belkind and Nissim Rootman said the same, and blamed Yosef for Absalom's death. If Yosef had not gone to the desert with him, he would never have gone alone, they said.

"If Absalom's family knew about his death, not one of them would take part in the work," Sarah wrote to Aaron, and in her desperation she begged him to forge a letter from Absalom to the Feinberg family.

"A letter in his handwriting and in his style? How could I do it?" Aaron answered her. "A letter like this would be a sacrilege. If you have no other way, tell the family the bitter truth. At any rate, please don't ask me to do that, Sarati, not that. You see that in many things I am a woman; just as you, my dear, are in many things a man, a strong man, whom one can be proud of."

Aaron's compassion for his sister was too great to express itself in sympathy. All he could do was to try and give her the strength to carry on. There was no question of Sarah not carrying on. "As you can see, I am working, and the danger isn't too great," she wrote. With every ship that got to Athlit she sent information more and more important. Thanks to it, those in Egypt were able to improve the situation which had been created after the defeat at the second battle of Gaza. When the Turks planned a surprise attack, they found the British ready to receive them. Instead of having the initiative, as formerly, they found themselves being attacked.

"The Turks are getting badly knocked around at Beersheba," Sarah reported, adding that the Germans were warning the Turks that there were spies operating in their midst. Still Sarah was not satisfied with what was being accomplished. She relentlessly lashed herself from place to place, laying the net again and bringing in more people. Everyone she passed on her way, she mentally summed up as a possible candidate. "I am beginning to reconsider the people in Zichron, and to single out the best from among them. We have some young men who are good swimmers, and brave as well, good chaps for work, who will listen to us, and be happy to work with us."

Little as Sarah could afford the time, she forced herself to keep in touch with all the rumours and the women's gossip and the pettiness of the place. She had to be able to counter the blows of their enemies inside the community. "Today they say so and so, and tomorrow something else. Our people here, particularly the family, immediately get alarmed about something which is of small importance, and think that because someone says this or that, one must immediately stop the work and bury oneself alive."

"No!" Sarah told them, quite definitely. "If they talk, let them talk. The work will be done. The settlement must get used to it that this is the way it's going to be, and their talking isn't going to alter the situation." They tried to frighten her as well. ("As though I were a little child," said Sarah, "and all they have to do to make me run away is to tell me that a big bear is coming to eat me up!")

"You don't know that there is a new army here now, brought from Anatolia," they told her. "Each one is a pure Turk, young, and strong as a lion, and a good shot. You won't be able to do much work now these soldiers are on the job."

But Sarah refused to panic. She made inquiries and found that they really had sent a patrol of ten such Turks to replace the Arabs, but they had arrived without weapons. The weapons and ammunition came almost a week later, together with their food. "You can imagine what energy and what enthusiasm they have for work," Sarah wrote to Aaron. "Some of the young men in Zichron told us that they no longer even guard the places that used to be guarded. I doubt if these new patrols will disturb us too much."

In spite of all her troubles and aggravations, there was no sign of it on Sarah's face. The malaria from which she had suffered all the time she was in Egypt had disappeared, and she never felt better in her life. "I work and toil, but forget everything," she wrote to Aaron. "Even though I were suffering from lack of bread, it would still be more pleasant for me here than in Egypt. Forgive me for speaking the truth, but you know your sister already. Everything that I feel, I tell you. And for that I am sending you another nice kiss."

By day Sarah worked without rest, and at night, when others slept and there was no more work that could be done, she wrote her reports and letters to Aaron and Liova. This relationship with Liova was the one ameliorating feature in the grim saga

Sarah in Egypt
with Yosef Lishansky
on right, and
Liova Schneersohn
on left

Alex
Aaronsohn

Sarah and Rivka in Arab Dress

unfolding around her. Liova, as Sarah had said, did indeed live in a beautiful world of non-reality. His love for her was undemanding, a thing of poetry and letters, lightening her heavy burden, and reminding her that she still had something in common with other young women of her age.

"I was very sorry that I wasn't at Athlit to meet you on Friday evening," she wrote to Liova. "Although I hurried back from Ramle, I came only on Saturday night, and then I dared to go with the group to the shore to wait for you. We waited until 1 o'clock, and no one came. I am very sorry, because the next time I will not go to the shore. I was alone then and we could have talked about everything freely. And on the 23rd your brother Mendel will be there. You will both have a lot to say to each other, and it will be difficult for me to say everything. Never mind. But if you wish to see me, and care to risk it, I will wait for you by the gate of the Station. Yesterday I prepared a nice big basket of grapes for you, and now they're getting spoiled.

"Yosef went north on Friday. The work still needs organizing, and it is going slowly, because it is very difficult to arrange anything now. You in Cairo have forgotten that we are not free, and they are persecuting us. Every step we take is watched, and everyone is talking terribly, although the excitement of our return is beginning to quieten down again. As long as they see me in Zichron they keep quiet, but if I stay at Athlit for a week, they begin to say again that I've run away.

"Write me sometimes and please send me what is written in your little notebook, because it also belongs to me."

Aaron had written that their brothers Alex and Shmuel were coming to Egypt from the United States. He had summoned them to work with him there, for he already began to see signs that his attention might be needed in another sphere.

"If I hear that my brothers are in Egypt, I will hurry to come to them. And probably my sister-in-law Miriam will come, although I do not believe that she's got enough courage to go there. I've already talked with her, and she's very nervous. And really, not every woman has strength and courage like I have. If I were permitted I would go to the shore every time, but Yosef forbids me. I only go when he isn't there."

Just as Sarah had promised Aaron in Cairo, once Yosef got back to Palestine he was his old self again, energetic, devoted to the work, and willing to be guided by her judgment. There was perfect understanding between them. "That's so important," Sarah wrote to Aaron. "You remember how hard it was until the English got to understand us?"

When Aaron wrote complaining of Yosef, Sarah took that for herself too. "I've told you many times that Yosef and I work as one, so whatever praise you give me I share with him, and whatever blame there is, falls on me too."

Aaron's complaints were only a reflection of the antagonism to Yosef which was growing in the ranks of Nili. No one's efforts satisfied Yosef, and he was outspoken in his criticism of the other members. His remarks were keenly resented, especially as he left no one in doubt as to who was bearing the brunt of the work.

"Liova writes that someone shot on him from the melon field," Yosef wrote to Aaron. "That's not a lie. They really did shoot twice one night. But not at Liova and Leibel, but at jackals. It was a mistake on their part to have returned to the ship, for we were lying on the other side of the field, only twenty metres away. Anyway, the field is free now, and those coming from the ship must remember that there are people, and among them Yosef, who are lying not far away, and at the first shout will go to their help, and they don't have to be afraid any more. Please explain this to Liova."

"The sister is good," he wrote to Aaron on another occasion, "but what concerns the rest of your men, even those most close to you, worthless, worthless, my friend!"

The quiet Zvi was his greatest opponent, for he had become almost maniacal in his resentment that Aaron should have entrusted everything to Yosef's control. There were others, outside their circle, who were also determined to see Yosef ousted from his position of importance. "Who is Lishansky, anyway?" was the common question. Everyone knew who Lishansky was, because everyone knew everyone, and everything there was to be known about everyone, in the tiny Yishuv. The question merely expressed the outrage that some one, not a leader of one of the national institutions, and never accorded any public status, should have become active in public affairs, and should be handling such large sums of money for the public good. Why, the man was an irresponsible upstart, and they lost no opportunity of producing examples of misconduct to prove their case.

To Zichron came stories of Yosef in fine clothes, riding about in carriages with women, sitting in cafés, drinking in the Hotel Fast, carelessly bringing presents for women friends with Egyptian wrappers still on them. Sarah and Yosef could not and would not go around answering or explaining that the safest way for Yosef to travel about was with the carriage and driver from the Station; that the Turkish officers he was treating to wine gave information in return which was worth far more to the Yishuv than the gold coin it cost; that Yosef was not wasting Nili money on presents for women; the chocolate and the stockings he had brought from Egypt were sent by Pascal to his wife and daughters in Petach Tikvah.

After the first big consignment of gold arrived, leaders of the Yishuv, among them Dizengoff, began to discuss the advisability of recognizing Nili. There were many who still disapproved of the espionage but were prepared to receive financial help from Nili and even to preserve friendly relations with a group that had an open road to the outside world at a time when a newspaper from abroad had not been seen in Palestine for over two years. A member of the Refugee Committee, ostensibly a sympathizer of Nili, appeared at the Aaronsohn house in Zichron to tell them the news. It had been decided that official opposition to Nili would cease, but only on one condition. Yosef must leave Palestine.

Why? There were two reasons. In the first place, Yosef had never been an organizer and therefore he was not capable of organizing anything as big as Nili. Secondly, Yosef was known to be at the head of Nili and was therefore a danger to the work. Yosef must go to Egypt and remain there, and the public leaders would choose someone who knew how to carry on the work and on whom no suspicion would fall.

Ephraim Aaronsohn and Zvi were astonished at this favourable interest on the part of the community and were ready to send Yosef off by the first ship. To her family's great disappointment Sarah received the news very coolly. She merely replied: "Is one permitted to discuss with those who sent you, or not? Besides, the matter is not in our hands. My brother Aaron also has a share in this. We must hear what he has to say."

When Sarah was alone in her room that night, she thought the whole matter over and wrote her conclusions to Aaron: "It would certainly suit them better, and be more convenient for them, if they could put someone from Ha-Shomer in charge of the work, so that all the work would be in their hands, and they would get the credit for it. That is why they are trying, in a diplomatic way, to show us that Yosef is bad for us, and that we must get him out of the country.

"If we have made mistakes, or spent more money than we should, we won't do it again. We already have experience. If we get someone new—new, which means someone who won't listen to Sarah's words, or your words either, and he comes with new principles, he will just make new mistakes, and new expenditures, and commit new stupidities. Why should we pass into new hands, someone we don't know, a party man, representing a whole group that has never been friendly to us?"

Sarah was desperately anxious to be dispassionate, to convince Aaron that she was pleading, not for Yosef's sake, but for the sake of the work. But her anger broke through her restraint, and she burst out: "It's just jealousy, jealousy; the whole thing rests on jealousy!" She quickly recovered herself, and ended lightly, "What do you think of all this gossip? Please let me know by letter with the next ship. We are awaiting the 'post' this evening, and will hand over to those who succeed in getting here, all the documents for you."

Chapter 15

A NEW GENERAL

ONE of the most heart-breaking aspects of Nili's work was waiting for the ships that did not come. "We waited and waited," Sarah complained sharply to Aaron in her next letter. "Then, just when we weren't here, the messenger arrived. These delays are making us lose many days. We can't leave the place when we expect you, and can't leave the documents all prepared, unless we are here, for that could lead to serious trouble. So we have to wait around and waste time. It is also necessary to speak to someone face to face sometimes, to know what your needs are, and what the situation is."

Although Sarah felt that their partners, the British in Egypt, were not taking the whole matter as seriously as she and her colleagues, they were not always to blame for the failure to arrive at the appointed time, as Raphael Aboulafia's diary reveals. He was on the *Monegam* at that time, together with Liova Schneersohn and Leibel Bornstein, who were the regular messengers.

For Liova and Leibel the descent from the little boat into the dark waves was a matter of routine now, but Aboulafia had come twice before without being able to muster up the courage to take the plunge. Preparations for the descent began in the afternoon. Everything that had to be taken was put into two small boats, and revolvers, rifles and knives were made ready. After supper they dressed in special grey clothes and waited for the night.

"The ship was scheduled to get there at 10, but now it turns out that because of the poor quality of the coal, we won't get there before midnight. What a shame. At such a late hour we certainly won't find anyone waiting for us at the meeting place, and we'll have to go to the Station. But this time I've decided there's no turning back. . . .

"11.30. We're getting nearer the place, and all is ready. We get into the boats. We are taking carrier pigeons with us, and some thousands of pounds for our unfortunate brethren. Our boat goes slowly. All is dark and quiet, only the noise of the waves breaking on the shore. The big ship vanishes from sight. On our right the ancient Crusader castle of Athlit rises up, and beyond it white shadows on the dark hillside indicate the Arab village. My heart bounds. Through the darkness we see the white foam of the waves. A sign that we're approaching the shore.

"We stand up. The two brothers—Scanda and Elias, Abdullah's sons—undress quickly, and drop into the water, naked. They take Liova and Leibel on their shoulders and plunge for the shore. Liova almost falls from the shoulders of the Arab and gets wet. In another moment one of them returns and takes me on his shoulders. A large wave sweeps by us. Both of my legs get soaked. At midnight I reach our land."

The first moment was the most difficult. They peered around on all sides, trying to penetrate the darkness. Then the three young men crept along the seashore and over the sand dunes, revolvers in their hands, hastening and lengthening their steps. At the Haifa highway they lay down for a moment and waited to see if anyone was coming; then they jumped up, crossed the road, and entered the Station grounds. At the house Aboulafia and Leibel waited while Liova ran up the stairs and disappeared. Ten minutes later he came down. There was no one in the house except Manasseh Bronstein. All had gone: to Zichron, Haifa or Damascus.

"Manassesh comes down. We give him the papers and he returns to the shore with us. He leads us by a shorter route. The situation in the country is very difficult, he tells us. At the shore we give a sign with our torch, and the boat, which has been floating at a safe distance, comes back for us. We should have handed over the money and the pigeons which were in the boat, but since neither Sarah nor Lishansky were at the Station, we didn't take them off."

They told Manasseh that they would return the next evening. and wait on the seashore for the people from the Station. They got back to the ship at two in the morning, changed their wet clothes for dry night clothes, and opened the big bundle that

Manasseh had given them. There was much material in connection with military affairs, and heart-breaking reports from
the Central Relief Committee to the Jews in Allied countries
regarding the plight of the Jews in Palestine.

All the next day the ship sailed around aimlessly while
Raphael worked with Captain Weldon translating the reports
which they had received from Athlit. Liova had got an attack of
malaria and was tossing in his bunk. The ship should have come
back the next evening at 9, but the captain "made an English
reckoning", as Raphael writes, and they didn't reach their
destination before 11.20. They lost nothing by their delay, for
when they anchored opposite the Crusader castle they found
the waves coming in so hard that they did not attempt to land
for fear the boat would be dashed to pieces against the rocks.
They decided to turn north to Famagusta and wait until they
could try again. The next night the ship approached slowly.
The coal was so bad that they could only make $4\frac{1}{2}$ knots instead
of 19. In the afternoon they began to prepare again for the
night, putting all their equipment into the boat.

"The moon set at 9.30, when we were still opposite the
Carmel. I lay down to sleep for a little. At 11.30 the Captain
came to tell Welden we'd reached the place. One Arab took
Leibel to the shore, and the second one took me. The fool had
not taken one step when he dropped me into the water, so that
my clothes and weapons were wet. When I got on to the land I
couldn't move because of the weight of my water-soaked
clothes.

"I suggested to Leibel to go alone, and I would go back to
the boat, but he didn't agree. As the Beduin proverb has it,
'The night has no friends.' I could have let him go alone, but
that wouldn't have been a decent thing to do. I tried to wring
the water out of my clothes, but in vain. Well, whatever
happens must happen.

"We crossed the sand dunes, came to a field, and from the
side of a little hill heard a low call, 'Nili'. We replied. These
were our people, three in number, who had been waiting.

"The first question was 'When will they come? Is the
redemption near?' What to reply to these unhappy men who are
suffering, and see all around them suffering?

"I answer them 'Be strong. The redemption is near. There is a new general. All around us they are working hard.'

"I took the group back to the sea. I gave a sign with my torch, and the boat came. We took the bags of gold and the pigeons, and went. The pigeons, may their names be remembered for evil, woke up and began to coo. The devil take them. I remembered the story of the geese who saved the Capitol. If the Turks had the luck that the Romans had, we'd all be buried.

"Leibel suggested that we should immediately quieten the pigeons by breaking their necks, but soon the pigeons quieten by themselves. We go stealthily. At the main road, we wait. Silence everywhere. Forward, friends. We go through the gate, and half the distance to the Station, and there is Sarah lying in the field.

"Shalom, shalom. Ah, there is a brave woman. She didn't show any surprise or excitement, when she saw me. How had I come? How had I got wet? 'Ain devar—Never mind. You'll be all right.' All this seems quite a natural thing for her, as if this is the way life is always lived. She understood everything with a word. What amazed me more than anything, she even understood beforehand what I wanted to say. I don't know how. By my eyes? By the look on my face? There is no need to say anything. Before a woman like this, one must bow one's head."

A new general has come! Allenby's arrival in Egypt a month before had jerked the army on to its feet and things were beginning to hum. Aaron was now in his element. Here was a man who could appreciate the very essence of Aaron's qualities. Here was a general who wanted the most a man could give him. Aaron had only met him two weeks before, but the vibrations were already being felt. The carrier pigeons Raphael Aboulafia had brought were to enable Nili to get information to Allenby's H.Q. in Wadi Gaza in a matter of hours. The mail-bag contained, for the first time, a number of specific requests.

The Turkish front stretched from Gaza to Beersheba. Twice the British had failed to capture Gaza, which commanded the historic coast road to the north. The new plan was to make a surprise attack on the Beersheba front, more weakly defended because the Turks never expected an army to penetrate the waterless desert route. Nili was now asked to ascertain the

Turkish strength in the Beersheba sector, indicating the weakest point. Sarah relayed the message to Naaman Belkind in the south. He passed it on to Absalom Fine, who worked as a carter with the Army around Beersheba, and Ronya Maze, a telephonist at H.Q., Beersheba area. Naaman also set to work on his many friends among the Turkish officers stationed at Rishon.

Nili's net was spread over the whole country. The Turks could no longer make a move without Nili knowing it and relaying it. Not only did Nili now have to supply more detailed military data, but requests came in for scientific material covering a wide range of subjects. Aaron spared neither himself nor Sarah in his attempt to satisfy the new Chief's insatiable thirst for knowledge on all things pertaining to Palestine. At night, released from the pressure and disturbances of the day, Sarah searched among the filing cabinets which embodied the essence of Aaron's methodical and meticulous labours during twenty years. From these she extracted pictures of rock formations to aid the engineers in finding the water which was more valuable than munitions in that desert campaign; records of air pressure in the Lebanon for the Air Force; charts from Aaron's malaria research survey for a bacteriolotical laboratory behind the front lines.

Wavell relates in his biography of Allenby[1] that while visiting a laboratory near Ludd, one day, Allenby saw some charts on the wall and asked their meaning. The bacteriologist told him that they were charts of the seasonal incidence of malignant malaria in the plain of Sharon. " 'I think that is the reason why Richard Cœur de Lion never got to Jerusalem. His army was nearly destroyed by fever, and I find that he came down the coast in September, when malignant malaria was at its height.' This sort of information was manna from heaven to Allenby, and he never forgot it. . . ."

Allenby's greatest enemy was the waterless, unknown desert which stretched before his army. In planning its conquest, no general could have had a more valuable ally than Aaron Aaronsohn. Like a modern Moses, Aaron had the ability to produce water where there had appeared to be only stony

[1] Wavell, *Allenby* (Harrap, London, 1948), p. 162

waste. It was then that the wells began to be sunk in the desert which Sir Basil Thompson had referred to. In the course of a reconnaissance sortie to acquaint the commanders with the territory which they would have to cover, Aaron revealed the existence of ancient wells on the sites of two long-buried cities. For some days before the big attack, the engineers of the Desert Mounted Corps, covered by a brigade of Anzacs, were engaged in digging out these wells for the use of the advancing army.

In putting his unrivalled knowledge and experience at the disposal of the military authorities, Aaron frequently ran the risk of captivity and death, as officers on General Allenby's staff later testified.[1] His boundless energy and forceful character attracted the Commander-in-Chief, and Aaron became a personal friend as well as one of Allenby's closest advisers.[2]

On July 20th, Aaron wrote to a friend in England: "I am at the Front, and hope to be amongst the first to tread the liberated national soil."[3] It seemed to Aaron that he had reached his zenith when he heard from Yosef Lishansky that the leaders of the Yishuv had decided to cease the opposition to Nili. "Today I can say that the task I undertook has succeeded," he recorded in his diary on July 26th.

Aaron considered not unreasonable the demands which were put forward as conditions for co-operation with Nili. They had been put much more diplomatically to Yosef than they had been presented to Sarah and her family. "The spies would send to Egypt two messengers who would see what was being done there, and at the same time make contact with America." One of the two selected for this journey was the honest broker, the man who had brought the information to the Aaronsohns, who, although a Shomer man, had always shown sympathy to Nili. The other "messenger", as they delicately put it, was to be Yosef Lishansky. If these two were convinced that the espionage was valuable for the Yishuv, Yosef would remain in Egypt, and the Security Committee of the Yishuv would take over the work of Nili.

---

[1] Brig.-Gen. G. Clayton, Chief Political Officer, E.E.F.—letter to Dr Eder, 27.7.19
[2] General Allenby—letter to Alex Aaronsohn, 14.7.19
[3] Letter to S. Tolkowsky

Yosef, less passionately than Sarah, also pointed out to Aaron the pitfalls in the offer, not for his own sake, but because of the danger to Aaron's authority and to the conduct of the espionage. Perhaps Aaron felt that his successes at Allenby's Command placed him in a position where he could control any personal opposition to him in the Yishuv. Sarah had promised him to come as soon as the work was organized again, and he hoped to see her safe in Egypt by every ship. To sacrifice Yosef in order to broaden the basis of Nili's work seemed to him no loss at all. And so instead of the reassurance about Yosef which her letter pleaded for, Sarah's battered brain received another blow in Aaron's curt enjoinder to Yosef not to antagonize people.

The greater part of Aaron's life had been spent in antagonizing people—in some cases, these very same people—and so Sarah would have been justified in returning a bitter answer and retiring from activity at least until Aaron made an effort to mollify her. But Sarah wanted neither credit nor consideration. All she wanted was to be allowed to do the work that had to be done. "We are not driving people away from us, as Zvi and the others are writing you. We can't accept the conditions they ask of us, that's all. The trouble is that people are rotters. For example, those who receive the money from us—do you think they permit one good word to pass their lips about us? They don't expose us, which is also something to be thankful for, but they haven't done a thing to alter the public's bad opinion about us. But, mah lesh, that too will come. There isn't much to complain about at the moment. The situation has definitely changed for the better."

But not in Zichron or in Sarah's own family. Everything suddenly changed for the worse. "I am not speaking to Zvi any more. He is now saying that Yosef killed Absalom, so that he could take his place, and other nonsense like that. Well, I will have to suffer from everyone, until the work is finished. Afterwards I will settle this business with him."

Zvi was beside himself with rage at Sarah's indifference to the open scandal which her close association with Yosef was bringing on the family, and he finally ordered her to leave Zichron and take Lishansky with her. He wanted to bring her to her senses and make her give up Yosef. But nothing would

induce Sarah to leave Yosef. Not that he would not work
without her, but, as she had explained to Aaron, "That man
hasn't a friend in the country. He is the sort of person who has
to have someone to turn to for discussion or advice; someone to
whom he can reveal his intimate thoughts about the secrets of
the work. I am the only such person Yosef has. If I leave him,
he will have to find other friends for himself. He is so simple and
sincere, when he talks to someone he reveals his whole heart to
them. It never occurs to him that anyone would deceive him,
and if he were alone, he would be certain to fall into bad
hands."

The Zichronites, her own brother Zvi, thought it was Yosef
that she was protecting in such a brazen manner. They could
not understand that Sarah was protecting the precious flame
which Absalom had entrusted to her, and which Aaron's genius
was shaping into a weapon for the Jewish people. She had
hoped that her family at least would understand and act
differently, but they hadn't.

Sarah stood looking at Zvi, her blue eyes wide and thought-
ful. "I will leave here, if you want me to," she told him quietly.
"Yosef and I will stay at Athlit. That will be more convenient
for our work, and better all round."

"But they are against this as well," Sarah wrote Aaron. "If
it is forbidden for us to live at Athlit, particularly Yosef, and at
Zichron it is also impossible, where are we to live?" The sudden
despairing cry which broke from her was immediately checked
as Sarah mastered her feelings. What did it matter now where
she lived? "The trouble is that these things interfere with my
work, and don't leave me a clear head to think. And all this
just at the time when the work is urgent, and we must get a
push on!"

"Concerning my return to you, dear, that is still impossible
for me. Until I see everything working as it should, and on a
solid basis again, I won't think of leaving this place. If there is
trouble when I'm here, what would it be like in my absence?
And in any case, Yosef can't do a thing any more without me.
He leaves it to me to make all his decisions."

The troubles and the interferences which were embittering
Sarah's life came only from a handful of people, who were acting

through panic or private malice. The rest of the Yishuv, Zichron included, had only the vaguest idea what the whole thing was about. All they had to go on were rumours circulated by people just as uninformed as themselves. Even the agricultural workers at the Experiment Station—both Jews and Arabs—knew nothing of what had been going on there during the past two years and were only then beginning to sense that the Station served another purpose beside agricultural research.

Secrecy had been essential to the espionage, but even more deeply rooted was Aaron Aaronsohn's lofty disregard for public opinion, originating, perhaps unconsciously, from the noble but patriarchal methods of the Baron de Rothschild, whom he had revered since childhood. Now, just at the time when it was important to have the whole Yishuv behind them, this secrecy was working against them. Not only were people totally unaware of the scope and importance of the work that Nili and Aaron were doing, but they refused to be made use of for what they considered Aaron's own interests.

"To be pawns in some man's dream, or to suit his private caprice? No, thank you. Who can be sure that the English will succeed? And if they do succeed, that they will get here in time to save us from being wiped out?" So said Aaron's implacable enemies, one of them a widely known and respected figure in Zichron, who began an agitation against Nili among the village committees of Samaria and Galilee. They in turn wrote to the Zichron committee: "These people are playing with our lives, and even worse, with that of the Yishuv. You are endangered more than we are, because those who are doing this work are in your neighbourhood. You must stop them!"

Some days after Sarah and Lishansky had moved to Athlit, they received a visitor in the person of Reuven Schwartz's father-in-law, Albert. As head of the Zichron Committee and the man most endangered by Nili's activities, he had been delegated to bring them an ultimatum and not to leave Athlit until they had agreed to it.

"We want you to promise to stop your work," Albert demanded of them.

"No," replied Sarah emphatically, "that we won't do!"

"Then we'll make you stop. We'll use force against you."

"Force? What sort of force?" asked Lishansky, pretending anxiety.

"We won't give you a chance to work. We'll come to Athlit and stay here, and interfere with everything you do."

Sarah and Yosef burst out laughing. "This is very funny," said Yosef. "How can you talk like that? Can you interfere in a private concern? And what if Athlit does not even belong to Mr Aaronsohn, let alone to us? Athlit is an American station, and if the Government can't even take it over, who are you to interfere?"

Albert replied that they would do it by force, in the name of the Yishuv.

"But we don't understand what you want from us," Sarah interjected. "How are we disturbing you?"

"You are disturbing our peace of mind, that's what you are doing," declared Albert. "Every time a leaf shakes, we think it is intended for us. You're ruining the Yishuv," he shouted.

After an hour's argument they got out of him that the Zichron Committee wanted to know who had given Nili permission to do their work, and who was working with them on the other side. Did Nili have the sanction of respected Zionists and public workers, or at least did such people know about the espionage?

They finally came to a compromise. Yosef swore never to appear in Zichron again. Sarah promised that the Zichron Committee would get a letter within forty days from some public committee sanctioning their work. In the meantime there was to be no interference from the community. Sarah also suggested to Albert that he might like to discuss the matter with Mr Dizengoff, who was administering the gold which Nili was bringing into the country at the risk of their lives.

Mollified at finding Sarah amenable to reason, Albert asked her, "If you can't give us the letter that we want, do you promise to stop this work and not continue?"

"Why should we talk now about what might happen in forty days?" retorted Sarah.

"With that we parted," Sarah wrote to Aaron. "And now, what do you think? I know if these rotters got a letter from the donkey G., or another donkey of the same calibre, they would be satisfied. But will these people put their signature to anything like that?"

Sarah was right to doubt it. "The donkey G." was the man Aaron had so brusquely thrust aside when he wanted to form a joint committee for handling refugee funds in Cairo a few months before.

"What is the situation with you, now? Have you succeeded in getting them to recognize you? Does Weizmann know that you are doing this work? And that the money is going to you, and that you are sending it by us to Palestine? They are confusing me so much here I've forgotten everything, so you must excuse me if I ask you stupid questions.

"Send us some newspapers, or circulars, if you have them, and we'll show them to these fools, and maybe it will quieten them a little. There is the fear that the Government will smell something here, and slowly and patiently work on it, until they find out what it is. But I'm not at all frightened of anything from the side of the Government.

"We've heard that our Yishuv is preparing a list of 100 names. We are amongst them, or rather, we head the list. They intend to hand the list over to the Government, if the Yishuv is attacked, and say, 'Here are the people who have been engaging in the foul work.' How true all this is, I don't know, but so much I do believe. They could do a thing like that, couldn't they? And now, again to what concerns our work. . . ."

Chapter 16

CALM BEFORE THE STORM

THE carrier pigeons were nothing but a source of trouble.
Either they had not been sufficiently trained, or they forgot
the way back to their station at El Arish. When the first pigeons
were sent off, one returned within a few days with the cylinder
containing the code message still attached to his leg. It had
evidently been wandering around in the vicinity of Athlit the
whole time. The next lot were hardly any better, and Sarah and
Yosef told Aaron not to send any more. They did not think the
pigeons were worth the danger involved, and it would be
impossible in any case to place them at the strategic points
throughout the country that Aaron had requested.

"Incapable as the Government is, it is getting stronger and
harsher," Sarah informed Aaron. "It is very hard now to work
on a wide scale. Slowly, slowly they are beginning to understand, particularly as the Germans are teaching them to be
careful." That didn't mean that the work wasn't going to be
done, Sarah assured Aaron, who in every letter now reminded
them that speed was essential. It just meant that they couldn't
work as quickly as before. The problem of placing agents at
Affulah station was an example. The young men were finally
found who were suitable for the job. You'd be surprised how
hard that was. Most people are frightened for their skins, and
they crumble like dry bread at the first pressure. And now we'll
have to waste three weeks more until we can get a permit to
open a buffet or a store there. And we need a barrack for this,
and there isn't one. Until we find timber, we have to lose time,
time. It's not like in Egypt. There you can go out and buy, and
cheaply as well. Here prices are terrible, and some things are
simply not to be had. The English themselves are not hurrying,
but they demand speed from us. And they are right, for every
hour wasted is a waste of opportunities."

During the whole period of her work, Sarah was never free

from worries about money. From the references in *Seven Pillars of Wisdom* to the uncounted quantities of gold thrown about among the Hedjaz Beduin every "pay day", one might have expected the British to have shown a certain leniency with regard to the expenses incurred by Nili during their dangerous operations behind the Turkish lines. On the contrary, Nili carried out its activities in face of a constant struggle against limited resources. Only the loyalty and devotion of Sarah and the other members of Nili made possible the brilliant results. At a time when Lawrence was spending more than half a million pounds sterling a month on the Beduin, Nili received some £300 to £400 a month.[1] With this paltry amount Nili's network of intelligence was spread over an area that extended from Gaza on the Egyptian border to Damascus in Syria. Surprisingly enough, Headquarters in Egypt provided even this amount with reluctance and demanded exact accounts. Sarah's constant concern about the expense of the work was a reflection of the complaints which Aaron received and passed on, whenever he presented the accounts which Sarah, in the midst of all her other worries, had to prepare for him each month.

Captain Smith, who dealt with the accounts, after checking the information sent in against the amount spent during the month, coldly informed Aaron that his agents were spending too much money and not exerting themselves sufficiently. Aaron passed on to Sarah the results of the conversation. Sarah was furious at the unjust criticism. "I immediately recognized that Smith was a swine! He doesn't know how badly we feel when we haven't material ready in our hands. No matter how much information we get, we are not satisfied that it is enough. I would like to see him in our situation. He doesn't even know our roads, or how much each journey costs. I would like him to watch us—from a safe distance, of course, with binoculars—driving to Petach Tikvah and Rishon, in the height of the heat. On the way, our wheel breaks, and we have to tie it up with string until we reach Rishon. What would he do under these circumstances? Do you think he would be able to say then that we were lazy in our work, after a journey of 24 hours, there and back, under bad conditions?

[1] *Sarah, the Flame of Nili.*

"There are no conveniences in the hotels in ordinary times, let alone now. All we can get when we get to a hotel is a glass of barley coffee instead of tea, but even then the expense is terrific. I'm not going, heaven forbid, to say that the work is too hard for me, or that you should raise our allowance. No, only that that swine should know the situation, and recognize what we are doing.

"For two weeks we ran after a permit in Haifa for the journey to Damascus, and in the end couldn't get a permit for a man, even if we gilded the Turks from top to toe. And so we have to use women. You can imagine what a journey to Damascus is like by train. We had to send Shoshanna, who is, after all, not Sarah. She is a lady, and not very strong either, but she came back with reports and information. Our work is going to be carried out and, whatever the situation, we will find ways of meeting it."

Actually, work was going very well now. The heads of the Relief Committee were taking the money like gentlemen, and those in Zichron had subsided for the time being. Sarah was free to concentrate on the espionage without time-wasting discussions and disagreements. Again she and Yosef travelled about the country together, as Sarah loved to do, bringing her woman's wit and her intuition to bear on the shifting circumstances. Free from the pessimists and the laggers, and face to face with the actual forces pitted against them, she was full of energy and optimism for the work. There was no problem that she failed to solve, no risk that she feared to take. Unlike Yosef, there was nothing dare-devil in Sarah's courage. Every move was carefully thought out, and based on decisions that were clear, logical and fearless.

People have compared Sarah to Joan of Arc. Although she too was an unsophisticated country girl, Sarah was no Joan of Arc. She was a heroine as women are heroines, never using or even suspecting the reserves of strength and courage stored within her until she felt called upon to fight for her endangered people, her brother, and the man she loved. The more the work became organised and expanded, the more it gripped her, and all her powers developed as the calls on her grew greater.

Like a voice from another world came a letter from her

husband, now in Holland. He sent her £20, and gave her permission to use £5 of it for the refugees in Zichron, if she wished. Recalling the humiliation and frustration of the year she had spent in Constantinople as a chattel in her hubsand's house, she wrote to Aaron: "The poor man doesn't know how many thousands of pounds are passing through my hands, and how many thousands of francs I hand out!"

But there was no past for Sarah now, only today and tomorrow and, if Heaven willed, perhaps next week. That was how Sarah wanted it. "I'm always busy, and my time passes without my noticing it. That is the best for me, because I haven't time to think and remember my troubles and our great catastrophe. If it weren't for the work, I couldn't keep going."

There was no Sarah any more who could be affected by fatigue, hunger, fear, a woman with needs and thoughts and hopes like other women. There was only Sarah, the flame of Nili, a flame which burned clear, steady and unflinching, a beacon of hope to the small band of weary, harassed workers who turned to her for their strength. Unlike Yosef, Sarah went about her work tactfully, unostentatiously, recalling the injunction of the sages to say little, do much, and receive all men with a cheerful countenance. Although firm in the needs of the espionage, she always found ways of encouraging her helpers and never failed to consider their many suggestions or to listen intently and seriously to all their problems. She was like a good, devoted sister moving among them, and they loved her and would have gone through fire for her. "I help relations between everyone. It is my luck that everyone has great confidence in me. Perhaps they are mistaken, but that is how it is."

Sarah expected risks and sacrifices when they were essential to the work, but could never permit her colleagues to be exploited unnecessarily. When Aaron let it be known in Egypt that provisions could be sent to Palestine, people sent all sorts of things, including bottled products, which broke and cut the shoulders of those who had to carry the sacks of provisions from the seashore. Sarah complained about this to Aaron, and at the same time told him not to send her or the family any food parcels. "The men shouldn't risk their lives carrying such luxuries on their backs. The work is holy, and one shouldn't

deal in frivolities. If you could send us guns, now, that would be
worth while. . . ."

Contrary to the stories of their self-indulgence on Nili gold,
Sarah maintained a strict austerity for herself and her helpers.
They used to laugh at the Station when they sat down to cups
of barley coffee sweetened with burned figs after their journey
to the seashore and thought of the kilos of sugar they had
secreted, to be delivered to some unknown recipient who was
probably hostile to Nili.

Giving urgency to their work was the poverty and starvation
which prevailed, particularly in the three main cities, Jerusalem,
Tiberias and Safed. "You must do everything you can to get
money, and not let our Yishuv remain with an empty treasury,"
Yosef wrote to Aaron. "You are the only one who can help us
now. If you fail us, we are lost."

When Yosef was unable to bribe officials to give him a permit
for Damascus, he went without one, trusting to his wits to see
him through. Travelling by night from Acre to Haifa, Yosef's
carriage was stopped by coast patrols. "Abu Farid threatened
them that I, the great man who had been Djemal Pasha's
engineer, would come out of the carriage to them if they didn't
go away, and they gave us the honour to which we were
entitled, and let us pass! In two places they stopped us, and at
both places we got through."

Eytan Belkind, Naaman's brother, and the engineer who used
to help them in Jerusalem were now working for Nili in
Damascus. Yosef returned full of information and suggestions.

"At Allii opposite the sea there are five long-barrelled
artillery guns together with five carriages for moving them.
There are only a handful of soldiers there. I could very easily
arrange for three ships to come and disembark lorries at
Beirut. I would be there, and at night could take the guns,
without a single person rising against us. Let me know now if
you agree to this, and I will arrange it." At Sidon he examined
a place he had in mind for Nili if they should be forced to leave
Athlit. "That is a fine place," he informed Aaron. "If only we
could acquire that place without arousing any suspicion, we
could really do our work well. The watch on the shore amounts
to nothing; that is to say, there *is* no watch on the seashore.

They patrol the road, which is close to the sea, but only early at night, and after that the only thing they look for is a place to go to sleep." At Tyre he learned from Abdullah's wife that two months earlier their ship had disembarked an old Arab, saying they would collect him again in another fifteen days. They did not come and the Arab was wandering hungry around the country, and the Government had got wind of him. "Our friends should hurry up and pick him up before he gets caught," Yosef wrote, "and don't bring him back to the country a second time."

Twenty-seven-year-old Yosef may not have been very successful in his relationships with his countrymen, but, as his reports showed, he was shrewd enough and he understood the Turks very well. "Habibi," he wrote to Aaron, "maybe it will seem funny to you that I, pappa, give you advice about the war, but for all that, we here in the country know what the situation is. The country is full of trenches, and even if you overcome the Turks at the front, they will retreat slowly, and again they will be entrenched in a defence line. That is their organization here. So this is my opinion: they should not delay attacking from the sea and capturing their mountains, which are free from soldiers, and so it will be a bloodless victory. If the English have the mountains as well as the sea, the Turks will be in the middle and they will have to retreat. Don't forget that if they enter the country now, the Turks won't have time to destroy things. The wheat is still in the country, and the English could take it.

"Of course, the landing from the sea must be done quietly and speedily; therefore we must be notified beforehand so that we can spy out the land well. In addition, it will be necessary to destroy the railway lines in advance."

More important people than Yosef were recommending this very programme, and with as little success. Churchill[1] writes that Allenby's success (in the Palestine campaign shortly to begin) "did not simplify the general problem. If, while Allenby held the Turks at Gaza, a well-prepared descent had been made at Haifa or elsewhere on the sea coast behind them, and if the railways by which alone they could exist had been severed in

[1] *The World Crisis*, p. 1181

September, the war in Syria would have been ended at a stroke."

Aaron's first reaction on the outbreak of war in Europe had been the right one. His place was in London, where the authority of his knowledge would have enabled him from the outset to press his plans at the highest levels. But would he have been able to break down the British tradition of disregarding the Jews as a military element to be reckoned with? When Joseph Chamberlain negotiated with Herzl in 1902 regarding the settlement of Jews in the Sinai Peninsula, he did so because he envisaged the Jews as a buffer between the Canal and Turkish expansion. Baring (later Lord Cromer) refused to consider the suggestion, preferring to rely on the local Beduin.[1]

And so the British continued to pin their faith to a Beduin revolt in a desert hundreds of miles from the Turkish forces massed against the British in Egypt, and the British attacking force in Egypt continued to be built up on solid, conventional lines. "The historian will not give to the E.E.F. campaign the extravagant praise which has been lavished upon it by an ill-informed public, ignorant as yet of the fact that in the field of operations the strength of the British to that of the Turks was that of a tiger to a tom-cat."[2]

That was written in 1922, but the public in Palestine knew the facts only too well, and in August 1917 Sarah was writing in disgust, "When are they coming, our liberators?" The rainy season would soon be upon them, with high seas and lashing winds. "To work again under those conditions—oh no, that's impossible."

It would not be long now, Aaron assured Sarah, and told her to find suitable young men to act as scouts with the British Army when the attack began. "We could give good Zichronites for the work," Sarah replied, "but the trouble is that their absence would be known, because they all depend on their parents. Nevertheless, there is one whom I want to try and get away, and that is Itzhak Halperin. He is a very good boy,

[1] H. F. Frischwasser-Ranaan, *Hebrew Encyclopaedia* (*Jerusalem*) vol. 6, col. 523
[2] Lt.-Col. J. H. Patterson, D.S.O., *With the Judeans in the Palestine Campaign* (London, 1922)

strong enough not to fear fire or water, and an excellent swimmer. I've invited him here so that the Zichronites should get used to the idea that Itzhak is working at the Station. We'll get him used to doing messages and all kinds of work, and one fine day, when his absence for some weeks won't be so noticeable, we'll send him off to you. And so, slowly, we'll begin to organize the other youngsters whom we can make use of on the day of redemption."

Not all those in Nili were lucky enough to have the tacit and unquestioning support of their parents that the Schneersohns had. Deeply religious people, the Schneersohn parents let their children follow their own conscience. If they were working for the redemption of Israel, they deserved the protection of the Almighty, the mother believed, and so she immersed herself in prayers on their behalf, while letting them go their own way without question. Liova had disappeared from home without a word of explanation some nine months before, and soon afterwards his young brother Mendel began to come and go on his mysterious errands, sometimes returning with guests whose presence in the house his mother was not even aware of.

When two German airmen were forced to land in a field near Hadera through shortage of petrol, Mendel arranged petrol for them and invited one to spend the night at his home. After a couple of hours' drinking he managed to extract from him several items of information which next day were forwarded to British Intelligence. In gratitude for the hospitality, the pilot offered to take Mendel for a ride in his plane. In the air a sudden impulse seized Mendel. How fine it would look if, at the point of his revolver, which he always carried with him, he would make the German fly straight over the front line and bring him as a prisoner to the British. He forced the idea out of his mind quickly, for the simple reason that just behind him sat the second pilot.

The reports from the agents came in every Sunday, sometimes brought in by Mendel and the other messengers, but usually collected by Sarah and Yosef on their rounds. They made every effort to get help from Jewish officers in the Turkish Army, but their only success was with the two or three who were related to Absalom or had been his friends from childhood.

With payment, however, they were able to get help from Turkish officers, some of high rank. Perhaps they were not real Turks, but members of the polyglot peoples who lived within the Ottoman Empire and hated Turkish rule for their own reasons. Such was the officer of Albanian descent who was Naaman Belkind's best source of information.

In the middle of August Yosef wrote to Aaron telling him that there was an officer who had information and plans and wanted to escape. "He is a close friend of N.B., but *I* for security reasons very much fear to show him our sea road. Let us know whether it is worth endangering ourselves through the sea, or should we take him through the desert route that they showed us the last time? Naaman guarantees that the officer is not a Turkish spy." Yosef then asked Aaron to send Naaman a present of a pen and a wrist watch. "It is necessary for politics."

Naaman had not ceased to give them trouble. He had joined Nili through his deep attachment to his cousin Absalom, and the mystery of his disappearance gave him no rest. First Yosef told him that Absalom was in Egypt. Later he told him that he had been sent to England on a flying course. Naaman used to write letters to Absalom, to be transmitted through Athlit. When he got no answer, he was sure that Yosef was not sending the letters on. He hated Yosef. He was sensitive to public opinion, which the others were not, and he was sure that Yosef's dare-devil method of conducting the business of Nili was going to bring trouble on them. Child-like and unreasoning, he had decided to get to Egypt himself and tell the whole story of Lishansky's misdemeanours to Aaron and Absalom.

Sarah was shocked at his demand to be sent to Egypt by the *Monegam*. They could do nothing without Aaron's permission, she told him. "Wait and we'll ask Aaron first, and see whether he says yes or no." But Naaman threatened that if they did not promise then and there to send him by ship, he would go through the desert.

"I don't agree to you going through the desert," Sarah replied quietly, "but, if you are determined to go, I can't stop you." All the young men of Nili had tried at some time or other to persuade Sarah to let them go to Egypt for a while, but she refused to consider it. "Where would we be with our workers

if they all thought they could go to Egypt when they wanted to?'
she asked Aaron. They too had threatened to go through the
desert if she wouldn't let them go by ship, but none of them
had been so incredibly foolish as to attempt it, and things had
always smoothed themselves out after a while.

A few days after the conversation with Naaman, Yosef met
him in Petach Tikvah. He had another talk with him, and
Naaman finally agreed to work in peace. Yosef thought a nice
gift from Aaron would keep him contented.

Towards the end of August Sarah received a jubilant letter
from Aaron. When he wrote it, Aaron believed that he had
reached the very pinnacle of all his dreams. It was only a
matter of weeks before the British Government would openly
declare its support for a Jewish National Home, and the High
Command in Egypt had been instructed to send "Major Aaron
Aaronsohn" to London for special political work in this
connection. Aaron no longer stood alone in his struggle for
recognition. The Zionist leaders disapproved of Nili, and it
was with the greatest reluctance that those in London had
agreed to work through Aaron in sending relief to the Yishuv.
For three months they had ceased to communicate with him or
answer his letters, and it had looked as if Nili's desperate effort
of the past two years was being sabotaged.

Now, wrote Aaron, he had just had an interview with the
British High Commissioner in Egypt, Sir Reginald Wingate,
who advised him to hurry to see the "great ones, and to explain
to them what we know and what they don't know; and he and
the Military Commander have authorized me to speak in their
name and to quote them as much as is necessary for our
success; for our future and their future are linked together.

"From today onwards we have the right to look on our
activities with confidence," Aaron wrote Sarah. "Up till now
we were just a few, isolated dreamers who endangered ourselves,
and even dragged others after us, against their will. Now at
last, when the highest authorities have given their official
approval of our work, no one can doubt the rightness of our
vision and of our action."

The pouch from Palestine had also brought good news.
"How happy we are to know that all is well. I set out on my

journey without doubt and without fear. I know that all of you will accept lovingly the added responsibility, now that our work is expanding and deepening just as we dreamed at the beginning."

Preparations for the big attack were speeding up. There was no reason now why Sarah should not return to Egypt. Very soon, in any case, the work of Nili would be drawing to a close, and all her colleagues would be joining the conquering army. Liova would give her details of the other magnificent news—that a Jewish fighting force was being mobilized in England and America for the freeing of Palestine, just as Absalom had visualized in the beginning. "We hope that soon their numbers will be great enough for them to be considered. And then I know one girl who has promised me to be a nurse. Please, Sarati, the girl that I love, remember this."

To come and say good-bye before he left—certainly, Sarah replied, but only on condition that she returned to Palestine immediately. "I want to be together with the others in the place of danger at the time of danger. I can't leave the work and the workers just at the time when the greatest difficulties are ahead of us."

The prospect that one day her work would come to an end, and she would have to return to—to what? That was something Sarah could not contemplate. "I don't know how I will get used to it, without the troubles here, and most of all, the work," she wrote to Aaron. "Do you remember Fontaine's fable of the dog who begged to have his collar put on again when they freed him? That's how I am."

Less than two weeks later the shadow of death began to fall on Nili.

Chapter 17

THE SHADOW OF DEATH

IN spite of their dissatisfaction with the pigeons, the group at Athlit used them from time to time. On one occasion the British were able to bomb Turkish troop concentrations near Beersheba within hours after Sarah had informed them by pigeon post.

On September 3rd, Sarah sent off several pigeons with messages. A little later, when she went down to bathe in the sea, she saw one of the pigeons standing by a water tank. She was surprised that it was still around, but concluded that it had not been given enough to drink. She threw a pebble at it and sent it flying off.

The next afternoon they got word that a pigeon had fallen into the hands of the Turks. It had come down at Caesarea, some kilometres along the coast from Athlit, where the Moudir, the head of the police, was feeding his own pigeons. He saw at once that it was a stranger, and when he began to examine it he found the little cylinder attached to its leg with the message in it. (A similar episode occurred during the First Crusade, in 1100. While the Crusaders were encamped at Caesarea, a pigeon was killed by a hawk overhead and fell near the tent of one of the bishops. The pigeon was found to be a carrier, with a message from the Governor of Acre to rouse the Moslems of Palestine against the invaders.)

The Moudir was unable to decipher the message, but he realized there must be a spy ring operating somewhere in the neighbourhood. The authorities now had their first practical proof of the existence of a spy ring inside the Yishuv.

As soon as the news reached Athlit, Lishansky killed the rest of the pigeons and ploughed over the earth where they were buried. They buried the reports and documents which were accumulating for the ship's arrival on the 10th and the gold they had on hand for expenses.

That afternoon they received a message from Naaman. They must come to Rishon and take the Turkish officer whom he had promised to get out of the country. The officer was adjutant to Kress von Kressenstein. Fearing, as the British attacks became more successful, that the Germans would soon track him down, he had deserted and put himself in Naaman's hands with the demand that he fulfil his promise.

Yosef had not heard from Aaron whether the Turkish officer should be trusted with the sea route, but they decided that nothing could be more risky than leaving him too long with the friendly and confiding Naaman, and so they set out immediately for Rishon. They took Toba Gelber and Nissim Rootman with them. The more people in the diligence, the less likelihood of the officer being recognized.

Furious at the danger that Naaman had brought on them, and certain that Aaron would hold him responsible if anything went wrong, Yosef wanted to kill the officer immediately. But Sarah refused to consider it, and so they took the young man (pale and nervous now, but well bred and very intelligent) to Hadera, where they left him in hiding at the Schneersohn house to wait for the next ship.

When the officer was disposed of, Sarah, Toba, Yosef and Nissim went to a photographer and had themselves photographed together. It was Sarah's idea. "Who knows how much longer we still have to live?" she said. "This may be our last chance to be together."

Sarah went on to Haifa, and Yosef was dropped at Athlit. The wretched business had lost them twenty-four hours, when they still had so much to do to cover their tracks. The next morning Sarah was back again. Sarah's and Yosef's reports had become almost running commentaries of their movements, in case they should suddenly find themselves unable to write any more.

"Morning light. Sarati appears," Yosef wrote to Aaron. "She left Haifa in the carriage before dawn. She paid half a bishlik (sixpence) baksheesh, and they let her pass. Can you imagine it, for half a bishlik our rulers let some one pass and, if they knew who it was, they would hang her! Isn't that a joke? Agreed: Sarah is driving to Zichron to arrange everything at home. But we still have these terrible provisions which we have to take care of, and deliver. That's all we need at a time like this!" The usual assortment of supplies had been brought with the last ship, and they had to be got out of the way immediately, before the searches began at Athlit.

Immediately after the pigeon had been discovered, the police started investigations in Hadera, the Jewish settlement closest to Caesarea. The farmers vehemently denied any knowledge of the pigeon. Whether any of them pointed in the direction of Zichron or not, is not known, but when Sarah hurried home on the sixth, as soon as she could free herself from Athlit, she found a mixed detachment of police stationed there and investigations under way.

"They are saying all sorts of things about the pigeon they caught," Sarah wrote Aaron. "That it knows languages, Yiddish, English and French. At the end they add 'Arabic', not to let on how much they suspect the Jews. They certainly know that the pigeon was sent by Jews. They say he was sent from London."

Once the note was deciphered, they would know everything. But they had not deciphered it yet, Sarah learned from her father. The old man, who had been so worried and nervous at every little rumour, was her staunchest ally now there was real trouble to face. Everybody wondered at his courage and devotion. He ran and he hurried and he helped wherever he could. He did not take time to eat, and he even forgot to pray. Most of the time he sat in the market place, listening to the rumours. As soon as he heard anything of importance, he sent a messenger to Sarah. "But in spite of this, he isn't very pleased with our work," wrote Sarah. "He wants the world to be quiet, so that he can have a little rest too. After all, he is of the old generation, an honest man, but simple."

Whether or not Sarah had seriously decided to go to Egypt, even to say good-bye to Aaron, she had changed her mind by the time the ship was due on September 10th. "I'm not ready to go this time," she wrote to Aaron. "I have a bad foot. I don't want to leave father alone in the house on the New Year. I am very busy. There, you have three reasons. But the real reason is that I am not prepared to take better care of my own soul than I am of the others.

"I am curious, too, to see the end of the war in Palestine. It seems to me that even if the English do come, there will not be an uprising, for the simple reason that there is no one left now to revolt. All the young men are in the army. If only they don't throw us out before the victory, as the army is demanding that they should do before the evacuation of Jerusalem.

"So far, everything around us is quiet. We are just waiting for an early redemption. What is the matter with the English? How long are they going to keep on like this? It is a scandal, really, with a lazy and starving people like the Turks, not to win. We are awaiting the New Year with curiosity, to see when the redemption will come."

Sarah did not tell Aaron why she was so busy. In desperate anxiety she and her father were working to save from the hands of the destroyer the records and the botanical collection to which Aaron had devoted so many years of his life. She took greater care in preserving them from the vengeance of the Turks than she did in saving her own life. She remembered how Absalom had trembled every time he thought of Aaron's beloved library and his collection in the hands of the Turks. She could do little for the books, but she and her father managed to save a large part of the herbarium.

They had to work by night, so as not to attract the attention of the neighbours or the gendarmes. The plants were carefully laid in a press and then concealed in the recesses of the natural cavern which stretched far beneath the Aaronsohn house. The documents went into the space between the double walls which separated the hall from the library. Aaron had had the walls built to serve such a purpose, a deep and ornate doorway camouflaging the unusual depth.

The ship they were awaiting so anxiously failed to arrive on the 10th. And they still had on their hands their dangerous guest, Naaman's friend, the Turkish officer. But the moon was still right. The ship would certainly stop on its way back from Tyre on the 12th. Sarah wrote to Liova:

"Liova, Shalom: This time we shall not see each other, because even if you would like to come to me, they will not let you, and they will be right. They are watching the shore more seriously now, and why should there too be much wandering around when there are gendarmes about.

"As you see, I am not accompanying you after all, and even if Aaron demanded it, I couldn't. My sister-in-law also cannot leave, for we have a more honoured guest whom we have to send with you.

"We don't know what to do with my sister-in-law, how to get her over. And if not? As soon as someone disappears they will begin to talk again, and interfere with us. And if I too should disappear, it wouldn't be passed over in silence. However, we will arrange this matter from here, somehow.

"When will it be finished? If we have to carry on this work in winter, it will not be at all agreeable. All eyes are turned on us now. Maybe it will pass, just like other things have begun, and then cooled down.

"Has my brother Alex come already? He must write to me at once, and I will come immediately." But she knew that she would not leave, and on second thoughts added: "Perhaps he would try the stunt once, and come to the shore at Athlit? But no, this is just silly. It is quite unnecessary, because if, God forbid, they should find me suddenly, you can understand what a black end there would be."

That reminded her of the Turkish officer, who was now their prisoner. "The man you will be seeing is a man who can tell you a lot, a lot, a very intelligent man, but you have to know how to get on with him, and Aaron must also try not to treat him like a prisoner. He is ready for anything, and is expecting difficulties, but not to be held as a prisoner. He has been told not to tell anything to the English, but he will see Aaron, and reveal everything to him, because why should *they* suck him dry? Aaron will do what he understands to be right, and what he wants us to do, he'll tell us, won't he?"

The ship did not come that night, nor on the nights following. Faithfully the little group of men crept silently from the Station to the seashore and waited there from nine until two in the morning, but in vain. Sarah waited up for them at the Station. When she saw their haggard, bitter faces, and the disgust with which they flung down the leather pouch, bulging with information which was already a month old, she sat down and wrote to Aaron the harshest words she had ever permitted to escape from her pen:

"Here we are, expending a fortune in money and in strength and energy to get our information, as you urge us to, because the information is very important, and the situation changes continually. How is it that you can't arrange to get hold of it immediately? As you know, the walk to the sea is always dangerous, and why should they endanger themselves for nothing? The English certainly wouldn't do that with their own lives. When the boat comes ashore, they are always in a hurry, and want to rush off as soon as possible. But when they have already got out to sea and safety again, our people still remain in danger, perpetual danger."

The members of Nili continually smarted under what they considered the Englishmen's disinclination to share any of the risks attached to their work. From time to time Sarah had suggested to Aaron alternative methods for handing over material which would not impose such hardship and danger on Nili. One suggestion, which came from Mendel Schneersohn, was to make contact by aeroplane instead of by sea. He had found a large, isolated field, not far from the coast, which he believed would be ideal. None of these suggestions were even considered.

In the meantime the cloud, which for the first few days seemed no larger than a man's hand, began to swell ominously. A special branch of the army had undertaken to find out where the espionage ring was operating. Nili was informed that the search had narrowed down to three places, Hadera, Caesarea and Athlit, with suspicion pointing most strongly to Athlit.

Hadera and Caesarea had already been searched. Why not Athlit? Sarah didn't like that. Were the Turks playing a game with them? Perhaps they were not going to search. Perhaps they were just going to keep watch quietly at various points along the seashore, until one fine day Nili would trip themselves up and fall into their hands.

Reuven Schwartz was informed that this was the plan, and he and Yehudah Zeldin, who were employed at the Station, approached Sarah and Yosef and demanded that the work of Nili should cease. Only for a few months. Just let the suspicion aroused by the pigeons quieten down, and then they could continue their work.

The atmosphere had been tense enough before that. On August 3rd Sarah had written to Aaron: "Our situation here in the country is getting worse and worse. It is completely impossible to get any arms, and what will we do at the time of danger?" There was no doubt about what the Turks, who were fighting a desperate battle on the Gaza front, would do to the Yishuv, if they discovered espionage going on behind their lines.

If Nili stopped functioning now, one of them could get away to be free to keep an eye on things and start the connection again when conditions were more suitable. Reuven suggested that Lishansky should be the one, since he did not belong to the area and his absence would not be noticed in Zichron. Reuven could not leave, even if he wanted to, because he belonged to Zichron and people would begin to talk immediately. The Turks would get suspicious as well, for he was known to be the accountant at the Experiment Station and he would be the first person they would want to speak to if they came to investigate.

Yosef pooh-poohed the danger and scoffed at Reuven for being afraid. Reuven retorted bitterly that it was easy for him to laugh. When the day of retribution came, Lishansky could run away, while he would have to remain as a sacrifice. Prophetic words. Sarah objected to Yosef's attitude. Certainly there was no point in getting frightened, but one could not just ignore the unpleasant facts, as he was doing. One had to weigh up the possibilities as well as the impossibilities. The situation was not favourable for their work, but it might only be temporary. The Turks were always very enthusiastic, to start with, but there was not a person in the area who was man enough to carry the investigation through to the end. She did not think there was any serious danger unless the business got as far as Djemal Pasha, which of course it could do any day.

The important thing was, did the English intend to keep on sitting there in Egypt? If so, then she was in favour of stopping the work for a few months. Winter was approaching. It was hard enough to work then, even under normal conditions, because of the difficulties of getting around the country to collect material, and of waiting by the sea in the heavy rains and high wind. Aaron was the one who had to decide. "We are brave, and we try to keep our spirits up," Sarah wrote to him. "All this is not going to turn us from our work, *if* the work is necessary. Is it really necessary to endanger ourselves every moment, and of course endanger the existence of the Yishuv as well? Because the moment Djemal catches on he'll kick us out, and send us to a thousand hells. He'll hang a few as well."

Loyal to Sarah, the band of faithful followers at Athlit agreed to wait for Aaron's decision. They were to wait in vain for Aaron's answer. Anger began to smoulder in them all, as once again the sea brought them nothing but disappointment. Their letters piled up in the bag, together with the information, while the dangerous guest whom Naaman had foisted on them hung like a millstone around their necks, tipping the already precarious scales on which their lives were balanced.

"Good-morning to you," Yosef wrote to Aaron. "I've already returned from the sea, very disappointed, and with empty hands. Except for kisses from hundreds of mosquitoes, and aching sides from the rocks that we lay on, we didn't gain a thing. And still with our passenger on our hands! One of these fine days they will come to *search*. I am not frightened of that. A hell of a lot they'd find, if you'd only take this miserable passenger off our hands. It will be very interesting if they come to search at Athlit, and find him, don't you think? And you people turn back and wait until the sea is so calm that you can pass through without wetting your feet! If, one of these fine days we find ourselves in the soup, I can tell you now that you people will be absolutely to blame, because you don't know how to organize your side of the work.

"Now, listen. Tens of people are risking their lives, working, and hurrying here and there, to get their material, and return to the Station with it, so that, Heaven forbid, they should not be late for the ship and displease our partners; so that our partners won't say that we are lazy (again heaven forbid!). But from your side, what? Under no circumstances can you manage to get two young people who know how to swim, *even* a *little*, to come and take the material from us. The whole operation takes twenty minutes, and no more. Believe me, the sea was very quiet all this month that we waited by the seashore, even though there were a few nights when there was a bit of a storm. But was that enough to stop anyone from landing? And what about our labour? Fifteen days of going round the country, and afterwards risking our lives lying on the shore night after night. And what is worst of all, returning home with empty hands. God of the Universe! And all that only because Leibel *wants to get rich* and demands a big sum for the trip to the shore. Tell me, isn't that enough to make you burst?"

So this was the secret of the ship's non-appearance. Leibel's wife had been thinking it over and had decided that patriotism was a fine thing, as far as it went, but £30 a month was not enough to recompense her husband's efforts and the risks he ran. Intelligence at G.H.Q.—or may be it was just Captain Smith—refused to pay the additional sum that Leibel demanded, and an attempt was being made to find someone cheaper. For more than a month, at the peak period of Allenby's preparations for the big attack which was expected to change the fortunes of the First World War, vital information about the enemy's movements lay wasted and unused. Someone had economized.

Why "they" attached such little value to the work of Nili at that time is hard to understand. Perhaps because the members of Nili were foreigners, and of an unaccountable and insignificant species, Palestinian Jews. And, of course, as Sarah had said, they had no idea at G.H.Q. of the risks and dangers and difficulties involved in getting the information, or how deadly serious the Jews were about it.

Lawrence, popping in and out of Cairo from the empty desert, had made it seem such a game, as in a sense it was, for he was just playing at war and playing about with a situation in which he was not personally involved. It was a struggle which even the people with whom he was associated—the Beduin—did not take too seriously. It was only later that G.H.Q. was shocked into realizing the work that Nili had voluntarily undertaken on behalf of the British.

Perhaps Aaron was to blame for this as well. He was so anxious to convince the British what valuable allies the Jews of Palestine could be, how faithfully and loyally they were prepared to serve the British cause, that he made it seem too effortless to them. Aaron could not realize, in that short time, the depth of British disbelief and their lack of interest.

Neither Aaron nor Nili are mentioned or given credit in any official or even semi-official account of the Palestine campaign. That is not surprising. They were spies, foreign spies, and, as Aaron had once said, "I don't see the English showering honours on spies." But Nili got even less than that. Captain Alex Aaronsohn, who entered Jerusalem with the conquerors, begged General Allenby, at the laying of the cornerstone for the Hebrew University, to say a word about the services rendered by Nili in the conquest of Palestine. The members of Nili, dead and living, were regarded as pariahs by the Jews of Palestine. The Aaronsohn family was ostracized, and the vilest accusations were being circulated against Sarah and Aaron. A word from Allenby, at this first official gathering of the new Palestine, would have saved the honour of Nili. But Allenby did not say that word.

For a week, day and night, Sarah remained on duty at Athlit, always ready in case the ship was sighted. At last she could wait no longer. It was September 16th, the eve of the New Year, and she had to be with her father in Zichron. "I have sinned enough against father, by leaving him until the last evening without a woman in his house," Sarah wrote to Aaron. "This also is an injustice on your part, that you didn't arrange things so as to let us free for the High Holidays, at least. As it is, all of us, from the biggest to the smallest, are remaining in their places, even though it is unpleasant for them to be away from home and family on the Holy Day. We are very cross, as you see. But perhaps there is a reason for this, and you are not to blame. Anyway, be successful. Who will give us our country for the New Year, so that we can be free people in our own land?"

Chapter 18

NAAMAN'S DOWNFALL

THE New Year at Zichron was observed in the traditional manner as a holy day, a day of deep thought and fervent prayer. The prayers were the prayers that the Jewish people had uttered from the depths of their being since their Exile almost 2000 years before. Never could they have been uttered more fervently than they were now by Sarah, as she sat, her head covered by the black shawl which had been her mother's, and pleaded for her family, her friends and her people.

"Forgive us, we beseech thee, O our Father! for we have sinned; pardon us, O our King! for we have transgressed. . . .

"O look upon our afflictions, and plead our cause; redeem us speedily for the sake of Thy name; for thou art a mighty Redeemer. Blessed art thou, O Lord, the Redeemer of Israel.

"O sound the great trumpet, to announce our freedom; and raise the banner to collect our exiles and gather us together from the four corners of the earth. Blessed art thou, O Lord, who will gather the outcasts of thy people Israel."

Sarah, dedicated to her people as she was devoted to her family, had absorbed these prayers with her mother's milk and had embedded them deep in her heart, so that her whole life was one continuous prayer for the redemption of the Jewish people. And now it was about to happen. Any day their freedom would be announced. Aaron had told her so. For all their sins, for all their transgressions, Nili had been an instrument in bringing the redemption nearer. And the English, when they did come, sooner or later, they too would be but an instrument. For the Lord was the Redeemer of Israel. Blessed was the name of the Lord.

In the afternoon Sarah walked slowly with her father through the one street of the village. They were taking their favourite walk to the old man's beloved vineyard on the outskirts. Once out of sight of the village, they quickened their pace. Their interest was not in the vines that day. They were hurrying to the watch tower, from whose open window a young man kept constant watch on the sea.

Nothing. Still no ship. Ephraim Aaronsohn returned to the synagogue, and Sarah went home. There, waiting for her, was one of their agents from the south. At sight of his face, she steeled herself for a blow. Naaman Belkind had been caught spying. Beduin had handed him over to the Turks in Beersheba. Yosef must hurry and come and bring not less than £400. The Wine Cellars at Rishon, where Naaman was employed, had already loaned £200.

Sarah quickly sent someone down to Athlit to bring Yosef to Zichron. They hunted up Nissim Rootman in Zichron, and the two of them left immediately with the messenger from the south. Sarah notified her father and then left for Athlit. Someone responsible had to be at the place, and the ship might be coming at any time.

Sarah's eyes were strained towards the horizon. She was waiting every moment for the "inquiries" to start, and her only prayer was that something would keep the Turks off until the ship had arrived. The next day she was summoned back to Zichron. The Village Committee wanted to say something to her. She stood before them frozen and unflinching, as the village elders addressed her in stern, passionate tones. They were no longer the friendly, homely farmers that she had known from childhood, but some medieval council, trying to exorcise the Dybbuk that had taken possession of one of their fairest daughters.

"In the name of our Committee, and the committees of Judea and Galilee, we have to inform you that you are working at unclean work, and that you are at the head of all this work. You are a daughter of this village. Your family stands to bear the brunt of the whole danger. We turn to you, not to Yosef, who is one day here, and one day there. This is the third time we turn to you. Today we don't want to hear any more explanations from you. Only one word, the right answer: Your promise to stop this work, which has gone beyond all bounds.

"We don't want you to endanger the whole Yishuv. Our leaders and our people do not want this imaginary treasure that you are getting for us. We don't want to endanger the small property that we have. The first building of our future homeland is already standing. We don't want the Turks to slaughter us and drive us out. We don't want to be hanged for a few people who want to endanger themselves.

"Stop your work. Remove all your services from Athlit, so that the place will be clean of crime. If you want to work at espionage, leave the territory and the lands of the Jews and go and work in some distant land. Otherwise, there will simply break out a war between Jews and Jews!"

Sarah gave no final answer to the Committee. She told them that since she worked with partners, she had to consult them. At the end of the month she would give them an answer.

"But a clear answer, and no dragging on," they told her.

Sarah was not alarmed at the verdict that had been passed on her, but all the way back to Athlit she wondered: "If the people are not able to understand the quality of our work, or don't want to understand, can we really force it on them? If people don't want to take risks can we force them to? They are perfectly justified in demanding 'Who is asking you to do this?' And if, God forbid, with all our care, we should fail, then not just a few of our leaders or twenty members of Nili will be hanged. All the Yishuv will be called to trial, and the judgment will be expulsion or hanging or massacres."

Sarah decided that they must stop the work for a time. They could see what would happen afterwards. She wrote to Aaron: "We must organize money here and pay all the workers a monthly salary, because wherever they turn, they will not get work. When I pretended to be naïve and asked, 'What do you mean by stop the work? What will be the sign?' they said to me: 'The sign will be that none of you will remain in the area of Zichron, Athlit or Hadera.' Perhaps you will send us such good news that everything will change. But it is difficult to rely on your Englishmen, so phlegmatic, so cold. How long will this continue? Even little children are mocking at the English. 'Why don't they come to take the country? Who is stopping them?' "

Three days later, the *Monegam* passed within sight of Athlit. The sea was stormy, but it quietened down by the next day. That night, waiting until it was dark enough to send the messengers to the shore, Sarah wrote to Aaron: "Our people are going down to the shore to wait. If, Heaven forbid, they return empty-handed, I am sure they will never want to go again. Don't forget that we have already been a month and a half without hearing from you. Our situation is very complicated now, and we need you. And there is not even any money in hand. Perhaps we'll find another hundred pounds in our cash box. And what to do if they don't come?"

As Sarah wrote, the enormity of her situation overwhelmed her. She was after all just a young woman, not yet twenty-seven and she had been left to pit herself alone against the monstrous gates of Hell which were slowly opening to engulf her and everyone connected with her. Yosef's recklessness, which had been so important to her when conditions were sane, was only a danger now. She needed someone solid now, with wisdom to balance his courage. She needed Aaron so desperately that she had to pretend that he was there, beside her, although probably he was not even in Egypt any more. "What will happen if the ship doesn't come? They have left us alone now for a month and a half. Perhaps they'll have some reason for not coming again tonight. Where will our help come from? To remain without a piastre in hand is also forbidden, for who knows what the day will bring? What will happen to us?"

Owing to the careful accounting, Nili was always kept so limited in funds that when they received no fresh supplies for a month and a half, they found themselves without money in this dreadful emergency. During the day another messenger had arrived from the south, and Sarah heard fresh details of Naaman's capture. It had been Absalom from his nameless grave who had wrecked the group that he had founded, and brought destruction on the ones he loved. Naaman could not rest until he had solved the puzzle of Absalom's disappearance. Against her orders, and without telling anyone, he had set out across the desert to get to Egypt, He hoped to pick up some news of Absalom in the desert, or get the answer from Aaron when he reached Egypt. He was accompanied by a Beduin guide. At Asluz, well into the heart of the desert, he became ill and went to a Beduin tent to rest. The Beduin seized them both, accused them of espionage, and brought them to their Sheikh.

The guide succeeded in escaping, but Naaman was handed over to the authorities in Beersheba.

For three days Naaman was kept in chains and deprived of food. But he stuck to his story, that he had been journeying south to visit his friend Ali Faud Bey, Commander of the 25th Division at Huj. Naaman would have been hanged, not because he had been found guilty of anything, but as a lesson to the spies in the country. The Germans intervened. They thought he might be more useful in helping them to track down the espionage ring. They told him that they were freeing him and that he would soon be able to go home. Ali Faud Bey had been notified, and he told them to bring Naaman to him. The Commander received him with great friendliness and entertained him for some days. From Huj Naaman sent a report to Sarah, saying that he was with friends. They were all very jolly and they would not let him leave.

During a banquet in his honour, the Turks plied him with wine, doped with hashish. Naaman prattled about his exploits and suggested that his friend Ali Faud should go over to the British. The Turks pretended to agree to his suggestion, and the game went on until they got all they could out of him. Then Naaman was put in chains again and taken back to Beersheba, where von Kressenstein ordered him to be tortured for more information and then hanged.

Yosef and the other members of Nili in the south did not know of the information which Naaman had unwittingly supplied to the authorities. As far as they knew, there was still hope for them, if they could get him out of the hands of the authorities. Money was flowing like water. But this time the Turks were taking the money and doing nothing.

Sarah's letter to Liova, who was expected that evening, was crisp and to the point: "Shalom Liova: I am enclosing a letter to Aaron, explaining the position we are in today, but first you must see the people who are our partners in our work, and tell them that we are in danger. We are trying with all our strength, which means, with the strength of our money, the gold coins, to quieten the affair, but it's going hard. It looks now as though it will be impossible. The cash box is empty because you haven't brought us anything for such a long time. Naaman has been in jail for eight days already, and he is ill, and they are torturing him, terrible tortures, to make him tell who is working with him. Von Kressenstein says he knows there is a whole group working with him. For the moment he is able to hold on, and is bearing it in silence. If they keep on with their falucca treatment, who knows what will happen? It is possible that he will talk, and then we are completely lost, and all the Yishuv.

"Therefore you must make your people understand that from this evening, every day, as often as the moon permits, they have to come, so that we can keep you informed about how matters stand. Secondly, without any excuse, you must come back tomorrow, because there is with us a man whom we must get on board. He is not with us now, because we are afraid to keep him with us, and therefore if we know that you are coming tomorrow, we will bring him to the Station. It is forbidden for him to stay with us a moment. Give Aaron the letters, immediately, if possible, and if not, then telegraph him the news of Naaman, and the position.

"Know that the business of Naaman has already cost us £600, and this is only the beginning. In our cash box there is £100 and no more. You understand conditions here, therefore try to help us with money. We don't know what will happen tomorrow whether they come and search amongst us, or what they intend to do. Yosef is in that area, and I must stay here and arrange matters. I am the only responsible person in the place. The fact that Yosef is over there worries me, worries me very much, because if he should be caught, they know him well in that area. He has a thousand things to arrange, and I couldn't persuade him, under any circumstances, not to go there. Somebody must work there, because everybody has lost their head since the business of Naaman. If he were the only sacrifice. But it looks as if he will pull more and more after him.

"If you could come yourself, that would be best, but at least someone from the ship must come tomorrow, without any excuse. If you don't, I don't know what will happen. The person who is with us can swim, and even if the sea is a little rough, it doesn't matter. Let down the little boat, and one of the Arabs can swim with him, because 'bread' of this sort must not be found in the house at Passover. If he, at least, did not lie on our shoulders, it would be less trouble. I hope the ship will come tomorrow. Or better still, I *order* it to come.

"For the moment it is quiet in Athlit, and after this, Allah knows. Keep well. Tell the English everything. They will see how people go into danger, searching out news for them. And in the end they don't come for five whole weeks. Get the post to Aaron, because it is urgent. We have to know his opinion and his decision.

"Shalom, and be successful, at least you, as I am blessing you. Sarah."

That night the *Monegam* came. Liova got to the Station and brought reassuring news. There was 40,000 in gold francs for the Refugee committees, funds for Nili, and the ship would return the next night and pick up the "passenger". Liova would remain ashore with them until the next night and in the meantime see what could be made of the situation.

Early the next morning a messenger went off to Hadera to fetch the "passenger" who had been concealed in the Schneersohn home. By late afternoon all were assembled and waiting for the night. Yosef had got back to Athlit a few hours earlier, after three days of frantic work. He brought news that Naaman was still holding out. Yosef had at first thought of taking six companions, dressed as Turkish gendarmes, and kidnapping Naaman on the pretext of removing him to another prison; but he gave up the idea under pressure. He returned to Athlit when he felt an attack of malaria coming on and was now pinned to his bed.

The stifling end-of-summer heat enveloped the Station at Athlit. The windmill began to turn, slowly at first, then more quickly. The rising wind brought no good news. If it did not drop by night, the boat might not be able to come. Inside the Station were people whose lives were hanging on a gust of wind. One was the prisoner, hidden away again in the little room upstairs, where once in the good old days Aaron used to work long hours in the night, evolving plans to make his homeland and all the desert places blossom like the rose.

The other was Liova. He sat beside Yosef, who was in bed with a soaring temperature, desperately needed in the south but too ill to lift his burning head from the pillow. The two of them talked together in low voices, trying to think of ways of saving Naaman, and how to save the members of their group. But the situation was as dark and nightmarish as the fever beating inside Yosef's head. Whatever plan for escape they made, it evaporated into nothing, for as long as they had a conscience, the Yishuv dragged them back with a thousand hands. Their sudden departure would endanger the community and leave those closest to them as hostages to the Turks. This is what had happened at Tyre. At the end of July, when the danger began to increase, Abdullah had removed his whole family, some sixteen people. The Turks arrested the notables of Tyre, and the latest news was that they had all been condemned to death.

The only decision Liova and Yosef could come to was that the ship should return on the 25th—in two days' time—and they would see what the situation was then. Yosef was determined to carry on, if only the affair of Naaman could be settled. They did not then know the extent of Naaman's disclosures.

"Their personal life is of no account to them," wrote Liova. "They have ceased to exist as people. They are carrying out a historic task. They are only clay in the hands of the potter."

Night came and the sea remained calm. Sarah dug up the reports and the letters, and Liova and the Turkish officer went off. The officer took with him a long, detailed report on higher policy, based on a visit of Enver Pasha, Minister of War, to the southern front. Beersheba had been evacuated, but houses and wells were mined. The road to Jerusalem was clear and Jerusalem was not fortified. Enver Pasha believed that the army at Gaza and Tel Sharia would be able to stand against the enemy, but not the army between Beersheba and Dhaheriye, which was the weakest point. Here was the answer to the question which Aaron had asked them in July, held up for three weeks.

A terrible depression fell on the comrades in Athlit as their friend Liova disappeared. His coming had torn aside for a moment the black curtain which was encircling them. With him went their assurance that they could ever be part of a normal, living world again.

Alex had replaced Aaron at G.H.Q. He, Raphael Aboulafia and Captain Smith were waiting for Liova when he arrived at

Port Said. Captain Smith immediately prepared money and made arrangements for an additional small boat to be available to take off six people, and the *Monegam* set sail again. Two days after he had left, Liova was off the coast of Athlit once more. It was September 25th, the eve of the Day of Atonement. The moon was in the ascent, and they could not come ashore until 1.30, which was cutting it fine, for any hitch might find them there in the light of dawn.

Nili's situation had grown critical since Liova had left. The Turks had just caught two young Christian Arabs from Nazareth spying. They had been brought from Egypt three weeks earlier and landed at an old Phoenician harbour outside Haifa. The young men admitted everything, even giving the names of the families they had visited and revealing that a French ship would be coming to pick them up on October 13th. The Turks intended to sink the ship when it came, and in the meantime had set a strong guard along the coast in the Haifa area. This had increased the danger for Nili.

But the real danger came from Naaman. It was known now that he had revealed everything. Naaman's mind ceased to be completely stable from the time he was given the doped wine. Or perhaps all the betrayals and the menace around him had broken his spirit. Like a simple child he believed everything the Turks told him. When they promised that he would be released and forgiven if he admitted all his crimes, he told them whatever they wanted to know. Even in the last weeks in Damascus, where he was finally sent, he said innocently and with child-like confidence to the judge: "I've kept my word to you. I've told you all I know. Now you must keep your word and release me." "Yes, yes, my son," the Turkish judge said soothingly, "you will be released. But I'm sure there is just a little bit more you can tell us first. . . ."[1]

The terrible thing for Sarah was that Absalom's name was again going from mouth to mouth, for Naaman had told them of his beloved cousin who had disappeared after founding the espionage.

"Our situation is getting worse," Sarah wrote to Liova. "Nevertheless, we cannot run away at this moment because a

[1] Dr Neumann's unpublished memoirs.

sudden departure will harm the whole Yishuv and, in particular, those close to us. We've decided to organize our affairs
so as not to cut off the connection between us and Palestine so
that we can steal back here one of these days and see what is
going on. Very likely this is a mistake on our part, and we will
be too late to escape, but we are endangering ourselves to the
last moment, and are keeping our people with us so that if we
can't get to the shore by stealth, we'll get to it by force of arms,
come what may.

"You must understand that we cannot remain in the country
much longer, because our hours are numbered, and so, without
any excuses, on the 27th of the month, immediately after the
moon sets, you must be by the coast, and we will be waiting for
you. Possibly with the family, or without them. We don't want
to take off too many people at one time, so that no great
suspicion should fall on the Yishuv. God be with you. And if,
with God's help, we are not caught before the day after tomorrow, then we will meet again at midnight."

When the little group of friends met at the Station that
evening to await the coming of the *Monegam*, they urged Sarah
to leave with the ship that night. "Sarah, get out while you can,"
Nissim Rootman warned her. "They'll start with you first,
because of Absalom."

Nissim would have been only too glad to leave. He did not
see how he could help anyone by staying. He had brought
Miriam, Sarah's sister-in-law, and her four-year-old son down
from Zichron. Sarah was determined to get her out of the
country, even though her disappearance should cause a stir in
Zichron. The others could not conceal their bitterness. Why
should she be saved in preference to themselves or their own
families, when she had taken no part in the work of Nili? Her
husband, Shmuel Aaronsohn, who had been in the States for
the past two years, had never been in favour of the espionage
and her own family in Zichron had kept themselves clear of it.
Sarah ignored their complaints. Although Miriam had no
connection with Nili, she bore the name of Aaronsohn, and
Sarah knew she would be amongst the first to be interrogated.
Who knew what she might not reveal in her innocence?

Sarah refused their pleas that she should save herself. "I want to be the last, not the first to leave," she answered. She wrote another letter to Liova: "I'm sending you my sister-in-law and all her property, that is, her son Yedidia. Watch over this property of hers and settle her and the child as well as you can. Try without fail to come on the 27th, for who knows if you will find us after that. The situation grows worse from moment to moment. I know the moon won't allow you more than a short visit, but we'll be ready and waiting for you."

The Naaman affair had not stopped Nili's activities, and with Sarah's letter went reports fresh from the Turkish front. They had been brought in that afternoon by Absalom Fine, who worked as a carter with the army around Beersheba. With his waggon and two horses the young man had free access everywhere, for most of the civilian carters had deserted by that time, fed up with working for bad pay and worse prospects. In spite of the panic and confusion among the agents in the south since the capture of Naaman, Absalom Fine managed to locate the hiding places of some dozens of machine guns on the Gaza-Beersheba sector. He knew that the *Monegam*, due that night, was not due again for another fortnight or more, and he had been travelling since dawn to bring Sarah the rough map he had drawn of the gun positions. He received his reward when Sarah said to him, "Absalom, you're doing good work, and you're very quick. Continue in that spirit, for you must achieve the maximum. Our days may be numbered. Every moment that we are not active is wasted. Who knows how valuable every moment of our work might be to the fate of our people?"

The reports that Liova collected that night at Athlit were handed over to the Intelligence officer on the *Monegam*, Captain Smith. The two of them immediately began to go through the reports together, as usual. When Captain Smith came across the slip of paper on which Absalom Fine had sketched his rough map, he jumped up and telegraphed immediately to G.H.Q. This was against regulations. He was obliged to report only to Intelligence, but he evidently considered the information too important to wait.

Captain Smith received a reprimand for communicating with G.H.Q. through unauthorized channels. Shortly afterwards he was promoted to the rank of Major. Whether his communication was also responsible for this is not known. What did Absalom Fine, or Liova, or Sarah get? Nothing. Liova put it quite simply. "Who asked us to sacrifice ourselves for the Yishuv? We didn't make any reckoning with the Yishuv or the English, and neither rewarded us for our pains."

Chapter 19

THE BRITISH TO THE RESCUE

WHEN Liova, on the *Monegam* in the early morning of the 25th, read Sarah's letter outlining their situation, he was filled with consternation. "Sarah demands most firmly that we return here in two days' time," he wrote in his diary. "That is the same as coming in the full light of day. No, no, that's impossible. Tell your friends, my dear, that they must wait. They must hold out until the 12th of October. May the Lord God of Israel be their help. Then we will come with Alex and we will save them."

The *Monegam* reached Port Said on the evening of the 26th, but Liova was not able to land until next morning, when he left immediately for Cairo. Alex and Pascal met him at the station. Liova reported the situation and showed them Sarah's last letter. They began to discuss and talk. Pascal had a wife, a mother and two daughters in Palestine, and Alex, who was high-minded to an extraordinary degree, had been in America for the past two years and was out of touch with the fiery furnace. The question that concerned them most was: "Can we possibly endanger the whole Yishuv to save the people of Nili?" They decided that this was impossible. Then and there, in the station at Cairo, they came to the incredible, the unforgiveable decision to ignore Sarah's order that they come to her rescue.

In all fairness it must be said that in any case the final decision rested with the British. They would not, as Liova had indicated in his diary, have considered anchoring off the coast of Athlit at the risk of being caught there in the light of dawn. Neither Liova nor Pascal nor twenty-nine-year-old Alex, fresh from the States, had the status to demand that the British take some risks to save the lives of a handful of men and women who had so often endangered themselves on their behalf. Only Aaron could have done that, and Aaron was already in London.

Seventeen days later, on October 12th, the *Monegam* was once again sailing along the coast of Palestine. Alex had come this time, and Aboulafia and Leibel Bornstein, who had agreed to work again. They all had guns and Very lights to signal to the two warships which had been brought to help in the rescue of the people, should their route to the sea be barred. The wind was high, and the *Monegam* seemed to dawdle along. They should have been opposite Zichron while it was still light, to see if the window up in the Aaronsohn vineyard was open. But the captain said he doubted if they would make it.

"And they call this an expedition of three men-of-war!" exclaimed Liova. "Wonderful!"

It was already dark when they passed Zichron and they could see nothing. The captain said it was no use approaching the shore, as the wind was too strong for a boat to be lowered. They drifted about that night and came back again the next afternoon. The window in the Aaronsohn vineyard was open. A good sign. They could see the settlement clearly and down by the shore two horsemen who hid in the sand dunes when they saw the ship. Otherwise there was nobody to be seen, neither in the Station grounds nor on the veranda. Suddenly they noticed something white waving on the roof, but it was difficult for them to make out what it was. Was it Sarah signalling? But what was the message?

Anxiously they waited for the night. They got to Athlit at 8 o'clock. They lowered two boats. Although Alex had been forbidden to land, he insisted on coming with Liova and Aboulafia. Captain Weldon came along as well. Liova was certain he had seen a signal from the shore, but when they landed there was no one to meet them. The cave on the cliff where they usually found their friends, when it was too stormy to wait on the shore, was also empty. A cold fear settled on them.

Slowly they crept across the stones and over the hill into the field where they had often met their friends coming to meet them. But no familiar shapes loomed through the darkness, and they strained their ears in vain for the whisper, "Nili!"

They dared not go inland to the Station. But they could not bring themselves to leave the shores of Palestine. Perhaps if they waited, someone of their friends might still appear.

Suddenly they were startled by a shot coming from the direction of the highway.

"They're shooting already!" exclaimed Alex. "What does it mean?"

"Perhaps someone is trying to cross the road, and there's a patrol, and they've shot at them."

"But who's shot at whom?"

"Perhaps the patrol has been killed, and we can hope that someone will get through to us?"

For almost an hour they sat in the field waiting. But beyond the one shot, all was quiet and nobody came. They returned to the shore and Alex stood silent, with head sunk, while Liova signalled the boat to take them back to the ship. Alex thought bitterly of the telegram he had brought with him. It was from Dr Chaim Weizmann, one of the two heads of the Zionist Organization in London. It had been dispatched on October 6th, immediately after Aaron's arrival, for the members of Nili through the High Command in Cairo: "We are doing our best to make sure that Palestine Jewish under British protection," it read. "Your heroic stand encourages our strenuous efforts. Our hopes are great. Be strong and of good courage until the redemption of Israel. Weizmann."

One thing remains a mystery. How was it that after Naaman had revealed every detail about the work of Nili, the visitors from the sea were still able to land on the coast of Athlit and move about freely for as long as they wanted? Could it be that the Turks were still too frightened of British naval power to think of resisting, whether a ship came by moonlight or even in the full light of day?

Chapter 20

THE DEATH OF SARAH

ON Yom Kippur, the Day of Atonement, Sarah fasted and prayed. The next day was the 27th. All day they watched the horizon for the smoke which would signal the *Monegam*. They watched in vain, and by nightfall Sarah knew that her name was no longer inscribed in the book of life. Calmly Sarah remained at her post, waiting for the disaster which nothing could now prevent. On October 2nd, the beginning of Succoth, the feast which marks the reaping of the harvest, the Turks surrounded Zichron.

It was late at night when the news of approaching cavalry was brought to the house. "Now they're coming for my soul," said Sarah. A wedding was being celebrated in one of the houses across the street. The young people danced and sang, not knowing what was going on until someone came and told them that the settlement was surrounded. The celebration dropped to a hush. As the young men and women dispersed, they saw Sarah standing at the gate of the Aaronsohn house, alone and quiet. They told her the news.

"What of it?" she said to the young people. "What is there to be frightened of?"

She had already sent into hiding in the vineyards the young men from Zichron most closely implicated in Nili. Yosef was concealed in the cellar. She and her faithful colleague, her good old father, and her brother Zvi, remained to await the Turks.

The searches and the tortures began in the morning. The Kaimakam of Haifa was in charge, Hassan Bey, hashish addict and notorious butcher. They came demanding Yosef Lishansky or Yosef Tuvin, as he had called himself in his false passport and in his negotiations with the authorities. Naaman had made it quite clear that Yosef was at the head of Nili. In the excitement Yosef, unnoticed by anybody, slipped out of the cellar and disappeared.

Zvi, Ephraim Aaronsohn and Sarah were arrested immediately. When they began to beat the old man to make him reveal the whereabouts of Lishansky, Sarah turned on the soldiers furiously.

"Why are you hitting my father, an old man of seventy? Do what you want with us, but my father doesn't know anything."

They saw that her father's suffering unnerved her. Throwing him on the floor, they tied his hands and feet to a rifle, and beat him on the soles of his feet, demanding that he reveal the whereabouts of Lishansky. Between his cries, the old man murmured over and over to himself, "Sh'ma Israel. . . . Hear O Israel, the Lord our God, the Lord is One."

Fearful that he would not be able to hold out, Sarah entreated him: "Be strong, Father. In any case you have not many years to live. All your life you were an honest man. Die honourably. Don't give in, Father, be proud. They did the same to our holy ancestors. Don't speak a word, Father." Even in his pain, the old man was moved to fury at his daughter. "Girl, do you warn *me*!"

They didn't touch Sarah that day. She stayed by her father's bed all night, calming him and easing his pain.

Reuven Schwartz, Manasseh Bronstein, Itzhak Halperin and Nissim Rootman had been hiding in the vineyards since the night before. They drew lots to see who would try to get to the village to find out the news. It fell to Manasseh. Crawling on all fours, he worked his way up the hill from the Wine Cellars to the back of the Aaronsohn house. Sarah was standing at the open window, as if she had been expecting him to come.

The situation was bad, she whispered. He was to find Yosef and tell him to get out of reach of the settlement as quickly as possible. "Wait a minute," she said and disappeared, coming back with a loaf of bread wrapped in a silk handkerchief, a bundle of paper money, some gold, and a small bottle of eau de cologne.

"Give this to Yosef, and tell him, if he's taken, he's to put all the blame on me. You understand? On me, on me, and nobody else."

Next day they started on Sarah.

"Where's Tuvin? Where's Reuven Schwartz?" demanded the

Kaimakam of Haifa. "Tell me, or I'll draw the words out of your mouth."

They took her outside, tied her hands to the gatepost, and began to beat her. The Anatolian soldiers tried at first to soften their blows, for it was not customary amongst them to give such treatment to women. But the Kaimakam urged them on with a ferocious, sadistic energy. He kept shouting at her: "Where's Tuvin, where is Schwartz? Where is Absalom Feinberg? What have you told the enemy?"

Sarah had warned all the members of Nili not to forget that they knew nothing, that they were simply workers at the Experiment Station. Whatever had been done was known to Sarah alone. That was what Sarah told the Turks, that the others, including her father and Zvi, knew nothing.

"You are murderers!" Sarah spat at them. "You are wild beasts, thirsty for blood. I saw how you tortured the Armenians. Their cries split my ears. You are cowards, rogues. You are torturing me in vain. You are torturing the innocent in vain."

They continued to beat Sarah until only the hands tied to the gatepost supported the sagging body. Then they untied her, and she fell unconscious to the ground.

In spite of the rumours which had been circulating about the spies, it was surprising how few people in the little village of Zichron actually were aware of what was going on in their midst. Dr Hillel Yoffe, who was also a member of the Zichron Committee, was waiting for a diligence to take him to a patient some distance beyond the settlement when he was informed that Turkish soldiers had surrounded Zichron during the night. "We thought at first that they were looking for army deserters," he recorded in his diary, "but we were told that they were looking for Reuven Schwartz, a clerk at the Experiment Station. The police have already arrested the Aaronsohns and Toba Gelber. Mrs Feinberg, who had just come from Hadera, was also arrested. They brought me to the house of the old man Aaronsohn, whom they'd beaten with murderous blows. He was very courageous. Sarah showed me whip marks on her body. The whole house is full of soldiers and police.

"For a long time the journeys of Sarah and Lishansky have

been causing us great worry. Perhaps because of dislike of inter-
fering in the affairs of others, we did not pay sufficient attention
to them. And then suddenly the carrier pigeon was caught at
Caesarea. We heard it from the Committee without realizing
that it had any connection with the Experiment Station. And
now Absalom Feinberg and Sarah are being talked about, and
people realize why Absalom suddenly came to stay in Zichron.
They are recalling how Aaron was always wrapped in secrecy,
and they are beginning to understand the life of Alex, and his
novel, *Forty Years of Espionage*.

"What a tragedy! Three brothers left the country one after
another, after they had organized all the espionage business,
and they left behind their sister Sarah, who was married and
rich, and never aspired to any public rôle. A place intended for
science and public use has been turned into a nest of spies. Now
one can understand why all scientists were kept away from the
place. And who is this Lishansky? And how did he come to
exert such an influence on Sarah?"

After he had been to the Aaronsohns, Dr Yoffe went to the
Kaimakam and protested against Sarah's torture. The Kaimakam said he had already severely punished the officer who
had beaten Sarah and it would not happen again. But he would
continue to beat the old man on the soles of his feet as long as his
daughter continued to refuse to reveal Lishansky's hiding-place.

In the afternoon they began on Albert, Reuven Schwartz's
father-in-law and head of the Village Committee. It was Albert
who had been sent to Athlit to beg Sarah and Yosef to stop
their work, because he would be one of the first to suffer. They
dragged him through the streets on a chain like a dog and beat
him with whips, crying "Where is Reuven Schwartz?"

The old man, shrieking in his agony, called on the name of
Reuven, begging him, if he could hear him, to return to the
settlement and give himself up. Reuven, hiding in the vineyard,
heard the cries and his blood froze. At last he could bear no
more. He returned to the settlement and gave himself up to save
his father-in-law.

Before the eyes of Sarah they began to torture Reuven
Schwartz, her cousin, her childhood sweetheart, and her
brothers' faithful friend. Then, one after another, before her

sickened eyes, they produced Manasseh Bronstein, Itzhak Halperin and Nissim Rootman. They too had given themselves up, unable to stand the cries of those who were being tortured for their sakes.

There were some who almost went mad listening to the cries of the tortured, but there were four women who seemed to be gripped by an obscene hysteria, and they ran in the streets shouting and rejoicing to hear the screams. They fell upon each new captive with blows and abuse, and ripped the coat off Nissim Rootman when he was dragged through the village.

A terrible fear fell on the settlement. The next day, which was Thursday, October 4th, the Kaimakam called a meeting of the Village Committee and told them that he knew that a spy ring existed in Zichron. There was no use for the Aaronsohns and the others to tell him that they knew nothing about it. And he did not want lies, such as the worker Zeldin had told him even under torture, declaring that he had been the one who always travelled with Sarah, whereas he, the Kaimakam, had often seen Sarah together with Lishansky. He knew from a reliable source that Sarah always travelled with Lishansky, and they should not try to lie to him.

He told them that he was prepared to punish a hundred innocent people to find one guilty man. He reminded the Zichronites of his activities in Armenia. With his own hands he had killed many Armenians, and his soldiers had killed thousands. He would leave no single house standing in Zichron, no trace of the settlement would remain, if they did not produce Yosef Tuvin within three days. He was now leaving the settlement in the hands of the Military Commander, who had his orders.

The elders of Zichron were shattered. Many of them could not remember ever having seen Yosef, for he was not from the area and it had been months since he had appeared openly in the village. As they left the meeting, they met the police leading Sarah Aaronsohn in chains.

"I asked her how she was," noted Dr Yoffe, "and she answered me with a wry smile. She knew they were leading her off to another investigation and new tortures."

Before her arrest Sarah had given the Village Committee £500 in gold from the money that the *Monegam* had brought on its last trip. She had given it to them to use in an emergency, and surely this should have been the time to use it. But not one of the Committee dared or even knew how to approach the torturers in order to soften their treatment of Sarah.

Toba Gelber, who was taken for interrogation at the same time as Sarah, was not tortured. When she was brought before the interrogation officer she took off her gold wrist watch and without saying a word placed it on the desk in front of him, out of sight of the two policemen behind her. The officer, also without speaking, adjusted the papers on his desk until the watch was concealed. Then he spoke some words to the policemen in Turkish, and not so much as a finger was laid on Toba, even when she was sent to prison later. Anyone could have been bought for a piece of gold.

But the people of Zichron had lost their heads, overwhelmed by the terrible catastrophe that had befallen their village. Each one thought only of his own life, and the safety of his family. It was a natural reaction. Most people in any country would react in the same way in the same circumstances. This makes even more remarkable the work of Nili. Not one of them but was prepared to sacrifice themselves, and even their family, so that their people might live.

In the midst of the inhuman chaos, Sarah suddenly remembered that the shutters of the watch tower window were open. When the *Monegam* came again on the 12th, the first sign they would look for would be the open window. It had always been kept open, because up to then there had never been anything to prevent them from coming ashore. The shutters had to be closed now to warn them of their danger. But how could she close the shutters? She was under guard all the time and could not do it herself. What was she going to do?

To get to the torture centre on the outskirts of Zichron, Sarah's captors had to lead her through the entire village. As they walked along, Sarah searched the faces of everyone she passed, greeting each one politely, as if that were her only purpose. Suddenly she saw a friend approaching who could help her. She shortened her steps, and began to sing lightly:

"In father's vineyard there is an open window with a ladder
hidden among the vines.
The shutters have to be closed because of the wind, and I, as
you know, have nowhere to turn."

The words were in Hebrew and the soldiers paid no attention
to them, except perhaps to think that her tortures had turned
her mind. The friend listened to the song. He had not caught it
all and, not being a member of Nili, he did not understand the
situation. But the words "shutters, ladder, vineyard" kept
sounding in his ears. He hurried to the Aaronsohn vineyard,
looked among the vines, and found a long ladder. He leaned it
on the wall and closed the shutters. Hiding the ladder, he
returned to the village, and loitered on the road opposite the
interrogation centre. Finally Sarah appeared at the window.
She called to him, "Shalom?" with a query in her voice.
"Shalom," he answered, in the affirmative.
But he had not fixed the shutters firmly enough, and during
the storm which delayed the *Monegam* they were blown open
again. Hence there was nothing to warn Alex and Liova of their
danger when they sailed past Athlit. It has never been possible
to find out what the white thing was which suddenly appeared
on the roof of the Station, and which Alex and Liova thought
was Sarah trying to convey a message to them.
Meanwhile terrible and unrelenting punishment was being
inflicted on Zvi Aaronsohn, his father, Reuven Schwartz and
the others. Everyone tortured saw the torturing of those dear
to him. And every one of them promised to forbear from re-
proaches if one of the others should find himself unable to keep
silent. The sense of mission which had sustained them during
their years of espionage fortified them now. When word was
brought to Reuven of his newly-born son, he named him
Asah-ayl—"God has done it". It was the will of the Lord.
Sarah was tortured worst of all. "Torture me," she told them.
"Beat me as much as you want. You won't get anything out of
me. You think that because I'm a woman, I'll be weak. I
despise you. No one but I did anything. Only I knew. I despise
you and death. Hit. Torture. I will be avenged. Your end is
coming."

Sarah's taunt was true. Because she was a woman, they thought at first they would get what they wanted out of her more easily than the men. When she withstood them, they refused to be defeated by a woman and increased their efforts. General Adrianus Bey, who had been called in to assist the "inquiries", was moved to pay her a grisly compliment. "She is worth a hundred men!" he declared.

They were all kept in the house which had once been Aaron's office, the home of Shmuel and Miriam Aaronsohn. When they were not torturing Sarah, they were torturing her father or her brother or her friends, so that their screams should unnerve her.

By the third day it seemed as though they had reached the end of their resistance. The groans of the men were terrible, and Sarah's body was one great, festering wound. Her hair had been pulled from her head, the palms of her beautiful hands were burned by irons, and her finger nails had been extracted with pincers.

"Mother . . . Mother . . . I can't stand any more," they heard her scream through the closed door. Then silence. The door of Aaron's old office was opened, and Sarah's limp body was flung on to the stone floor of the ante-chamber, where the prisoners had been huddled together without food, without drink and without rest since the tortures began.

As Sarah came to, she heard the rumble of carts outside the house and saw her old father and others of her comrades being dragged out by the police. Not being able to extract any information from the suspects, the Turks had decided to move them all to Nazareth, where interrogation could be continued under the supervision of the infamous Hassan Bek, Chief Medical Officer of the Turkish Fourth Army. Even though the structure which Nili had built up had fallen in ruin about them, Sarah never for a moment lost her clarity of mind or forgot her goal. She knew that if they suffered more, their bodies might force them to turn traitor. Some way had to be found of giving them the strength to hold out.

In the proud spirit of her ancient forefathers, Sarah came to her decision. This was such a moment as Josephus Flavius had described, the climax of the siege of Massada, the rock fortress in the wilderness of Judea, where the last defenders of Jewish liberty held out for three years after the Roman conquest of Jerusalem: "Neither did Eleazar once think of flying away, nor would he permit anyone else to do so; but when he saw their wall burned down by fire, and could devise no other way of escaping or room for further courage, and setting before their eyes what the Romans would do with them, their children and their wives, if he got them into their power, he consulted about having them all slain. This he judged the best thing to do in their present circumstance. . . ."

So it was with Sarah. When she saw there was no room for further courage, she decided that the moment had come to make her final sacrifice for Nili. She asked permission to go to her home and change her blood-soaked clothes for the journey to Nazareth. Bound with chains, she walked through the streets of Zichron for the last time. Every window was shuttered, but she knew there was not a person in the settlement who was not watching her through the slits. She held herself straight and proud in spite of her agony. She wanted to comfort her friends, to confound her enemies, by showing that her spirit was still unbroken. At the gate of her father's house she stood for a few minutes and looked up and down the street, where she had spent almost all the years of her short life. Then she turned and entered the courtyard.

The guard remained outside while she went into the bathroom. There she wrote a letter giving instructions for the care of the families who would be left bereft because of Nili. She forgot no one and no detail. "If the workers of the Station are freed, let them continue to work there, and they can live from the wheat and barley which is there. Give them 30 francs a month. If the Government forbids them to work at the Station, give everyone 50 francs compensation, and let them go. I heard the Moudir give the Commandant the names of four women. They have simply informed on us. We are now in a terrible position, and I in the worst of all, because I have taken all the blame on myself. I've been given the most murderous beatings. They have tortured me with terrible tortures. They chained me with iron chains. Remember to tell of our sufferings to those who are coming. I am certain that our friends will be victorious, and you will see my brothers. Tell them everything, and tell them that Sarah lays on them the duty of avenging her blood. Don't have pity on them, as they had no pity on us.

"I haven't the strength to suffer any more. The tortures are something terrible. Better for me to kill myself than to remain any longer in the hands of these beasts. They say they are going to send me to Damascus, and there they will certainly hang me. I have a small weapon. I don't want them to defile my body. It was terrible seeing my father suffer so. But no, we will not speak. In vain did they try all kinds of tortures on us. We do not speak. And remember them as heroes, those who died without informing on us.

"We've sacrificed ourselves, but we've saved our people, and liberated the country. Don't pay any attention to the words of the scandal-mongers and informers. I aspired to save my people, and if my people are not able to understand. . . ."

She gave instructions that after the army went, they must look for Yosef in the mountains and give him her last order. "Tell him from Sarah: Never give yourself up. Kill yourself, but don't give yourself up. They are coming. I cannot write any more."

Taking a pistol which she had hidden behind a secret panel, the same pistol which she had asked Aaron to send her from Egypt, she shot herself through the mouth. But her strength had failed her, and she only succeeded in wounding herself horribly.

Dr Yoffe recorded in his diary: "On Friday, October 5th, Nidderman, the Mukhtar, called for me in the morning, shouting: 'Sarah has committed suicide. Hurry to save her!' I quickly took my instruments and went to the house. I found Sarah lying unconscious on the floor of the bathroom. Her pulse was slow and heavy. Blood was flowing from her lips. Consciousness returned only after an injection of caffeine. She recognized me, and begged me in God's name to finish all this. 'I beg you to kill me. I cannot live and suffer. I cannot.' I carried her to the bed and examined her. The bullet had passed through the tongue and had lodged in the spine. Her arms and legs were completely paralysed." There were left to her three more days of agony before she died.

On the day Sarah shot herself, the Nili prisoners and many of the people of Zichron who had been arrested in the round-up were taken to Nazareth. A price of £50 in gold was put on Lishansky's head, and fourteen elders of Zichron were retained as hostages until he should be handed over. A time limit of two days was set.

That evening, as Sarah lay dying, all the men of the settlement assembled in the synagogue, and in the light of black candles before the open Ark swore to hand over Lishansky. There was bitter weeping, for it was a terrible thing to put on a man the mark of Cain. Henceforth Lishansky would be hunted like a dog.

On Saturday, October 6th, Dr Yoffe again saw the military Governor and informed him of Sarah's condition. "I told him that I refused to treat her if there was no security that they would not start torturing her again. The Governor rose, shook my hand, and said, 'In the presence of the government officials who are here, I give you the word of a soldier that she will not be touched if she gets better." I demanded that they take Sarah to Jerusalem for operation, to which they answered that they also had Turkish surgeons, and there was no need for this. All evening young men and children have been going from house to house looking for Lishansky. The whole business is strange and terrible."

Few of the people of Zichron dared to come to Sarah for fear of falling under suspicion, But Zvi's wife was with her as much as her own family cares would permit. Yardena, her eight-year-old daughter, came too to be with her beloved aunt Sarah, who had always been so gay and loving and was now in such terrible distress. When Sarah saw Yardena's red eyes, swollen from weeping, she called her to her bedside. "Don't cry. There is nothing for you to cry about. It will be all right." Then she whispered to her: "Try and find my blue skirt. There is a letter in the pocket in the belt. If you can destroy that without anyone seeing, I'll be happy."

On Sunday, October 7th, Dr Yoffe recorded: "Sarah's temperature is mounting. Her condition is terrible. She begs ceaselessly to be given poison. In the evening I gave her an injection of morphine. In the settlement, complete panic. The period for handing over Lishansky has expired, but Lishansky has vanished.

THE DEATH OF SARAH

"Monday, 8th of October. Sarah's condition is very bad. I visited her three times at night. She keeps pleading to die. Consciousness is limited. At three in the morning Sarah cries out that she is frightened she is going mad.

"Tuesday, 9th of October. All Sarah's relations come to bid her farewell. She begs them to look after her poor old father. Her last wish is that they should free her father, because he has never been guilty of any crime. She sits up for a moment, then falls on the bed without moving."

So she lay until 8 o'clock in the morning, when she died.

That same day Sarah's tortured body, swathed in mosquito netting from the windows for lack of other material, was laid to rest beside her mother. The hysteria, the fear and the panic which had gripped Zichron as though in a nightmare suddenly vanished, and in spite of the threats of the Turks all the inhabitants of the settlement followed her coffin to the grave.

According to the Hebrew calendar it was the 23rd day of Tishri, the day after the reading of the Law has made a complete cycle and the new cycle begins. In Jewish tradition there is no end, only fresh beginnings. As the grave closed, the sky became overcast, mist covered the sea, and a light rain began to fall, the first rain of the new year.

Chapter 21

AT NAZARETH

WHEN the Turks besieged Zichron, they invaded Hadera as well, searching for Lishansky and other members of Nili. Hearing the noise around midnight, Mendel Schneersohn got out of bed and went to investigate. In his pyjamas he found himself herded together with a group of men and women under arrest. To his horror he remembered that in his pyjama pocket was a letter from Liova. It had been left on Liova's last visit a few days before, and had been transmitted to him only that day.

With one hand he began to work off bits of the letter, rolling them into tiny cylinders between his fingers, and when no one was looking he transferred them to his mouth. As the bits of paper softened, he swallowed them. It took him an hour to dispose of the letter.

After standing in the open road for some hours, while one after another was taken off and interrogated, Mendel was finally told to go home and wait there. He hurried back and began to destroy every document and scrap of paper in the house that might cause trouble.

Although both Zichron and Hadera were closely guarded, the terrifying details of the Zichron interrogations and Sarah's suicide quickly reached them. Mendel recalled the last words Sarah had spoken to him. The comrades were at the Station at Athlit on the night of the 27th, waiting for the ship which they knew might not come. Sarah was standing near Mendel, playing with a small revolver, a present from Aaron. Suddenly she said to Mendel, with a smile on her lips: "Where is the safest and surest place to fire to be killed instantly, should one decide to commit suicide?" Mendel replied, also with a smile, "Just put the barrel in the mouth, pull the trigger gently, and all is over in a flash."

Mendel expected to be arrested every minute. It was impossible for him to hide. Nobody would conceal him. Many even refused to speak to him, lest they be suspected themselves. The police left him at liberty. Mendel wandered around like Dante in the nether world, almost longing for arrest to put an end to his feeling of being null and void in the realm of the tortured and the suffering.

He was evidently being watched, for a few days later, on his way to visit his fiancée at Karkur, two mounted policemen suddenly appeared and ordered him off his horse. He was bound hand and foot and taken off to Zichron without an opportunity of letting anyone know what had happened to him. They increased his dejection by informing him that Lishansky had already been caught. (This, as it happened, was a false alarm.)

At sunset they reached Zichron. Mendel was led by a rope along the main street to the interrogation centre at the end of the village, conscious of the hundreds of eyes looking at him with deep sorrow. Only against the Aaronsohns and Lishansky had the people of Zichron their fierce, bitter hatred.

The Turkish sentry bashed him in the face with his fist. "You English spy", he shouted. "I wish I could kill you like a dog." In the prison, another guard came in, gave him a beating and started to rifle his pockets. Mendel had £20 on him, which he hoped to use for his escape, and he began to shout for help. Demanding to see the commanding officer, he showed his bruised face and told him that if any of the guards touched him again, he would do just what Sarah Aaronsohn had done.

Torture was a means of extracting information, but to cause the death of a prisoner was a criminal offence. Sarah's death had already begun to cause reverberations, and the police at Zichron must have felt that they would do well to be more circumspect. Mendel's threat accomplished its purpose. The officer said something in Turkish to the guard, and Mendel was left in peace for the night.

In the morning he was taken off to Nazareth. Leaving the prison, he saw heaped up in the hallway and in the courtyard the books and manuscripts of Aaron's treasured library. On the way to Haifa they passed along the highway which had so dangerously separated the comrades of Nili from the visitors from the sea, who were to bring the news of the redemption they had worked for so faithfully. They had outwitted the Turks for two years, but their fate had caught up with them. Absalom dead. Sarah dead. Lishansky captured and certain to be hanged. This would probably be the fate of them all, with a nightmare of torture ahead of them before the end. And where was the redemption?

Mendel could have let himself sink under the weight of the sadness which fell upon him, but he did not. He was of a practical and optimistic disposition, unlike his introspective and poetic brother Liova. He began instead to notice the beauty of the Galilean landscape—the silver olive trees, the grey rocks, the green bushes, the cultivated fields, interspersed with patches of yellow daisies and white narcissus. Here and there were drops of red, the flower known in Hebrew as "Blood of the Maccabees", because it is everlasting. And over all the brilliant sun which cast a golden glow.

The prison in Nazareth, formerly a French convent, contained only Jews, picked up from all over the country. Not a single town or village but had its representative in the prison. Many of Mendel's friends were there, their green faces full of grief and pain, their feet bare, chained and bleeding. As he passed slowly by them, some whispered words of encouragement and appealed to him to be brave.

In his cell was Abu Farid, the Aaronsohn coachman, his feet and hands a bleeding pulp. And indeed the loyal man who would not betray by a word the doings of his beloved master Aaron and his sister Sarah remained a cripple for the rest of his life. Another cell mate was a young men whom Mendel knew in connection with Nili, dejectedly holding his head between his knees. Neither of them showed the least sign of recognition. The rest were strangers. That night terrible cries and groans penetrated through the wooden floor from below. They were the cries of the old man Aaronsohn, who was being bastinoed there. He was beaten first slowly, then with increasing rapidity. Between the strokes he continued to pray, as he had done from the beginning, "Sh'ma Israel. Hear, O Israel, the Lord our God, the Lord is One."

In charge of "investigations" was the infamous Hassan Bek.

Mendel's name had been given by Naaman Belkind. Hassan Bek asked Mendel if he knew Belkind.

"His name is well known in Palestine."

"Are you not an intimate friend of Naaman Belkind? It is what he said himself."

Mendel replied: "I suppose I saw him once or twice a long time ago, but he was never a friend of mine."

"And what about Absalom Feinberg from Hadera? He must certainly be one of your best friends for you worked together to betray the Turkish Government and sell us to the English? And Yosef Lishansky, alias Tuvin. . . . And Sarah Aaronsohn?"

During the beating he received, Mendel remembered Sarah and the old man Aaronsohn and this enabled him to bear up. He wore thick glasses. During a pause he picked up his glasses from the floor where they had been thrown, and thrust them before the inquisitor. "Examine my eyes," he said. "How could a person as short-sighted as I am do the things you accuse me of?" The veins of Mendel's eyes must have been alarmingly distended by his falucca treatment, for Hassan Bek, after looking at them, let him be.

Prisoners kept coming into Nazareth. One was a staunch farmer from a settlement in the Emek. As soon as Hassan Bek opened his mouth, the man interrupted and said: "Look here, Hassan Bek, I am certain that you do not want to ask me anything of importance to you. Your only purpose is to torture and bring suffering on everybody who has the misfortune to fall into your hands. Here are my soles ready for the whip, and let my feet talk instead of my tongue!" With these words he stretched himself upon the floor.

A coachman brought money and parcels of food and clothing from the people in Zichron. Mendel sent a message with him to Hadera asking for £50 in gold. He knew his family did not possess so much, but they would find it somehow. Without money people could starve in prison. He also needed money to buy himself out. He had heard that those accused of espionage would soon be sent to Damascus where a court-martial would be held. Each prisoner had to make his own plans for escape.

With small bribes he was able to come face to face with the commandant of the prison, to whom he gave £25 to cross his name off the list of those to be sent to Damascus. Thirty-two were sent. Mendel was one of those freed.

When he got back to Hadera he found that his father had been arrested and removed to Zichron. Soon after his arrest he was ordered off to the torture camp on the outskirts of the village. Mendel's father pleaded for time to sustain himself. The soldier, thinking that he meant he wanted time to eat, began to drag him off. The Moudir of Caesarea, who had known Schneersohn for many years, told them to leave him for half an hour. The old man, descendent of many generations of Hassidim, spent the half-hour in prayer. Strengthened, he marched off to the torture place. At the entrance he was met by the Moudir, smiling.

"You are a very lucky man. I have just received a telegram from Damascus to stop all the inquiries here at Zichron. I am glad you have avoided the tortures. Your God has heard your prayers."[1]

Lishansky had been captured, Schneersohn was told, and had confessed everything.

[1] From Mendel Schneersohn's unpublished memoirs

Chapter 22

MAN HUNT

LISHANSKY, when he fled from Zichron, hid in caves in the mountain above Faradis village. He had no food beyond the loaves of bread which Sarah had sent him that first night, and after three days hunger drove him out. He was wearing his Arab kaffieh and abbaya, and he intended to escape to his friends, the Druze or the Metuwallee, up in the Lebanon.

It was not yet dark. Working his way through the gorse until he came to the plain, he met an Arab with a cart. He stopped him, told him he was looking for Lishansky, and asked to be driven to Karkur, a communal settlement behind the Haifa highway, a few kilometres from Hadera. Mendel Schneersohn's fiancée and her family lived there.

Yosef went to their house and asked for food and a vehicle—any kind of vehicle. He pulled out his bag of gold coins to pay for it and even thrust his gun in the farmer's face when he refused. But the farmer would not budge. Everything in the settlement was owned in common, and he could do nothing without asking the other members. Yosef would have to wait until the next morning.

Yosef was sitting there with his bag of gold and his pistol on the table beside him when Mendel's fiancée returned home at 4 a.m. She had tried to get to Hadera to see what she could find out about Mendel. But the road to Hadera was sealed off by gendarmes and soldiers and everywhere they were looking for Lishansky.

She gave a start when she saw Yosef sitting there, and drawing her father aside, she whispered something in his ear. He turned to Yosef and said curtly: "You'd better go. There is no place for you here."

Yosef went out of the house and wandered around the fields of the settlement, not knowing what to do. When dawn came, he hid and remained hidden until nightfall. When he appeared again, he heard a vehicle coming. It was a diligence with three people in it. He recognized two of them, Zvi Nadav and Shmulik Hefter, men of Ha-Shomer from Galilee.

They were smuggling arms for the defence of the Jewish settlements in Galilee. The exposure of Nili could not have come at a worse time for the Yishuv. As the situation at the front became more threatening for the Turks, so the situation became more critical for the Jewish community. The Turks had made no secret of their intention to leave ruin and destruction behind them as they retreated, and the Jews knew that the Arabs also would not fail to make good use of their opportunities for loot and massacre.

The Palestine Office provided whatever funds it could lay hands on, and Ha-Shomer, like ants, penetrated to every part of the country, buying up arms and transporting them to strengthen the defences of the isolated communities. Arms were transported in carriages and in work carts, hidden in sacks like provisions. Now that the search for spies was on, any vehicle driving along the road was likely to be stopped and searched.

Another dangerous crisis had arisen among the representatives of the Yishuv. That very month Nili had handed over 40,000 gold francs to the Relief Committee. When the authorities began their investigations after the discovery of the pigeon, they began to pick up stories about gold being smuggled into the country for the use of the Jewish community. Police made a surprise visit to the Palestine Office in Jerusalem and sealed up the safe, until the authorities could come and inspect it.

The 40,000 gold francs were in the safe. Some of it had been minted as late as 1915. If the authorities found it, they would confiscate the money and arrest the heads of the Palestine Office. A desperate call was sent out to the teacher of metal work at the Bezalel School for arts and crafts. He took a wax imprint of the seal, made another one in the shop, and they were able to replace the gold with Turkish paper money. When eight representatives of the Turkish authorities came to inspect the safe, they found the seal intact and no gold inside.

In the meantime the gold was hurriedly sent off to Petach Tikvah, the chief provincial centre since the expulsion of the Jews from Tel Aviv and Jaffa. Petach Tikvah was all Jewish, and normally there was no need there to fear informers, or Turkish Mukhtars, or the gendarmerie. But the capture of Naaman Belkind had left no place safe any more, and the head of the Relief Committee in Petach Tikvah refused to accept the money. He demanded that it be taken off his hands immediately, or he would throw it into the Yarkon river.

Ha-Shomer decided that they would take the gold that the frightened community heads wanted to get rid of. Two of their members were sent to Petach Tikvah to collect it, together with a load of arms for the Shomer headquarters at Tel Adas. It was this vehicle, hurrying north with its doubly dangerous load, that Lishansky stopped at dusk on the highway outside Karkur. Yosef called out, "Zvi, stop! Take me with you!"

Zvi called the driver to stop, and got out of the diligence. He knew that the Turks were on the track of the spies, and his first impulse was to take Yosef. Then he remembered the money and the arms. He consulted Shmulik, but Shmulik was against it. They could not carry the gold and Lishansky at the same time, and anyway he did not want to have anything to do with these people. But Zvi Nadav could not bring himself to leave Yosef stranded, and finally, much against his will, Shmulik agreed to take Yosef with them to Tel Adas.

At Tel Adas the next morning everyone was anxiously awaiting the return of their comrades with the arms and the money. The exposure of Nili had spread terror in Haifa and the Emek. The dread name of Hassan Bek was on everyone's lips, and no one knew where the investigations and tortures would spread next. The whole of the Shomer work was endangered, the getting of arms and the preparations for the critical moment when there would be a change of rule in the country.

One of the women members was stationed at the window to watch. Suddenly she saw a diligence rocking down the road to the settlement. The driver was nervously beating the horses to greater speed. The vehicle swept through the gate, and they all gathered in the yard as Shmulik jumped out, tense and excited. "We've brought the money and the arms, and on the way, by Karkur, the tachshit (the jewel) Lishansky appeared, and Zvi said we had to take him."

They were horrified. Tel Adas was at the foot of the Nazareth mountains, close to Turkish headquarters. The punitive battalions might be turning up at any moment.

Some hid the arms, others hid the gold. "We must hurry and get the gold to a safer place." "But I've got to count it first," Shmulik grated out between clenched teeth. "They want an account, and we've got to separate the gold coins made during the war, so we'll not be caught out by them. If it wasn't for the discovery of these spies, we could have done great things with that money. Now it's only an added danger to us." If it hadn't been for the spies, the money wouldn't have been in the country, but they were in no mood to think of anything like that.

The young woman returned to the house, and once again she stood at the window on the second floor of the ramshackle wooden barrack, this time looking in the direction of Nazareth. Would they have time to hide the arms? Would they have time to get rid of the money? Zvi Nadav came up the steps. They looked at each other in grim silence for a moment, then he said to her: "Lishansky's here. We're bringing him up to you, and you'll have to look after him until we can take him away. He's changing his clothes now. It's a terrible night we've had. When we left Tel Aviv we took the officer Riklis with us, for greater security. Who would have thought that on the way we'd run into the tachshit? It's a miracle that we were able to make the whole journey by night. He never stopped talking in a loud voice, boasting of his deeds. He seemed to believe that the British navy was waiting for him on the coast."

They had intended to keep Lishansky hidden behind the ancient ruins opposite Tel Adas with Zvi to guard him, while they decided what was the best thing to do with him. But try as they might, they could not make Yosef keep himself concealed. "I begged him, 'Sit beside me quietly. Shmulik will certainly get us water and something to eat,' Zvi told Rachel. "But he couldn't control himself. He was like a baby. 'I'm thirsty, I'm thirsty!' he cried. I tried to hold him, but he tore himself away from me and ran towards Tel Adas. He doesn't seem to understand that he's running straight into danger."

They heard heavy steps and Yosef appeared. He was already dressed in work clothes and torn sandals. Rachel looked at him with disgust, noting his full, round face, shaven head, and the gold rings on his fingers. "The man doesn't yet feel his bitter fate. Very strange. He's in high spirits, excited, chattering, jumping from one subject to another, boasting about his escapades. Once he was in Egypt, then he was in Zichron, then in the desert."[1] Yosef assured them that if they hid him just for a little while the British would pay them for it. Pay them in gold. He would pay them too from the gold he had buried around Athlit. He did not notice the looks of pitying contempt they exchanged. This penniless watchman, this boaster, for whom they had never had an ounce of respect because he always talked big and never did anything, was still boasting and running off on his flights of fancy. Like everyone else, the Shomer had heard stories about Nili's deeds, but they did not believe half of them. They had put them down to wishful thinking or plain bluff.

Within an hour Zvi Nadav had Lishansky out of Tel Adas and was heading north with him to Poriah, the Shomer head-quarters perched on the crest of grim black hills high above the Sea of Galilee. There, in one of the cluster of weatherbeaten little shacks, they debated the situation. "By this time the authorities must know about his journey to the Emek. Best that we go to them, and explain that he just got into the diligence, and this will stop any suspicion falling on Tel Adas."

Israel Giladi, one of the founders of the Shomer and its undisputed leader, said: "If he's caught with us, we'll all be reckoned as spies. If we hand him over, we'll still be suspect, because they won't believe us. We must keep him with us, and guard him."

"Lishansky won't stand up to torture. If they get him, he'll pull us all after him. Can we take on the responsibility of guarding him? If we can't, then we've got to finish him!"

Giladi replied that there was no need to kill him in panic. They had him, and if there was any danger of him falling into the hands of the Turks, and he really was a coward, they could help him out then by saving him from Turkish torture. They decided that Zvi Nadav should take Lishansky up to Hamrah, on the Lebanese border, where he must be kept under guard. Beit Gan, the little community which Yosef had helped to

[1] *The Book of Ha-Shomer* (Tel Aviv, 1957), p. 193

213

found, was only a kilometre or two away in the hollow of the hills. While his fate was being decided at Poriah, Yosef was at Beit Gan, guarded by one of the Shomer men who lived there. Near by lived a cousin, his closest relative. On the pretext of going to the outhouse, he slipped away to her house and begged her to let him hide in the little cubby hole under the roof until his pursuers were thrown off the scent and he could get away to the Lebanon. But her husband refused to let him stay. He had never been in sympathy with the espionage, and he had warned Yosef against it many times. He was not going to get mixed up with it now.

On all fours Yosef crept through the field at the back of the house to the farm of a friend of his. His friend was full of compassion when he saw Yosef, with red-rimmed eyes, ravenous and hunted like a dog. Yosef slipped into the barn and hid among the sacks of barley, while the farmer sent his seven-year old boy out with a parcel of food for him. But he could not let Yosef stay. He was Mukhtar of the village and the father of four children. Whatever trouble arose, he would have to pay for it with his own body.

The Shomer people were already out searching for him, and Yosef returned to the house. In the middle of the night Zvi Nadav and another Shomer man came to get Yosef, and together they set off northward to Hamrah. They went on horseback, following the mountain tracks and so avoiding Tiberias, which was surrounded. The horses, used to travelling in the mountains by night, trod quietly and easily. The wide, rolling hill country of Upper Galilee was Lishansky's district. Always one of the best horsemen among the Shomer men, he now took the lead. He had calmed down, and it was almost like the old days, when they had ridden patrol together.

But when it got light, Yosef became nervous again. His voice was loud and hysterical, and his companions could not get him to talk quietly. Suddenly, to their horror, he said that they must go back. He had to get to the seashore. Zvi Nadav thought he had become unbalanced, for he insisted that, at a sign from him, a ship would come, lower a boat, and take him off to Egypt. "He promised me everything, if I would go back with him," recorded Nadav. "If I disliked him before, he sickened me now." Lishansky was handed over to the people of Kibbutz Hamrah, who were instructed to hide and guard him.

Meanwhile other men of the Shomer were turning up at Tel Adas, and they were far from satisfied with the situation when they heard about it. Among them was Nissinov, Mukhtar of the area. Older than most of the others, he was taut as a bow string and devoid of all sentiment. When a group of young men from Zichron arrived to beg them to hand Yosef over, he realized that it would not be long before Lishansky was tracked down. Nissinov went straight to Turkish headquarters in Nazareth and got a statement from them that he was authorized to bring them Lishansky alive or dead. He then arranged with an Arab police officer that, if Lishansky were found dead, the officer would say he killed him and receive the £100 reward now offered by the Government. Nissinov sent a messenger to the people of Hamrah telling them to watch Lishansky well and, if he tried to run away and had to be killed, to leave his body on the main road above the waterfall. Nissinov would come with a carriage and pick up the body. He then set out for the north in a carriage with two other men of the Shomer and the Arab police officer.

"We were certain that everything would go as desired," he recorded, "but it didn't turn out like this. Later we were told that Lishansky had a suspicion of our intentions and ran away. They shot at him, wounded him, but it was a dark night and he succeeded in escaping. When I heard that, I felt that we were lost. If Lishansky was captured now, he would take his revenge on us."[1]

Lishansky did not know that they intended to kill him, but he did not trust them and wanted to get out of their hands as soon as possible. He told the people at Hamrah that he wanted to get to the Druze in the Lebanon. They made no objection, but as he crept up through the ravine towards Metullah, one of them who had been lying in wait appeared from behind the waterfall and shot him. Yosef fell into the ravine. They thought he was dead and went to fetch a cart to take his body to the main road. But Yosef was only wounded in the left shoulder. He crawled along until he reached the stream. There he washed

[1] *The Book of Ha-Shomer.*

his wound and bound it with a silk handkerchief which he had transferred from his other clothes before they were burned. It was the handkerchief that Sarah had sent him.

Yosef crept on towards Metullah, hoping to find refuge with his family there. He did not know that they had been under watch by the Shomer since the Turks had put a price on his head. He entered the grounds of a cottage three houses away, jumped over the intervening fences, and entered the Lishansky house by the back door. The Druze servant girl, who was sleeping in the kitchen, woke up but remained silent. He started for the room of his niece, who was also his foster-mother. She was many years older than he was, and had brought him to Palestine and reared him with her own children.

In the room leading into her bedroom two Shomer men lay asleep on the floor. Yosef crept between them and entered his foster-mother's bedroom. She lay asleep with her own daughter and the daughter of a neighbour. She woke up and saw Yosef trying to hide himself in the clothes cupboard. She stifled her scream with the back of her hand and shook her head violently.

"The outhouse," she whispered. "Stay there until I come."

Yosef crept out again between the sleeping men and hid in the outhouse. His foster-mother decided to go and get the advice of a relation who lived near by. Her bedroom window overlooked the barn.

"My cow, my cow!" she began to cry. "I've lost my cow." She rushed out of the room and got to her cousin.

Before she could return dawn had begun to break and Yosef did not care to wait until daylight, lest he be caught. Hungry and weak from loss of blood, he got to the house of a little hunchbacked tailor whom he had known from his youth. The tailor had pity on him, gave him food and a hiding place in the rafters of the roof. There he rested for a day and a night. But the word went round that Lishansky was in the north, and that the delegations from Zichron and the other settlements were after him. The tailor gave him a loaf of bread and sent him on his way.

Lishansky no longer had the strength to go unaided into the wild Lebanese mountains to contact his friends the Druze. There were two alternatives open to him. One was to hide in the country until the British came; Liova had said that they would not be long. For this he had to find somewhere in the south, close to the front. The other alternative was to get to the coast at Athlit by October 12th and get to Egypt. In either case he had to escape from the north. But could he make it? What about food? And his wound? The man hunt was on all over the country and so he could get no food from Jew or Beduin. How could he make it? How *did* he make it?

That same night, under cover of the high grass and the shrubs, he fled. He rested by day and then crept through fields and vineyards at night. He must have come across an Arab or a Beduin who helped him, for some four nights later he found himself, around midnight, on the western slopes of Carmel, north of the Experiment Station. He gave the Station a wide berth and staggered down the mountainside towards the coast. He saw a light glimmer for a second and disappear. Was it the ship? Or was it a firefly?

He automatically halted and listened as he came to the Haifa highway. He heard the sound of a patrol. He dropped behind the rocks. His foot slipped and a pebble rolled. A shot rang out and then there was silence. Weeping with impatience and excitement, and grinding his face into the rocks to muffle the sound, he waited for the footsteps to die away. Then he staggered across the wadi Dustera. Weak and starving, he fell among the rocks in his hurry and his wound burst open. He still had half a mile to go. Picking himself up he staggered on, his hand pressed against his shoulder to stem the blood and ease the pain.

When he got to the shore he saw nothing, no one. The ruins of the Crusader castle loomed up, silent and deserted. Against the dark horizon he thought he saw a dark shape moving southwards. The ship? In despair, he started to walk into the sea, as he used to walk to the boat. Let the waves cover him! Then he realized where he was. One of the hidden caches of gold was not far away.

He groped among the rocks until he came to the hiding place that he had dug with Sarah. He found the place open and empty, and spat into it. But there was another place. Feverishly, without caring for Turkish patrols, he crawled to the next one, across the dunes in the direction of the Station. Here the earth was undisturbed and, digging with a sharp rock, he found the tin intact. He bashed it open and filled his pockets.

With the feel of the gold his confidence returned. His luck was in again. He would outwit them yet. By the time it was light he was at Givat Ada, where he bought some food from Trans-Jordanian Beduin encamped with their herds and flocks in the lush grass of the swampland. He bought a horse and set out for Petach Tikvah where the Pascals lived.

Yosef did not know it, but he was walking right into a trap. The Turks were keeping a close watch on this, the biggest Jewish community in Palestine. The settlers had protested their innocence, and after the first search by Turkish gendarmerie they were keeping their own watch against the hunted man. Women, children, beggars, all sorts of people were engaged in counter-espionage by the Turks, and terror reigned in the settlement.

Peretz Pascal was in Egypt. Mrs Pascal, her mother and her two daughters were sitting at home one terrible night, when a hand knocked at the window. They sat frozen, no one daring to stir. Then the little girl, Loret, went and came back with Lishansky. He had left his horse on the outskirts of the village and had crept there under cover of darkness. He was hungry, thirsty, sick, and trembling with fever. The women fed him, bandaged his wounds, and hid him for ten days, although the penalty was death.

But the strange horse wandering around the outskirts of Petach Tikvah attracted attention, and once more the word swept like wildfire, "Lishansky is here!" A house-to-house search began, and the Pascal women got frightened and could keep him no longer. Mrs Pascal procured Beduin clothes for him, and he set off on foot at night, to seek shelter with a Beduin tribe in the south beyond Rishon, where the Sheikh was a friend of his and would shelter him until the British came. Daylight found him near an Arab village in Nebi Rubin not far from Rishon. He approached one of the huts to seek shelter for the day. The Arab recognized him and called others. Together they stripped him of his clothes for loot, then bound him and handed him over to the Turks for the money on his head.

Yosef was taken to Ramleh, where the Governor received him with a blow on the face and telegraphed to Jerusalem that he had caught the dangerous spy. Then he produced a whip to begin the usual tortures. Yosef stopped him with a sharp command. "Don't hit me until you have heard what I have to say." Yosef was not tortured. He was quite willing to talk.

"Who are your friends?" was the first question.

"Only the Shomer," he replied frankly. "I had no other comrades in the spy work." And he gave them the names of every person he could remember, together with their descriptions and nicknames.

The Zichron hostages were freed with Yosef's arrest. He was sent by special train to Jerusalem with a battalion of soldiers to guard him. Then to Damascus, where he found Naaman Belkind, completely broken; he had been told that if he confessed everything he would be released. And now he was going to be hanged. Other members of Nili were there too, and dozens of other people, members of the Shomer, settlement heads, and leaders of the Yishuv.

One night, after midnight, Manasseh Bronstein and his friend Yitzhak Halperin woke up. In the corridor they heard the creaking of chains. They knew that people who went out like that never returned. It was Naaman Belkind and Yosef Lishansky. When Lishansky passed by their cell he called out to them, "Shalom, comrades"; and after an hour's silence they heard his cry from the gallows: "Long live the English redeemers!"

The next day they learned that Allenby had captured Jerusalem.

Epilogue

ALL the members of Nili in Palestine were tracked down and arrested. In the prison at Nazareth they were subjected to prolonged torture, but not one of the group revealed the secrets of Nili. Reuven Schwartz was beaten to a pulp. His jailors, fearing that he might succumb to his wounds, hanged him from the bars of his cell window to make it seem that he had committed suicide.

Ephraim Aaronsohn fell ill with the typhus that raged in the prison and was left to die. But he refused to die, and within three months was sent back to Zichron under guard. The Aaronsohn house had been looted, and Aaron's vast library and the results of his scientific research had been scattered or destroyed. The only thing that remained was the collection of plants which the old man and Sarah had been able to hide in the last days of Sarah's life. Weak and wounded though he was, the old man managed to evade the Turkish soldiers who guarded the house, and crawled into the cellar at night from time to time to protect the cherished collection from rats and insects. He later returned to work in his vineyards, preserving the secrets of his children until his death at the age of ninety.

With the exception of Mendel Schneersohn, all the men of Nili were sent to Damascus for court-martial. Zvi Aaronsohn spent almost a year in the prison hospital there as a result of his tortures, and returned to Zichron an incurable invalid. Eytan Belkind escaped the fate of his brother Naaman only because of his age. He was nineteen years old and legally too young to be hanged. Nissim Rootman, Manasseh Bronstein, Dr Neumann and the others were kept imprisoned under the impression that they were to be hanged. When the British took Damascus, they were freed by Captain McRury of Advance Intelligence, under whom Liova Schneersohn and Alex Aaronsohn had been serving since the fighting began in Palestine the year before.

Alex tracked down the murderous Hassan Bek in Aleppo and

had him brought to trial in Jerusalem. He was charged with Reuven Schwartz's death, and sentenced to a long term of hard labour. Norman Bentwich, then the Senior Judicial Officer of the British Military Administration, has provided the rather disturbing information that, when he saw the prisoner later, "he looked mild and gentle".[1] Hassan Bek's sentence was later reduced to a few months on the plea of Alex Aaronsohn. "Vengeance is the Lord's," Alex assured his family. And, indeed, not long after his release from prison, Hassan Bek became paralysed and never walked again.

Mendel Schneersohn returned to Hadera, which was in confusion with demoralized Turkish soldiers retreating before the British attack. Although the authorities renewed their search for him, Mendel in disguise hid in a village on the Turkish front for several months, waiting his chance to steal across the lines to the British. When he did get across, he brought with him data and maps of Turkish positions along the front.

At G.H.Q. they looked with astonishment at the modest, bespectacled young man who produced his valuable information in such a matter-of-fact manner. To test his authenticity, Mendel was immediately taken up in a plane, and from the air, with Turkish anti-aircraft shells bursting around him, he indicated all the points described in his notes and maps. The next day he spent two hours in a front-line trench, verifying his information in more detail with the aid of a camouflaged telescope.

Mendel joined his brother Liova and Alex Aaronsohn in Advance Intelligence, and was appointed Intelligence Officer in an area adjacent to the front, which included Rishon le Zion. Familiar with the people and the area, he was able to do useful work in intercepting the flow of weapons from the Arab villages to the Turks and in tracking down ex-Turkish army men who were making anti-British propaganda among the population. He continued to serve in the army until 1920, when he returned to farm at Hadera. As Liova Schneersohn has said about the members of Nili in general: "In time of war a simple farmer can be a hero. When the need passes, he stops being a hero and returns to farming."

[1] In letter to author, London, August 30th, 1957

The only recognition Mendel ever got, or expected to get, from the British was a contract from the army to plant trees along the roads of Sarafand, the big British military centre in Palestine. Liova Schneersohn was awarded the O.B.E., and Alex Aaronsohn, who served at Allenby's Headquarters and reached the rank of Captain, received the D.S.O., "in recognition of gallant work carried on in the interests of Intelligence in 1918."

Aaron's fate, like his whole life, was a stormy one. Not until January 1918, when he was in America on his mission for the Zionist Organization, did he receive the news of Sarah's death and the fate of Nili. "The sacrifice has been paid," Aaron recorded in his diary, and grimly continued with his work of mobilizing support for the Allied war effort and for a British Mandate over Palestine.[1] All that Aaron had foreseen and struggled for was coming true. The conquest of Jerusalem and the Balfour Declaration had, in his own words "thrilled the souls, quickened the blood, and stirred the hearts of millions..."[2] But once again, like Tantalus, Aaron found his reward snatched away from him. His aim to stand behind the scenes and to bring his ideas to bear on the new programme of building up Palestine his perpetual hope of achieving a recognized status to enable him to press his policies, these he could not achieve even though high-ranking British officials could declare that "the Jews must remember that no man has done more than Aaron to make the conquest of Palestine by the British possible",[3] and hope that his people would not forget "what this great soul suffered and undertook when Zionism was scarcely born, and how very largely he contributed towards making Zionism a practicable proposition".[4] Yet when Aaron came to London from Egypt asking to be co-opted to the political committee of the Zionist Organiza-

---

[1] Letter from Dr Weizmann and N. Sokolow to Aaron Aaronsohn, London, November 16th, 1917, Weizmann Archives, Rehovoth

[2] *Julius Rosenwald* by M. R. Werner, Harpers (U.S.A.), 1939, p. 100.

[3] Statement made by Col. W. H. Gribbon, assistant to the Director of Intelligence, the War Office, 1917-1918, at a dinner given by the Z. Delegation at the Paris Peace Conference, and quoted in the unpublished diary of S. Tolkowsky, member of the Delegation.

[4] Colonel R. Meinertzhagen in letter to Dr Eder, Cairo; 11.11.19. Published in *Appreciations of Aaron Aaronsohn*, p. 61.

tion, where his background and his connections could be of most value, he was refused. The tortuous path which he had chosen to follow in the belief that it was the only way to save the Jews of Palestine from the fate of the Armenians, and the means by which he had helped the British to their remarkable victory were turned against him. "How can we have on the Zionist Executive a man known to be a British secret agent?" they asked.[1]

And so Aaron's lot was that of the political exile in ancient Greece of whom Pindar wrote:

> *The bitterest fate of all, men say*
> *Is his, who clearly hath descried*
> *The right thing, and no part may play,*
> *But stands, perforce, aside.*

It was Aaron's tragedy that in spite of the safe and rewarding refuge which the scientific world offered him he could not stand aside. He could not free himself from the burden of responsibility which weighed upon him. He felt that it was he, and not the accredited leaders, the Zionist theoreticians from the Continent, who held the key to Palestine's future.[2] When Sir Mark Sykes begged him not to quarrel with the recognized heads of the Zionist Executive in London, Aaron replied that he did not want to quarrel but only to tell them their mistakes and to show them the way to do things properly.[3]

Dr Weizmann, himself a scientist and the member of the Executive who conducted negotiations with the British Government, valued Aaron for his abilities and for the implicit faith which people in the highest ranks of the Government had in his judgment. He attached Aaron to the Zionist Commission which left for Palestine under his leadership, and so in April 1918, five months after Allenby's conquest of Judea, Aaron found himself travelling along the railway which the British Army had built from Egypt to Palestine through the Sinai desert. To cross that

---

[1] S. Tolkowsky to author, July 1957.
[2] Ibid.
[3] Letter from Aaron to Alex, quoted in *The Realities of American-Palestine Relations*, Frank E. Manuel, Public Affairs Press (Washington), 1949, p. 182.

desert on horseback or camel was thought to be great bravery only a few years before. "We are now crossing without danger or difficulty, that same evil desert that has taken from us the fresh life of our Absalom," he wrote to Rivka. "Our opponents can say what they like, but Absalom has his share in the success of the English, and the approaching realization of our aspirations."

In Egypt Aaron had heard the details of his family's fate from a prisoner of war. He had been told that his father too was dead. "What he tells about the heroism of Sarah and our father, and how they rose above their great difficulties, is on such an exalted plane, it is so great, that it is almost impossible to understand. It is impossible to imagine where this thing came to them, and however much they suffered, one is filled with pride to know that if they were sacrifices, they were great sacrifices.

"To pour salt on your wounds," he continued, "I must also tell you that with regard to the Station, nothing remains of the work of the last twenty years. . . . It will be necessary to start everything afresh." So wrote Aaron, not yet forty-two years old and, like Samson, confident that there was neither bond nor boundary that could withstand his iron will and his phenomenal strength. Five years later his devoted friend Dr Judah L. Magnes, then head of the Hebrew University in Jerusalem, was writing to the Rosenwalds in America, who had severed their connection with the Experiment Station when Aaron's espionage activities were revealed to them:

"I am sending you two roses from Aaron Aaronsohn's 'grave'. My wife and I drove there recently. The stately palms line the road into the Experiment Station's grounds, but the road itself is all overgrown with poppies and thistles and daisies and weeds, as though no one was so poor as to trouble to enter this graveyard of many high hopes. Camels and asses were grazing over the experimental fields, and the camels had nibbled off almost all the young leaves of the fig orchard. The windmill still stands, as do the buildings.

"In the lower rooms of one live a few Arab women, who gathered armfuls of flowers for us in their delight at having someone come there. In the shed American farming implements are piled in disorder, useless, rusting. We climbed the rotting stairs and looked through a boarded window where eleven years ago we had been happy and full of plans over some cups of tea. There the test-tubes were all in order along the wall, and at the other end specimens of wheat, some of them strewn along the floor. At the back of the house we gathered lavender and roses from glorious bushes, and as we picked them Aaron never felt so near or so dead.

"Dear Friends: May I not appeal to you to do something to clear Aaron's good name? He sacrificed everything—his debts, his name signed to checks for the Experiment Station that have never been honoured. I do not ask that you help to re-create his work, although it would be fitting that in his death he might have some part in the new budding life here in the land he loved. Please help to pay his debts and keep his name from ill-use and contempt. Do this, if for nothing else, for the sake of those old days, so long ago, before the war filled men's souls with bitterness and disappointment."[1]

But in the meantime Aaron saw his life stretching ahead of him, and the war, which was filling men's souls with bitterness and disappointment, was still going on. As soon as the Zionist Commission arrived in Egypt, Aaron had felt the first blast of the fury which raged in Palestine against him and against Nili. The public leaders who had come to greet the Commission refused to sit at the same table with "the man who endangered the Yishuv".[2] They even tried to stop him from entering Palestine.

But had Nili really endangered the Yishuv? Contemporary accounts support Nili's claim that there had never been a time, from the first months of the war, when the Jewish community in Palestine was not in danger.[3] One of the active public figures of the time, while writing harshly of Nili in her memoirs, corroborates in other sections of her book the fact that the Yishuv was in a drastic state, and unknowingly reveals that the only things which saved it were the events to which Aaron and the members of Nili had dedicated their lives.

[1] *Julius Rosenwald*, p. 101
[2] *The History of Zichron Yaacov*, A. Samsonov
[3] Among other accounts, *The Realities of Am-Pal. Relations*, p. 127

"For three years the Yishuv was without any foreign news-papers or any definite knowledge of what was going on on the European Front. Rumours of events on the Egyptian Front were also vague and contradictory. Everywhere there was starvation, illness, and cruel authority. The power to suffer had almost ended. The Jewish population was declining in the most alarming manner. . . . All our achievements were on the verge of destruction, and help there was none. In this state of despair, a great thing befell Israel, the Balfour Declaration."[1] And later: ". . . if the campaign in Palestine had been carried out at the slow tempo with which the fighting had been carried out in the three years before the conquest of Jerusalem, there would not have remained a refugee or remnant of what the Yishuv had built up. . . ."[2]

Yet in Palestine they called Aaron "spy". "Traitor," they called him, although they themselves had welcomed the British victory, and were now working for the overthrow of the Turks, in spite of the danger which their activities brought to the Jewish settlements still under Turkish control. If their indict-ment of Aaron was against all reason, there was nevertheless a vestige of logic in this implacable antagonism. Aaron had been false to the new spirit which was struggling for birth within his own people. The Jews were looking to Zionism, not merely for rescue but as a means of independence and self-expression. They were no longer prepared to remain passive while two or three self-appointed people (no matter how capable) interceded with the great of the world on their behalf.

It was this new spirit in the Jewish masses which had caused the revolt against the Baron de Rothschild's bounty and which now flared up against Aaron. It would accept no leadership by putsch. The people had to be reckoned with. There could be no short cut from the long, time-wasting procedure of committee meetings and parish politics.

Aaron soon saw that work with the Zionist Commission was not for him. He devoted himself instead to the question of the future boundaries of Palestine, which up till then had been part of the administrative area of Syria, and to his plans for

[1] *Chapters from Life*, Sarah Azriahu (Neuman, Tel. Aviv, 1957), in Hebrew, pp. 143-4   [2] *Ibid.*, p. 149

reclaiming the waste lands of the Negev, which would bring untold benefit to both Jew and Arab.

Like Lord Plumer, who was later to become one of the very few successful British High Commissioners in Palestine, Aaron believed "there is no political situation, don't create it". But the Military Administration, which was controlled by the men who had headed the Arab Bureau in Cairo, decreed otherwise. Although prepared to co-operate with Aaron personally and to accede to his requests on behalf of the Yishuv, they remained unrelenting enemies of Zionism. General Allenby had refused to permit the Balfour Declaration to be announced in Palestine, and the members of his Administration were making full use of their considerable opportunities to undermine it.[1]

Whatever Aaron's feelings at finding the work of Nili discredited by the Jews, and the Arabs of Palestine the only apparent beneficiaries of their bitter sacrifice on behalf of the British, his optimism and his fighting spirit never flagged. "All right then, we shall have our country, not only because it is right and logical, but because we will it," he declared, and in the summer of 1918 he left to mobilize support in England, France and America for the struggle which lay ahead.

Aaron attended the Peace Conference in Paris, where he was an indispensible assistant to Dr Weizmann,[2] his connections, his influence and his vast store of knowledge giving him an entrée everywhere. "He was, I believe, the greatest man I have known," W. C. Bullitt has written of him. "He seemed a sort of giant of an elder day—like Prometheus. He was the quintessence of life: of life when it runs torrential, prodigal and joyous. Many men, no doubt, are as great as he was intellectually, though I have never known his peer, but if they are great intellectually, they are not also great emotionally, as he was; great in courage, in sympathy, in desire, in tenderness, in swift human understanding; great at once in dealing with statesmen and children, with scientists and artists, great at once in humour and constructive imagination.

[1] There are many books on this subject, among them *The Great Betrayal* by Stephen Wise and Jacob de Haas; *Trial and Error* by Chaim Weizmann.
[2] Letter from Aaron to Dr Weizmann, Paris, February 16th, 1919. Weizmann Arch.

"Aaron, to me, was not merely the flaming embodiment of the determination of the Jewish race to have a home and to be again a nation, but rather a captain in the foremost company of that small army of humanity which marches ever against ignorance, superstition and hatred.

"I remember him in Washington—how the diplomats sat open mouthed, astonished by his knowledge and his insight, and were warmed by his picture of the Zion that was to be. I remember him in Paris at the Peace Conference—how from the first he foresaw the end of that tragic drama, how unerringly he picked his way through a thousand diplomatic pitfalls, how wise he was in counsel and how strong in friendship. And withal how human. Almost my last memory of him is of a talk in the Crillon, when he told me that he expected to appear before the Council of Four to plead for Zion and asked if I thought Clemenceau, Orlando, Lloyd George and Wilson would understand if he should ask that a particular five-acre field should be included in the Zionist State, because it contained a unique specimen of a wild plant, which would be preserved for the service of science and would be tended by the Jews, but might be neglected by the Arabs!"[1]

Every national group which had lifted a finger on behalf of the Allied cause was furbishing its claims in order to extract maximum concessions for its people. This was the time for the Nili episode to be brought forth in all its splendour. But Nili's work was never mentioned at the Peace Conference. When the time came for the Jews to specify their claims to Palestine, there was no one there—except the British—who knew the value of the aid which the Jews of Palestine, through Nili, had rendered in the Palestine campaign.

Aaron had returned to London to prepare his report on Palestine's boundaries. With this report and with all his documents relating to the war effort, Aaron left by British Army plane to return to Paris. The plane disappeared in a mist over the Channel, and Aaron Aaronsohn was never seen again.

[1] *Appreciations of Aaron Aaronsohn*, p. 61

Appendix

THE LAWRENCE-SARAH MYTH

MANY people have said that T. E. Lawrence fell in love with Sarah Aaronsohn, and that she remained the only woman in his life. It is also believed that Sarah is the mysterious "S. A." to whom *Seven Pillars of Wisdom* is dedicated.

If Sarah and Lawrence ever met, if could only have been during the time that Sarah was in Cairo in the spring of 1917. Even if he did not meet her personally (Aaron was formal in his relationships with the British and introduced his sister only to those people with whom she had work in common), Lawrence might still have seen and admired her from a distance, as did other officers of G.H.Q.

The possibility is ruled out by the fact that Lawrence was not in Egypt or anywhere in the vicinity during the whole of the time that Sarah was away from Palestine—that is, from April 28th to June 18th. From at least the third week in March until the first week in July, Lawrence was circulating in the Hejaz or adjacent desert, engaged in the two activities which have added most to his fame.

On March 27th, 1917, he went on his first mine-laying operation against the Hejaz Railway.[1] He occupied himself in the area for the next month, and on May 9th joined a body of Arabs which set out from Wedj to capture Akaba. Fifty-eight days later they reached Akaba, which had just been taken.[2] This was early in July. Lawrence then left for Cairo, where the report which was circulated of "his" victory caused him to emerge, for the first time, as one of the outstanding figures in the Middle East campaign.

Lawrence had made a brief study of the Crusader castle at Athlit in pre-war days. It is always possible that the curious and enterprising young man, having heard from the Intelligence in

[1] *Lawrence and the Arabs*, by R. Graves, Cape, 1927, p. 153
[2] *Lawrence of Arabia*, by R. Aldington, 1957, 4-Square ed., p. 180

229

Cairo of the young woman who headed a spy ring operating from that vicinity, decided to drop in on her from the sea. (There is no reliable evidence that Lawrence or any other Englishman penetrated into Central Palestine by land until the last period of the war, by which time Nili had stopped functioning).

Since, as Sir Leonard Woolley has explicitly stated,[1] Lawrence himself never worked with Nili, he would have had to have the co-operation of Aaron to reach Athlit from the sea. All British contacts with Nili were made through Aaron. Aaron, who meticulously noted all encounters and conversations in his diary, has only two references to Lawrence during the course of that year.

Lawrence had already been sent off to work with Feisal in the Hejaz when Aaron arrived in Cairo at the end of December 1916.[2] It was not until February 1st, 1917, that Aaron notes in his diary that he met "Second-Lt. Lawrence of the Arab Office."[3]

Lawrence may have been able to impress people unacquainted with the Arabs and the Middle East, but not someone like Aaron, who had actually grown up there and had a specialized knowledge of just those subjects about which Lawrence spoke so glibly. Aaron's further comment on the occasion of that first meeting is short and expressive: "A little snot," he wrote in French.

Sir Wyndham Deedes, who valued Aaron and worked very closely with him at that time, has said that Aaron was startlingly blunt, but he never said anything behind a person's back that he would not say to his face.[4] Aaron probably did not mince words when Lawrence turned up at G.H.Q., where he had been the expert on the geography of Palestine and Syria, and began making facile statements about the Turkish Army (another "speciality" of his), "the Arabs" and similar subjects. The relationship between them would have been far from cordial.

Aaron's next diary reference to Lawrence comes more than

---

[1] Interview given to Leonard Woolf and reported in letter of June 11th, 1957, to the author.
[2] R. Aldington, Ibid., p. 154
[3] Notes to *The History of Jewish Self Defence*
[4] *Appreciations of Aaron Aaronsohn*, p. 70

six months later. On July 10th Lawrence had appeared in Cairo, where an official version of the "capture" of Akaba by Lawrence and Feisal's troops was prepared and circulated.[1] He had been made a Companion of the Order of the Bath and was recommended for the French Croix de Guerre. With his new toy (the Arab Revolt) and its stimulating possibilities Lawrence was as bombastically enthusiastic as a schoolboy about the prowess of "his side". On August 12th Aaron recorded a second conversation with him, when Aaron attempted in vain to explain how important it was for Great Britain and the Middle East to have a Jewish revival in Palestine. Lawrence was only interested in the Arab revival, and declared that if the Jews did not support the Arabs, they would be butchered. Aaron wrote that it seemed to him that he was listening to "a scientific Prussian anti-Semite speaking English".[2] This is borne out by Lawrence's own letters referring to encounters with Jews in the Levant[3] and his later references to the Balfour Declaration. Whatever His Majesty's Government may have felt about the subject, Lawrence viewed the Declaration with something considerably less than favour.

A record of Lawrence's feelings and intentions in this respect is to be found in the reports of William Yale, American Agent in the Middle East. Extracts from many of his reports are quoted in *The Realities of American-Palestine Relations*. On page 190 the author, Frank E. Manuel, writes that in a conversation with Yale "Lawrence expressed his distress at the recent pro-Zionist policy. Balfour in London was Foreign Minister; but Lawrence was directing a war of his own in Arabia, and Yale was a good pipe line to the U.S. if he needed aid for his private struggle with Downing Street policy makers."

Among the Arab Office publications which were supplied to Yale were fragmentary notes under the heading, "Syria, the Raw Material", which Lawrence had prepared in 1915. Mr Manuel refers to ". . . its gross misinformation about the Jewish colonies, and its dose of contemporary anti-Semitism",[4] and

[1] R. Aldington, Ibid., p. 187
[2] Notes to *The History of Jewish Self Defence*
[3] *Oriental Assembly*, T. E. Lawrence, pp. 57-8
[4] Manuel, Ibid., p. 188

quotes Mr Yale's comment on the document: "T. E. L. in a few words suggests the bitterness which exists in southern Palestine against the Zionists . . . and recent developments only tend to aggravate the natural hatred of the Palestinians for those Jews who come to Palestine declaring the country to be theirs and acting as if such were the case."

In view of the fact that the Aaronsohns were among the most unabashed exponents of this idea, it seems most unlikely that Lawrence ever thought of contacting Sarah at Athlit, or even suspected during her lifetime that this insignificant little group of Jews was doing something so remarkable that he would attempt to claim their achievements as his own later on.[1]

It is irrelevant that Lawrence later became an avowed Zionist and worked closely with Aaron at the Paris Peace Conference.[2] Lawrence had come to see Zionism as a help for Feisal's kingdom, which by 1919 needed some bolstering against the French and the Syrians.

Apart from the title "To S. A.", there is nothing in the dedication of *Seven Pillars* that could apply to Sarah.

> *"I loved you, so I drew these tides of men into my hands*
> *and wrote my will across the sky in stars*
> *To earn you Freedom."*

If Lawrence did do these things, it could not have been for love of Sarah. Presumably he is referring to the Arab revolt, and he had neither met nor heard of Sarah in December 1916. No one in the Arab Office or in the Intelligence at Cairo had. Furthermore, the suggestion that the aim of the Arab revolt was to obtain freedom for a Jewess or for the Jewish community in Palestine is hardly borne out by the book itself.

If it is ridiculous to suggest that Lawrence had Sarah Aaronsohn in mind when he was doing his political work with the Hejaz Beduin, it is equally ridiculous to suggest that it was for Lawrence that Sarah carried out her espionage work in Palestine, as has been freely asserted in British publications in the course of the last twenty years. There is no mention in

---

[1] *Seven Pillars*, p. 394
[2] S. Tolkowsky, ibid.

Sarah's detailed reports and letters of any contact with Lawrence by her or any member of Nili in Palestine. Nor are there any facts about Lawrence and his activities in the Middle East which would lead one to believe that Sarah would have been favourably impressed with him if she had met him.

Lawrence could have dedicated his book to Sarah Aaronsohn without knowing her, just as other imaginative young men dedicate poems to Grecian urns. But even this possibility is repudiated by a statement from an authentic source, that the whole story of the connection between Sarah and Lawrence was started at least a year after Lawrence's death.

By a remarkable coincidence the story of this fancied love affair originated in America, the country which also gave the world—through the kind offices of Mr Lowell Thomas—the fabulous Lawrence of Arabia. Sometime in 1936, four people were sitting in a hotel in California, discussing Palestine, where Arab rioting had broken out. Two of them, one an author and the other a newspaper man, were about to leave for Palestine. The other two, a professor and his clever young daughter of sixteen, knew something about the country and had connections there. The conversation veered to Lawrence, and the three men began to speculate about the identity of the S. A. to whom *Seven Pillars* was dedicated. The young lady then proceeded to solve the mystery for them. It happened that she and her father were connected with the Aaronsohns of Zichron Yaacov. Under the hypnotized stare of the three men she calmly evolved her theory. Lawrence had once visited the Crusader castle at Athlit. He would have met Sarah there or at Zichron. When Sarah started her espionage work, what more reasonable than that their paths should have crossed? Naturally he had fallen in love with the woman spy whose feats were as daring as his own, and the S. A. to whom he had dedicated his book was, obviously, Sarah Aaronsohn.

The journalist immediately telephoned interested people in England, and was authorized to spare no expense to obtain a signed statement that Sarah had indeed been a close friend of Lawrence. Taking the professor and his daughter along to make the introduction to the Aaronsohn family, the whole party, without a moment's doubt, set out for Palestine. To their horror

Sarah's sister, Rivka Aaronsohn, the only person there who was able to speak with authority on the matter, flatly and categorically denied that Sarah had had any contact whatever with Lawrence, let alone a romantic association with him. The people in England who had a right to know were notified, and the story was dropped by the visitors.

The writer in the group was Ladislas Farago, and in his book *Palestine at the Crossroads*, published in 1937, he makes the following statement (on pages 159-60): "It is said with conviction, even today, that Lawrence was seized with the passion of love only once in his unsentimental life, and that the object of his passion was the tragic Sarah. I tried to discover the truth of this and was able to certify that Lawrence had never seen Sarah and hardly knew anything of her existence. Their romance is nothing but a mournful legend."

The American journalist also dropped the matter, but he must have dropped some (probably innocent) remarks as well. It was the time of the riots in Palestine, and the King David Hotel was filled with newspaper men sitting around and waiting for something to write about during the lulls in the shooting. In 1938 the London *Daily Express* carried the following story under the headline: "Woman in Lawrence of Arabia's life was a Spy."

"Lawrence of Arabia, enigmatic archaeologist turned soldier, all his life shunned women. Evidence has now been discovered that he dedicated his famous book, *Seven Pillars* to a woman. She was Sarah Aaronsohn, a red-haired Jewess, who, while still in her 20's shot herself rather than betray him to the Turks, after she had been tortured. She was head of the British Secret Service in Palestine. Whether they were lovers probably no one will ever know. But Lawrence wrote in his dedication (then follows the first verse).

"The revelation that S. A. was Sarah Aaronsohn was made when an American journalist, Stanford Grunberg, recently wrote to her father in Haifa for news of his family in Palestine. Sarah was Grunberg's cousin, a friend of his childhood. The *Daily Express* correspondent in Jerusalem writes:

" 'During the war a group of young Palestinian Jews formed their own secret service behind the Turkish lines. They crossed the Sinai Desert to Cairo, where, it is believed, Sarah first met Lawrence.

" 'She became head of a secret office outside Jerusalem which was his clearing house. In March 1918 German agents . . . tracked down Sarah to her home in Zichron.' "

Not long afterwards a magazine carried an article on the same lines. I did not see it, but I was told about it and so heard for the first time of the connection. I was very pleased, for I thought it might make the British take a kinder view of Zionist aspirations in Palestine. When I moved to Israel some ten years later, I decided to visit Zichron and get a story for an article on Lawrence's friendship with Sarah.

I slipped off there one day, allowing myself an hour to get the story. But the fog of mystery which surrounds the Aaronsohn family is almost as impenetrable as that surrounding Lawrence, and it took something like four years before I could get a definite and conclusive statement that the whole story was a myth. The origin of the myth and its date, many months after Lawrence's death, were then explained to me by Rivka Aaronsohn.

Confident that I could speak with assurance, I embodied the statement in an article which appeared in the *New Statesman and Nation* of December 22nd, 1956, under the heading, "The Mysterious S. A." When I opened the *New Statesman* the following week, I felt something of the shock which the American visitors to the Aaronsohn home must have experienced when they learned that Sarah quite definitely was not "S. A." Only this time the procedure was reversed. There, in clear print, was a letter from Mr Douglas V. Duff, stating that Lawrence himself had told him that *Seven Pillars* was indeed dedicated to Sarah Aaronsohn. I wrote to Mr Duff for further details and received the following reply, dated June 4th, 1957:

". . . The meeting (with Lawrence) to which I referred took place outside Thear's Garage in the wide East Street of Bridport in Dorset, in the last few months of his life.

"That morning I was filling my petrol tank at the garage, when a large Brough Superior motor-cycle roared up and I saw, without his seeing me, that it was Lawrence. I knew he hated recognition, and so made none, but I heard him ask the pump attendant who I was and my name given. Then Lawrence, a small man, came up and spoke to me in the strange way he had of using soldierly language, *very* soldierly. He asked me if I had written a recent book on Palestine which I had dedicated to Sarah Aaronsohn. I was very flattered to think he had read my work and said so. The conversation went like this (without hoping to be verbatim):

L: So you know who I am?

Me: I do. Col. Lawrence, of course.

L: Shaw's my name and I'm no —— colonel.

Me: I beg your pardon—I'm afraid you'll always be Lawrence in my mind. I apologize for saying so aloud.

L: Did you know Sarah Aaronsohn while she was alive?

Me: I'm very sorry that I did not. I'd have given my right arm to have done so.

L: Why?

Me: Good Lord, man, if ever there was a Joan of Arc in our days, it was Sarah!

L: Strange we two men should be here in this little town, both of us with a book dedicated to her, without either of us ever having seen her alive.

Me: Why, judging by that sonnet of yours I was sure she and you were partners in the old days.

L: We were—but without meeting."

Two weeks later, according to Mr Duff, he saw Lawrence again, who made the only other reference Mr Duff heard him make to Sarah: "If she had had a man for a husband, she might have been the leader of a Hebrew return with glory. It must have been hell to have been married to her when one was so unable to appreciate her."

As if this was not confusing enough, while looking through newspaper files in the office of the *Jerusalem Post*, I came across an interview with the faithful old friend and coachman of Aaron and Sarah, the Maronite Abu Farid. He had been tortured by the Turks but had refused to speak a word which would incriminate his beloved employers. In an interview which he gave a few months before his death in 1941 (he must have been well over 70 then) he is reported to have said:

". . . Once a fortnight a submarine used to wait some miles off Athlit. Sarah got in touch with it by signalling, and the submarine used to send a boat ashore during the night. My main job was to carry the 'mail'. I had to get to the shore, deliver the letters, and receive a bag of cash in return.

"I started this job after a rather momentous meeting. One night T. E. Lawrence came ashore with the boat and stayed some hours with us at the Station. I was asked into the room where they were sitting, and Aaron said to Lawrence: 'This is Abu Farid. He knows all our secrets and we can trust him.' Lawrence turned to me and said, 'Take good care of Mr Aaronsohn' ."

Mr Duff's letter leaves me puzzled. One can only conclude that since Lawrence (as quoted) had indulged in a little wishful thinking when he said that he and Sarah were partners in work in the old days, his statement that he dedicated *Seven Pillars of Wisdom* to her was also an afterthought.

The next statement attributed to him is a mixture of banality and bland ignorance. "If she had had a man for a husband she might be the leader of a Hebrew return with glory." Sarah had two great men to work with and inspire her, the heroic Absalom Feinberg who originated the idea of Nili, and her brother Aaron Aaronsohn. Quite what "a Hebrew return with glory" means is not clear, unless it means that when the British conquered Jerusalem, Sarah should have raced in at the head of Nili and taken it for the Jews before the main army got there, much as Lawrence arranged the capture of Damascus for Feisal. As even Lawrence must have learned before he died, there is little permanence and less glory in a national revival which is based on such hit-and-run methods. A national revival is a long, slow process. The Hebrew revival began before Sarah was born, when her parents and other people like them turned farmers to restore the fertility of their ancient homeland. It continued and grew in volume after her death. Glory, like beauty, is in the eyes of the beholder. There are some who can see glory in the Hebrew return which, from such humble beginnings and on such puny means, developed into an independent State in sixty-six years.

The details of Abu Farid's story are, of course, incorrect. No submarine was used to contact Nili at Athlit. The coachman was never taken down to the shore to meet the boat, for this part of the work was kept a close secret, unknown even to many members of Nili. There was no gold or letter service until eight months after Aaron left Athlit. Once he left, he never returned to Athlit. He could not have been there with Lawrence, since they met only some ten months later. Apart from this, there is no record or any mention in the voluminous diaries and letters written by Nili members that Lawrence or any other Britisher set foot on the coast of Athlit during the period of Nili's activities.

Then why should Abu Farid have spun this story? The probability is that he was being loyal to his beloved employers to the end. He knew that no matter how courageous their deeds or how important their service, no story about the Middle East during World War I would amount to a row of beans unless Lawrence could be dragged into it somehow.

Index

239

INDEX

INDEX

INDEX